Praise for *The Honey Thief*

"Elizabeth Graver i[s] ... [one o]f our finest writers on the grand ... [Her] vision is magnificently det[ailed ...] ... [rea]ders a memorable and sustained gl[...] ...e mysterious machinations of life itself." —*Chicago Tribune*

"Graver's writing remains both vivid and understated. Remarkably finely tuned, it maintains a consistent delicacy and precision." —*The New York Times Book Review*

"Intense, lyrical . . . Elizabeth Graver's beautifully fluted prose—slipping fluidly between past and present, and as sensitive to the nuance of thought and feeling as it is to place and landscape—makes each word a joy to read." —*The Times* (London)

"This novel is so absorbing that when I had to set it aside to contend with life, I moved in the fog of someone physically in one place but mentally in quite another. I counted the hours until I could pick it up again." —*Newsday*

"Have you ever read a novel that absorbs you so completely that you have to swim up out of it to reality? This is such a book. Poignant, well written, and thoroughly engaging . . . This is a great story about growing up, coping with loss, and the tenacity of the human spirit." —*Library Journal* (starred)

"Engaging, quietly suspenseful . . . The characters gently win our sympathy as they reach out for love and friendship. Graver has written a fresh, moving tribute to the human spirit's ability to survive." —*The Boston Globe*

THE HONEY THIEF

Also by Elizabeth Graver

Have You Seen Me?
Unravelling

THE HONEY THIEF

ELIZABETH GRAVER

A HARVEST BOOK
HARCOURT, INC.
San Diego   New York   London

For Jimmy

First published by Hyperion in 1999

Library of Congress Cataloging-in-Publication Data
Graver, Elizabeth, 1964–
The honey thief / Elizabeth Graver.
p. cm.
"A Harvest book."
ISBN 0-15-601390-8
1. Mothers and daughters—Fiction. 2. Problem children—Fiction. 3. Ithaca (N.Y.)—Fiction. 4. Bee culture—Fiction. 5. Beekeepers—Fiction. 6. Girls—Fiction. I. Title.
PS3557.R2864 H66 2000
813'.54—dc21   00-038896

Designed by Kris Tobiassen
Text set in Goudy
Printed in the United States of America
First Harvest edition 2000
J I H G F E D C B A

To make a prairie it takes a clover and one bee,
One clover, and a bee,
And revery.
The revery alone will do,
If bees are few.

EMILY DICKINSON

The apple trees were coming into bloom but no bees droned among the blossoms, so there was no pollination and there would be no fruit.

RACHEL CARSON, *Silent Spring*

1

What Eva would remember later, looking back, were the honey jars, how she was riding her bike down the road, legs churning, hair whipping across her face, not far from home yet (if this new place could be called home) but rounding corners, moving fast, until there they were—six jars of honey, maybe eight, each with its own curved belly and white lid, sitting on an old wooden card table in the grass. And perhaps it was the way the sun caught them or how unexpected they were, but she stopped her bike that afternoon and simply stared. She'd seen honey before—they had it in the city—but not lined up like this, not outside for anyone to take, a light-filled golden orange color like a prescription pill bottle or her mother's amber necklace from her father, the one with ancient insects trapped inside its beads.

And though Eva didn't know yet that all across the country, the honeybees were dying, she felt the honey, still, as a rare thing. Propping her bike against a tree, she walked up to the table and looked around—nobody—then reached a finger out to touch warm glass. She saw the sign, HONEY $3, and the box with a slit in its top. She touched the sign, touched the box, then the honey again—carefully, as if it might give her a shock. She wore a brown T-shirt and black cutoffs, a city girl, and her hair was dark and curly, escaping from her bicycle helmet like something live. Standing there, she felt her throat clog with longing—for someone to step out from behind a tree and speak to her, or for the honey; she wasn't sure.

But no no, she wouldn't take anything, wouldn't mess up. All this way, they had come, for her. Country air, safe streets, a place to make a good life, her mother had said. Eva had a new used bike, and long days to fill, and an old-lady babysitter sleeping on the porch as if Mrs. Flynn were the baby and Eva the sitter. A babysitter, though she was eleven, too old to need one. A good life, she figured, meant learning to be good, but she wanted to snatch up one of the honey jars, tuck it under her shirt and sneak it home. It might be a present for her mother, a way to get her to laugh in some old, forgotten way, a gurgle of surprise, her head tipped back.

But she knew it wouldn't work like that. Where did you get it, her mother would ask. Was Mrs. Flynn with you? Did you pay for it? And Eva would find words spitting from her mouth—*I hate you, leave me alone!*—and run crying from the room. She remembered, then, the man with the big stomach and walkie-talkie, his hand gripping the hood of her sweatshirt as they waited for her mother by the checkout at Love's. On the counter, her loot: a fluorescent green pen, some fingernail polish, a mood ring. I don't know, she had said, only half lying, when her mother shook her and asked why. And later, both of them crying, something her mother almost never did. Be good, be good. She had promised both her mother and herself.

So she took nothing, just got on her bike and left, weaving down roads of dirt and tar, past barns and cows, tilting houses

2

and rusting shells of cars, coming home thirsty and dusty to find Mrs. Flynn still sleeping on the porch, as if no time had passed. She stole nothing, but that night as she lay in bed, the honey returned to her anyway, slow and thick as a river she might dream of, a place where things hung suspended or inched slowly, slowly toward her hands.

Mornings in the city they'd had rituals; here they had none. In the city, Eva would wake first, pull on her jeans and sweatshirt, grab the dollar bills from the table, lock the door behind her and head downstairs, her eyes still glazed with sleep. A newspaper and coffee for her mother, a bagel for each of them; she didn't even have to ask. A dim, sleepy smile for Hal in the coffee shop, Hal with his gleaming bald head and ears sparkling with gold rings. "Eva my diva, don't ever leava!" he'd call, and sometimes he'd point her out to other customers: "See this cupcake? I've known her since she was a babe in arms." Then back upstairs, her mother in the shower, the radio tuned to jazz, Eva late again. She'd wolf down her bagel, vaguely run a comb through her hair until it got stuck in her curls, put on a clean shirt for school, maybe a bracelet even, the one she'd made from leather and glass beads. And Miriam would be out of the shower by then, dripping in the hallway, wrapped in a towel. "Comb your hair," she might say, but she didn't really care. They were flying by then, both of them, with things to do, places to be, the city singing out below them, horns, voices and the grinding of gears.

Here, most days, Eva woke to silence. Sometimes she tried to rouse herself when her mother did, but the house was so big, the walls so thick, and she couldn't always hear Miriam getting up. Plus her mother set her alarm so early, nervous about the used car she had just learned to drive, about the half-hour drive to work and work itself, the job new, the people, well, different, was all she would say. Mean? No, not at all mean—nice, actually, especially the other paralegal, I just. . . . And Miriam would sigh.

I want to do well, that's all, she'd say, and Eva would know she meant I want *us* to do well, or *you*, really, because wasn't Eva the reason they'd come here in the first place, to this nowhere house?

Eva would wake to a slant of light on the pale striped wallpaper of her room; it started by the ceiling and ran past Jesus to the floor. Her mother had wanted to take down the cross on the wall but Eva had said no, please leave it, and her mother had let it stay. Each morning, now, Eva got out of bed and walked slowly downstairs, trailing her fingers on the walls. In the kitchen she'd switch on the clock radio and look at the pictures in yesterday's *New York Times*. Once in a while, out of a mix of habit and stubbornness, she turned on the TV. They had no reception without cable, but still she sat straining to hear words through the static and seaching for shapes that might be people through the snow.

Each morning at nine, Mrs. Flynn showed up, lowering her stout body onto the porch chair, pulling out a pile of bills, or *People*, or a crossword puzzle book that she did in pencil so she could erase it and do it again. "'Lo, Eva," she'd say. Low low, and she just sat there like a bulldog until five o'clock, the skin on her neck all loose and soft, her ankles and fingers bloated as if she'd been stewing in water.

"I don't need a babysitter," Eva told her mother after the first week. They were eating dinner on the front porch, balancing their plates on their knees. "I don't like her. Why didn't we get somebody younger, who'd *do* things with me?"

Miriam finished chewing. "She has excellent references. I had to hire someone at the last minute and she seems responsible. She said you played Scrabble yesterday. Wasn't that fun?"

"I'd rather have a teenager."

"I wouldn't."

Eva rolled her eyes. "You're not a baby—that's why you don't have a babysitter. Hmm, that's funny—neither am I."

She could see her mother trying not to smile. "Listen," Miriam said. "You never know what a teenager will do, and we need

4

someone who can drive in case of an emergency. It's just for now. I'm still trying to find you a camp but you have to be patient. It's almost August—even if camp doesn't work out, school will start before you know it."

Eva stabbed her fork into a stalk of broccoli and left it there. It was barely July. "What *is* this?" she asked.

"Risotto. You don't like it? We used to eat it when you were little. It's Italian. I think it's delicious."

"It's slimy," she said, but in fact she was hungry and did kind of like it, so when her mother sighed and shut her eyes, she had some more. "Why did I like it?" she asked.

Miriam opened her eyes. "What?"

"Why did I like risotto when I was little?"

"I don't know—I guess you thought it tasted good."

Why did I think it tasted good, Eva wanted to ask. Did my father eat it? Did he make it for me? So many questions came to her, but no matter how many times her mother answered, the answers never satisfied. She tried to see herself in a highchair, her fists full of the slippery smooth grains. Her mother's eyes were shut again; she always came home exhausted from her new job.

"It's not even dark yet," Eva said loudly. "And already you're going to sleep."

Miriam opened her eyes and yawned. "I'm not, I'm just resting for a second." She stretched. "But you're right, let's do something. Let's . . . no, you decide. What do you want to do?"

"Hang out with Charu."

"Please, Eva. How about we . . . I know—we could take a walk."

"Where? There's nowhere to go."

"Oh come on, goose." She waved at the field in front of them. "Look."

Eva looked. The field was lit gold with early evening light. A bird she couldn't name flew overhead. Her mother stood and reached out a hand, then dropped it to her side. Eva put her plate down and stood, too. She could try to be nicer. She could. "Which way?" she asked.

"You decide."

She pointed over her shoulder. There was no road in that direction, just a high, dense wall of trees behind a field where a shed sat filled with broken things.

Her mother turned and looked. "That way? Really? Are you sure?"

They didn't get very far that evening; there were too many bugs and Miriam was afraid of getting stuck in the dark. Eva would have liked that—to make a roof of trees, a bed of grass, to settle into the curve of her mother's arm like she had when she was small. Instead, they came back while it was still light, but they did pick flowers, a floppy bunch of them, and put them in a coffee pot on the kitchen table. The next day Miriam came home from work with a book called *A Field Guide to Wildflowers*, a green shovel and a packet of seeds. Eva read the instructions on the label—Plant late May/early June.

"It's too late," she said.

Her mother took the packet from her. "You're right. How stupid of me. *Damn*."

Eva almost said, It doesn't matter, almost said, Thanks, it was a good idea, but something kept her silent.

"I'll get you different seeds," her mother told her. "They must have ones that can be planted now."

But Eva knew she never would.

And then, one day, after they'd been there for another week, the bike.

"I stopped by a white elephant sale," Miriam told her, "and bought it for a song."

White elephants? A song? Her mother was starting to talk funny and kept filling their fridge with food from the health food store near her new job—fake, rubbery hot dogs called Not Dogs and drinks in cardboard boxes marked Rice Dream. But the bike was red with tassels on the handlebars and came with a rack over the back wheel and a silvery blue helmet for her head, and if she couldn't make a garden, Eva could ride a bike; her mother's friend Sarah had taught her when she was six, in Central Park.

"You can use it to explore the countryside," said Miriam, but in her mind Eva was already leaving, riding down dirt roads, over highways, through the city, down to the East Village. There—Second Street, their grubby, smelly, crowded, windblown block, and on one side the iron fence with the surprising green graveyard behind it, and she would peer through the slats to the ground where she liked to think her father lay, though she knew it wasn't true. And Hal winking, and the outside door and the door to the apartment, three keys in all—turn this one, then that, press up and in at the same time—and Charu downstairs, the smell of curry rising yellow through the floor, making Eva homesick for India, a place she'd never been.

"With a bike you can get to know the neighborhood, as long as you're careful," her mother was saying, but Eva didn't think it was called a neighborhood if it had no people, and already she was miles from there inside her head, remembering the smallest things (already she knew to hold onto them), vivid as tastes on the back of her tongue: the hollow clop-clop drip of the faucet in their apartment; the height chart inside the closet door, showing how she'd grown; the way her bagel steamed in welcome when she sliced it open; Charu leaving her notes under the milk crate in the hall.

But forgetting, too. The stealing—how empty, how *furious* her hands had felt before she filled them, how jagged her thoughts until her fist closed hard around an object and the world smoothed out. The stealing, but also other things: the way Hal in the coffee shop was looking sicker every day; how it was so hard to sleep in their Second Street apartment, the new people upstairs fighting in the middle of the night, Eva's mother opening the creaky medicine cabinet to get a sleeping pill, or putting the kettle on to make tea.

* * *

The day after she spotted the honey, she decided to go back. It was a soupy, cloudy morning, the air thick with rain that hadn't yet arrived. Mrs. Flynn stayed inside on days like this, stretched out on the couch.

"Lousy weather for my bones," she said as Eva passed by. "Where're you going, hon?"

"Just for a quick bike ride."

Mrs. Flynn pulled herself up with a groan. "Remember, you're not supposed to go far. You think your mother wants you out in the rain?"

"It's not raining. I'll wear a jacket."

"There might be a lightning storm coming on. If you ever get stuck in one, you know to lie low, right, away from metal, not on the bike? Those storms can split a tree right down the middle, like an ax. You ever see that?" She massaged her arm. "You better stay inside."

Eva squirmed as she stood there in the weak light, pretending to let this woman babysit her. Some days they hardly said a word to each other, but now and then Mrs. Flynn grew bossy and talkative, and Eva had the dim sense that there was a whole person sitting in front of her, with unexpected corners to her mind. Other times, Mrs. Flynn tried to be friendly, to get her to play a game or talk about New York or, once, to learn how to crochet.

"I'll be back before it rains," Eva said.

"I don't want you caught out there, getting a cold or who knows what."

"I won't, I just need—my mother wants me to get exercise, it's part of why we came here. She said to ride my bike every day."

Mrs. Flynn heaved her thick legs back onto the couch. "Lucky girl, to be able to run and play. Used to be I was the fastest one around. When I was your age, I took care of the younger ones, never mind having a babysitter myself. In those days I—"

"Be back soon—" Eva called over her shoulder, and was out the door.

* * *

At first, as she rode, she worried—the honey wouldn't be there, it was only a one-time thing; she would arrive to find it gone. She couldn't say why she cared so much, knew only that she did, the way in the city she'd see some small thing in a store—silver-pink fingernail polish, a chewy brown caramel with a sugar center—and know she had to claim it as a charm.

Then, as she reached the end of the driveway and turned down the dirt road, she worried that the honey *would* be there and she'd have to steal it. You should've brought money, she told herself. Back at the house, she had a red wallet with thirty-seven dollar bills inside that she could never bring herself to spend. But no—it was far more likely that she would steal the honey and her mother would find out and they'd be back where they started, Miriam looking at her sadly, her voice about to break: Don't you know how hard I try?

As Eva kept riding, her legs pumping hard, something stretched out inside her head. She rode the bike well, steering around potholes, taking the bumps, and she knew where she was going this time, had learned a route through the neighborhood, if you could call it that. In Manhattan she hadn't exactly been a latchkey kid since her mother paid Charu's mother to watch her after school, but Ratha also had the boys to care for and let Eva and Charu play outside for hours at a time. The two girls roamed the neighborhood like cats, poking here, sniffing there; this was their turf and they knew its every corner. But Charu was good, would never steal, got to piggyback her baby brothers, had a father who spoke to her in another language and wore white, soapy-smelling shirts. Eva pictured Charu next to her on a bike, the two of them tourists, laughing at this place. Except Charu didn't know how to ride a bike, and meanwhile, Eva was supposed to *live* here, and now the dirt road crossed with a tar road and for a second she was unsure which way to go, but then she remembered and turned left.

Above her, the sky was bloated. A slight breeze came toward

her through the heat. She hadn't brought a jacket but she didn't care—if it rained, she'd just open her mouth and have a drink. Or maybe lightning would strike, splitting a tree in two. Metal, Mrs. Flynn had said; the lightning would want her bike. She pictured herself lying stiff and dead and pedaled faster. Her mother would find the body, start to cry: *I'm so sorry; I shouldn't have made you move.* And they would bury her on Second Street, ashes to ashes, dust to dust, in the stubborn green grass.

Rounding a bend, she came to the place where the honey had been and saw that it was all still there—the table, the money box, the jars. The table was peeling, its legs stuck deep into the ground like it was growing there. She rode past the first time, then circled back. There were other things she hadn't noticed the day before: a red mailbox missing its door, a dirt driveway and, in the distance, a small white house and big gray barn. There were five jars of honey, one or two fewer, she thought, than there'd been before, though she wasn't sure. And something else, something new—a jar with a label that said TASTE in crayoned letters, and next to it, a stack of wooden sticks like the kind the doctor used to make you gag. She put down her bike and went to see.

At first when she put the stick in her mouth, she could only taste the honey—a thick taste, it was, almost too sweet, a little sickening, like cough syrup or the smell of flowery perfume. She licked the stick clean, looked around her again but saw no one, checked over her shoulder for her bike. It wasn't raining yet, but the air was so full it almost hurt. She screwed the lid back on the honey and held the stick to her mouth like a cigarette.

"Dahling," she said, flicking her wrist toward Charu, who wasn't there. Her voice surprised her, sounding louder than she expected. "Be good," she whispered, then. The honey jars were full and gleaming. Some of the honey was pale yellow, the rest a deeper orange, and she wondered why it wasn't all the same. The money box was held shut with a silver padlock. Three dollars was all it would take to buy a jar; she had so much more than that at

home. As she stood staring at the table, a raindrop landed on its surface. She looked into the pine forest to the right of the table, pushing her hair off her face. Just for a minute, she told herself, to see what's back there. Maybe a girl lived in the house and played outside, or there might be a dog she could take home, or a store in the middle of the woods, its shelves stocked tight with things.

What she found instead, when she walked through the trees to the field beyond, were the beehives. At first she didn't know what they were, these big wooden boxes on cinder blocks, painted gray or white and stacked on top of one another. Glimpsing shapes through the trees, she thought she might have come across a playground or construction site. Each stack of boxes had a faded brick on top, sometimes two. The rain was coming down faster now, making it hard to see, but as she got closer, she noticed darting shapes and saw that the ledge at the bottom of each stack was specked with crawling bees. A bee flew toward her, its buzzing loud enough to hear, and she flinched and stepped away. Breathing in, she realized that the air smelled of honey, or was she just smelling the inside of her own mouth? She moved forward again, hoping to find a way to look into a hive, but another bee flew angrily in front of her, then looped off.

The sky had opened up while she stood there; the temperature had dropped. Her shirt clung wet to her chest, and her hair dripped water in her mouth and eyes. Go home, she told herself. The bees, she saw, were crawling out of the weather, disappearing inside a dark space at the bottom of the box. *Come in*, their mothers must have been calling. Thunder sounded from the sky, an empty, thudding noise. Eva knew she should be scared but found that she was not. In New York, sometimes, it was like this, too: an ambulance would pass by and she wouldn't even blink, just stand there picturing a woman on a stretcher, maybe gasping, maybe dead, nothing to be done. A sudden death, I'm so sorry, cards and casseroles, or no, maybe the woman surprises them.

There was a bright light, she says, sitting up (on TV she was pretty, with a wide mouth and startled eyes). A long, red tunnel. A peaceful feeling. Then somebody called my name.

Again the thunder clapped. Still Eva stood in the field. Maybe, she thought, a girl struck by lightning would split down the middle and become two girls, and then she'd have a friend. She held out her watch with its metal band, to call the lightning down. She wouldn't tell Mrs. Flynn about the hives and honey, wouldn't even tell her mother. She had done nothing wrong, after all, had stolen nothing.

The lightning did not come to her; nobody came. As she walked through the rain to her bike, she prayed to Jesus for a live girl with hair the color of honey, who would open up a hive to show her what happened inside.

2

It was a last resort. Miriam knew it, and she was sure Eva knew it, though neither of them ever said so out loud. It wasn't hard, after all, to come up with plenty of good reasons for leaving the city: metal detectors in Eva's school; the smog so thick you had to scrub it off your face before bed; the rat they found in the bathroom, its claws skittering across the tub. The needles lying in the gutters, the endless shrill of noises from outside—sirens and car alarms, radios and horns, people yelling insults or talking to voices inside their heads. The roaches in the kitchen, the triple-locked door with its peephole too high for Eva to reach. How stretched they were for money, Eva begging for this, begging for that—a computer (*my teacher says it's a learning tool*), dance lessons, karate lessons, ninety-dollar sneakers, when some months Miriam could barely make the rent.

Excuses, they were. Excuses all.

The first time a store manager called about Eva, Miriam had

thought it was a mistake. "She's a good kid," she told the woman. "She gets an allowance, we have candy at home, she wouldn't need to—" The word too hard for her to say, only that day she'd had to say it—*steal*, like stealing away, like the look on Eva's face when they got home, steely, closed, and Eva hadn't said it was a mistake or cried and crawled into Miriam's lap. She had stared at her feet and muttered *sorry*.

"Never again," Miriam had told her, her mind already leaping ahead—*it all started when she stole some candy*. "All right, Eva? I need you to promise."

"Okay," Eva had mumbled, sucking on a lock of hair. The next time was a stationery store, and not candy but a child's pair of left-handed scissors, and Eva not left-handed, though both her parents were. The theft-sensors blaring, Eva standing at the front of the store in handcuffs, a huge, impassive security guard at her side. Handcuffs, on an eleven-year-old. For half a second, until she saw the terror on her daughter's face, Miriam had found the whole thing almost comic. Then she'd felt a stab of anger—at the guard, for treating a kid like a dangerous criminal, at Eva, for messing up again.

"Why are you doing this?" she had asked when they got home. "You need to tell me. You—" Her voice too fearful, her tone all wrong. She caught herself and tried again. "Please?"

Eva shook her head, first defiantly, then in a manner much too grim and tired for a girl her age, tears finally starting down her cheeks. I know, Miriam wanted to say, and gather her up. I'm sorry—I am, if you only knew. But Eva might have started crying in earnest then, let loose a flood of tears, a flurry of hard questions. Careful, their gestures said to each other. Most of the time, they knew how far to go. So she had reached for a tissue and wiped Eva's nose, made her some hot cocoa, let her watch afternoon TV. She hadn't said clean your room, wash your hair, be cheerful and helpful the way you used to be. She had raised Eva's allowance by fifty cents though they were short on money and she understood that money was not the point here. Why scissors, why left-handed, why *stealing*, she had wanted to know, but Eva had offered nothing and Miriam hadn't pushed.

After that, she made an appointment to see the counselor at school on her lunch break. Eva, she told the counselor, was caught stealing. Not uncommon at her age, the counselor said. Was she making passing grades? Was everything all right at home?

"Fine, yes," Miriam answered and wondered if she meant it. "She likes school—or at least I think she does. She has lots of friends. Her father died but that was . . . I mean, it was years ago, when she was six." She noticed a wedding band on the counselor's hand. "After that, she saw a therapist for a little while but she seemed, I don't know . . . I thought things were pretty good until fairly recently. I—I guess I hoped she was doing okay."

"Could be plain old prepubescent acting out, or maybe those early events are rising up in her again," said the counselor, and Miriam pictured mercury rising and felt her own skin grow hot.

"Do you think," she asked. "I mean, might it be a sign that something's really wrong? I've read—" She glanced toward the closed door. Outside, the shrieks and whoops of children echoed in the hall. "Should I take her to a doctor? I don't like doctors much, I'd rather not, but if—"

"You mean a psychiatrist? I wouldn't, not at this point. She's probably just rebelling. If you make her think something's wrong, she'll do it even more. They get like that around her age, in order to, you know—" The counselor checked her watch. "All children need to separate," she recited mechanically.

The counselor looked dazed, her lipstick smeared, stacks of paperwork and a bottle of aspirin on her desk. The girl is lucky she even had a father to lose, Miriam could hear her thinking. A pair of scissors, a chocolate bar—small potatoes among the woes of the children at this school. Wait, Miriam was tempted to say, yet already she was rising, slinging her purse over her shoulder, hearing her own voice recount the meeting to Ratha: I'm so relieved—the counselor said she's fine.

But then it happened a third time, and a fourth, and that last time Miriam stood outside Love's pharmacy, shook Eva by the shoulders and lost control. "Stop it!" she found herself yelling, and because it was New York, people glanced their way but no one intervened. "Don't you hear me, Eva? Are you trying to ruin our lives? They take away children who act like this! Didn't you hear that man? Weren't you listening? He said next time it's Juvenile Court!"

She screamed, not to teach Eva a lesson but because she couldn't help it. Because how could Eva sabotage all her hard work, all those years of keeping food in the fridge, clothes on their backs, and more—books and bedtime stories, trips to the Bronx Zoo, the herb garden on the windowsill, the glow-in-the-dark galaxy she had stuck star by star on the ceiling at a time when she'd barely had the energy to brush her own teeth? And under her rage, an unspeakable, nearly unthinkable fear. Because what if this was only the beginning, the snag in the stocking that leads to the run, the computer virus (it had happened in the law firm where she worked) that becomes visible too late? Eva still just a baby, only here she was, turning twelve in a year.

That night, after they went round and round again and Eva stormed off to her room, Miriam sat up at the kitchen table and tried to talk to her own mother: What do I do, please tell me what to do? Her mother, who had died of cancer when Miriam was twenty-two, but even now, without even trying, Miriam could call up a picture of her hands taking out a splinter, her eyes so dark brown they looked black, her level, knowing voice. *Too much*, she could hear her mother say, as Eva's sobs in the bedroom went on and on. *You need to start over, take her someplace better, someplace new—it's crazy how you live.*

Miriam tried to imagine a safe, clean, quiet, uncrazy place. On a mountain? By the ocean? In the desert where there was nothing for Eva to steal? Tucson? Boulder? Cincinnati? Her mother's sister Doris lived there; so did two cousins Miriam hadn't seen since her mother's funeral, fourteen years ago by now. Once a year, Aunt Doris came to New York, took Eva and Miriam out to dinner, gave them a check for six hundred dollars and suggested that Miriam join a temple—for community, for spirituality, to (I won't beat around the bush with you, sweetheart) meet men. Not Cincinnati. Maybe Portland, Maine, or Martha's Vineyard, or Chapel Hill, North Carolina, where her college friend Sarah had moved to practice medicine. Sarah had a custom-built house, a doctor husband, three-year-old twins who were already (or so the last card had claimed) speaking French. What would Miriam do, rent a space over her garage? *My old friend Miriam just showed up here. She's not exactly a self-starter and she's had a string of bad luck. We go back a long way; I felt obliged to take her in.*

As she sat, she heard Eva's sobs grow softer, turn to hiccups, stop. She waited a few minutes before she went into the room. Eva was curled over herself, her bottom in the air, the way she always started out in sleep, though Miriam kept expecting her to outgrow it. The covers were tangled at the foot of her bed. Her hands were fisted at her sides, gripping a treasure (stolen?) that Miriam couldn't see. Or maybe she was holding nothing at all, cupping the invisible with all her might. For a moment, Miriam stood watching her, then covered her with a quilt.

They would leave. The apartment, the city, maybe the state. She decided in a manner utterly unfamiliar to her, in ten brief minutes while her dead mother spoke to her and her daughter slept. Other people, she knew, did things like this, made decisions that changed their lives. If other people did it, so could she. She would take Eva somewhere with clean water and actual, visible stars, a place (if there were such a place for them) where a child's body loosened and unfurled at night, abandoning itself to sleep.

The next day she bought an atlas, and a magazine listing America's One Hundred Most Livable Communities. With Eva at her side, she read. Madison and Bloomington, Atlanta and Kansas City—good schools and good bike paths, good food, affordable housing, fountains and farmers' markets, low crime, high SAT scores. Safe safe safe. Sitting there on the floor with Eva, she pictured Francis shaking his head: Mim, it's a *magazine*, what do you expect to find there but middle-of-the-road America? Next to her, Eva scrolled through the atlas, excited, suddenly, though later she would resist the move with all her might. Idaho, she called out. Colorado. Silver Springs—that sounds pretty, huh? Watery places, she was drawn to: Grand Rapids, Salt Lake City, Great Falls.

When Eva got to New York State and called out the Finger Lakes, Miriam remembered that she had visited a friend at college in Ithaca, New York, walking from the university to the town below down a long, winding path alongside a gorge. It had seemed to her a faraway, exotic place, the university perched high on a hill, its lawns immense, its buildings columned, ivied—a private school for the rich or very smart. Her friend, lonely and unhappy there, had tried to convince her to apply as a transfer student. They have scholarships, she told Miriam. I got one—you could, too. Miriam had said no, she liked Queens College just fine. She was a city person, she'd go nuts in all that green. She hadn't mentioned her mother starting chemo, wearing a wig, making the best of it: Look at me, sweetie, like a *Hasid*—I think it suits me, don't you? Even leaving for that weekend had felt like a guilty pleasure, though her mother had commanded her to go.

Had she liked it there? She couldn't quite remember. The town had been filled with hilly streets, students carrying backpacks, clapboard houses with cupolas and porches. Anyway, the name was nice—the Finger Lakes, like a hand that might beckon them, a place that might hold them, and it wouldn't mean leaving everything all at once, still the same state, not so far away. Let me see, she had said to Eva, lifting the atlas into her own lap. The lakes were long and thin, scars left by glaciers pushing their determined way across the land. The towns were, well, everywhere, and how did you tell one town from another, and could she find a job with a salary they could live on, and would she really do this, just pick up and leave? In the end, she had decided to take a few days off from work and go out there in the spirit of a vacation, for a look. Eva's school year had just ended and the bus tickets were cheap. And just as it had been Eva who found the Finger Lakes on the map, it was Eva who saw the flyer on the bulletin board in the health food store: FURNISHED COUNTRY FARMHOUSE FOR RENT, $500. No picture, no description, just the bare facts punched out on an old typewriter, the O's not open in the middle, but dark, filled holes.

It turned out that the daughter of the people who had owned the farmhouse was renting it out because her parents had died. She met Miriam and Eva in front of the bus station and drove them in her spotless Pontiac—out into the country, first on tar roads, then on dirt, through green and rolling countryside like something in a postcard, sheep and cows nibbling the hills. I'm Kate, she told them in the car, and offered them each a licorice stick.

"Look Ma, horses!" Eva said on the way, a regular kid again.

Let's not get our hopes up, Miriam wanted to tell her. It'll probably be a dump and look nothing like what we've imagined. But then the car turned down a long, dirt drive, and they curved past an orchard and a rough shed, and there was the house, like some odder yet truer version of her image of it—steep-roofed and painted blue, its wide front porch as big as their living room in the city.

Inside, the house was sparsely furnished with cheap, wood veneer furniture and smelled slightly musty, and she felt a first flicker of disappointment. Where were the patchwork quilts, the kitten licking milk from a bowl, the hand-carved rocking chair? On the kitchen wall, instead, hung a shellacked plaque covered with a yellowed photograph of seagulls and a saying printed in slanted calligraphy: *Hold fast to dreams, for if dreams die, life is a broken-winged bird that cannot fly*. And there were other things wrong: the cigarette burns on the counter, the dingy mustard-colored flowers on the linoleum, the flypaper hanging, pocked with insects, from a nail. But the table was made of old tin and scrubbed a clean, bright yellow, and the kitchen windows looked out onto a leafy world.

"It's kind of bare," Kate apologized as they followed her through the rooms. "My son just got married and they needed furniture to set up house in Albany, and then we got rid of a lot of junk and had the place professionally cleaned. It's a good old house." She patted the wall. "My inheritance, with my brothers. I grew up here. My brothers wanted to sell it straight away but I said let's wait a little, maybe one of the kids'll decide to move back. I guess we should have left more inside it. Would you be bringing your things?"

"Some things, I guess," Miriam told her. "Our place in New York is a closet compared to this. We don't have that much."

"You have family out here?"

Miriam shook her head.

"Are you coming for a job?"

"For me," Eva tilted her head and gave Kate a wide smile. "I want to learn how to ride so we're moving to the country."

"No kidding. Is that right?"

"I'm going to be a jockey. If I stay short enough."

Kate laughed. "You've got a pretty nice mom, huh, to move like that just for you."

"It'll be good for her, too," Eva said. "The city's really bad. My friend Stacey got mugged last week, on Tenth Street, she was coming out of—"

"I think," Miriam broke in, "that we'd like to take it, if you'll have us. We could come in early July, as soon as I . . . I just need to work out a few details. I might be able to write a check right now, depending on how much—"

Eva glared at her. Kate hesitated, wanting, or so it seemed to Miriam, to ask more questions: Is there a father, do you have a job, can you make the rent each month? But there they were, standing side by side, this mother and daughter from the city, something (Miriam felt it as a warmth, a pressure) lighting their eyes from behind. Miriam put her arm around Eva: *Ask me no questions, I'll tell you no lies.* Kate stared at them for a moment, and then she must have decided they were all right, because she nodded and said yes.

No security deposit, no finder's fee, no last month's rent, not even a lease. A signed check passed from hand to hand. And so their lives began to change.

As they took the bus back to the city that night, Miriam grew more and more excited, Eva less and less. But what about my friends, she kept asking. Where will I go to school? Are there other kids? What'll I *do* in the country?

"You can ride, like you said," Miriam told her. "You can train for your career as a jockey and then eventually we'll move to Kentucky for the derby."

"No really, what'll I do?"

"You'll . . . you'll make new friends and breathe in the fresh air. I'll find you a summer camp. Once I get a job and save a little, you can take dance lessons like you've always wanted to, or riding. It'll be so much cheaper there. And you'll learn about new things."

"Like what?"

"Like, I don't know, all about living in the country and the names of things in nature and on farms."

Francis had known such things, from books he'd read and the summer camp he'd gone to as a child, and because he had that sort of mind. It had always impressed Miriam, that he could turn to trees in the park and know not only the obvious ones, but the others, too.

"What if we hate it there?" Eva asked as they neared the city.

"We won't."

"Are you sure?"

"I'm sure."

But though her head was filled with images of haylofts and horses, really she was anything but sure. How do I raise you, she would have liked to ask Eva. How do I make you safe and healthy and keep you from stealing from stores? A life, Miriam knew, could go either way: climb steadily toward its better possibilities or spiral down. As Eva's mother, it was up to her, and her jaw and shoulders were tight with the burden of the responsibility. She wanted (but how? She remembered Francis scoffing at what he called the Geographic Cure) to weed her daughter's brain, to take out the choked, unhappy parts and let the good parts grow.

The bus was making its way down the interstate, past the immense concrete apartment buildings of Co-op City; inside one of them, Miriam's Grandma Rose had lived. She remembered getting lost one day when her grandmother sent her out for milk, losing her bearings because all the buildings looked the same. She had stood on the pavement with her head flung back, her neck growing stiff as she tried to tell one looming, blocky building from the next. Inside one of those high rises, she had known, behind one of those windows, sat her gentle Grandma Rose among all that was familiar—the card table painted with roses, the Shabbat candlesticks, the velvety green couch, the pictures of Miriam's mother and her sister Doris as dark, solemn-looking girls. Had somebody helped her find her grandmother? Had she asked for help? Even then, she had wanted to do things silently and well. Somehow she had made her way back that day, but she couldn't remember how.

Eva leaned her head against the window and let out a tired little moan.

"You want to rest your head on me?" Miriam asked, but tentatively; she never knew, these days, when Eva would turn on her or jerk away. This time, though, Eva snuggled down.

"We're almost home," said Miriam, and tried to think of home as someplace new. They would get a local map and find the school, the supermarket, the hospital. She would buy a cheap used car and get her driver's license. She felt a tightness in her chest, a narrowing of her throat; for years she had made it her main project to keep change at bay. But then she remembered herself at nineteen, how she had used a portion of her waitressing earnings to go to Mexico with a friend. She had danced through the Day of the Dead, lost her virginity with a tour guide, lied to her mother by telling her that she was on a project to build houses for the poor. And stolen something; the memory arrived unbidden. A matchbox covered with pictures of the Virgin Mary, and inside, two tiny dolls, a grain of corn, a metal horseshoe the size of her thumbnail. She had seen it in the market in Oaxaca and it wasn't as if she didn't have the money—she had *wanted* to steal it, had liked the thought of the Jewish girl making off with the Christian charm, and the way nobody knew her there so she could, for a moment, be anybody at all. She had slipped it in the waistband of her skirt where it might (though she didn't believe in such things) bring her luck.

When she was twenty-four, she met Francis, who had grown up in an apartment filled with images of Christ. She *stole* him—the phrase came to her as she sat on the bus. But stole him from what? How quickly they had gone forward (it didn't seem like you, Sarah would tell her later)—the moving in, the getting pregnant, the city courthouse wedding after she started to show. She didn't want to go back to that kind of suddenness—the thought made her seize up—but this move was something in between, a loosening, an adventure, and, more than anything, good for Eva. And for yourself, too, she could hear her mother saying. Her Self. She tried not to pay it much attention. She would need to sublet the New York apartment and find a job; there had to be paralegal positions in Ithaca. And enroll Eva in school, and pack their stuff, and take driving lessons, and find a car they could afford.

Eva stirred and opened her eyes, her face lit by neon and streetlamps as they moved through the city and night fell. Miriam smoothed her forehead, drinking her in.

"I dreamed I really was a jockey," Eva said, yawning.

"You did? Was it fun? Were you good?"

She shook her head. "The horse was huge. I fell off after just a couple seconds and it stomped on me."

Miriam stiffened. "Oh baby, are you okay?"

Eva frowned. "It was a dream."

"I know, but it sounds like a scary one."

Eva sat up and rubbed her fists over her eyes. "When will we be home?"

"Soon, I hope, but it's rush hour. Do you want some juice?"

"I want—" Eva looked out the window at the blinking lights, "to be home."

3

Someone was stealing his honey. He had no idea how long it had been going on; he didn't keep close track of the stand. But one morning, as Burl turned into his driveway after making a delivery in town, he noticed that the jars were lined up in a neat row like soldiers standing at attention. He pulled over, figuring one of the widows must have come by, bought a jar and done a little housekeeping. He had started helping them with odd jobs after their husbands died, and now they seemed to see him as a fix-up project of their own. But when he went over and shook the cashbox, he found it empty. There were six jars that day (for some reason he counted), with three inches between each jar and their fronts perfectly aligned, the sample jar standing in front of them like their captain.

The next day he walked down the driveway with three more jars—honey from last year's flow, but people knew the season was about to start and would be stopping by. This time he found four jars set apart from one another in two neat pairs, with the sample jar off by itself.

"Looky here, an *artiste*," he said to Lissa, who was sniffing after something in the grass. Two jars sold, he supposed, only when he shook the cash box, he found that it was, once again, empty. "I take it back. Someone took them. Who would do that?"

It wasn't a big deal, only six dollars and each year he gave away pounds of honey anyway. Probably the person had been out of cash and would bring the money by later. At the end of the day, though, he checked again—still nothing. Anyone who knew him would have left a note scrawled on the back of a napkin or old receipt—Hi B. IOU 6. No, this visitor had fiddled around with his jars, then taken two.

That night, as he lay bored and hot in bed, he began, like Lissa with a good bone, to gnaw. It wasn't just a few missing jars that were the trouble; it was the state of things in general. You couldn't sell on an honor system anymore, not even out here. You had to wholesale to the supermarkets, but they'd only buy from Sue Bee, which mixed its honey in giant vats so the color would be the same bland shade in every jar. It was the economy, the pesticides, the land-use laws, yet the confusing thing was that it was nature, too, creatures so small you could barely see them, red specks the size of a pinhead, hairy shells with eight tenacious legs and jaws that could bring down the world.

It was opening up a hive he'd thought might make it through the winter and finding it strewn like a war zone, dead bees everywhere, the green honey uncapped, bee carcasses drying out. Aristotle had placed bees higher than humans on a scale, believing that in bees the laws of nature were expressed far more perfectly and firmly. Burl had pondered that after he read it. Did it mean that the bees' ways were simply starker, less muddied, an engine aimed entirely at the survival of the group? He wasn't sure, knew only that over the years he had found a deep pleasure, even a comfort, in his bees.

He loved watching them in spring, seeing the field bees leave the hive and head into the fields, how they left empty and came back with their bellies full, their rear legs loaded up. He loved walking toward his bees on a July night and picking up the scent of nectar before he reached the hive. Inside, the bees were fanning water from the nectar; if he stood near enough, he could feel a draft play around his feet. He loved the way the pupae were curved like human fetuses, glossy white except for the purple splotches where the eyes would be. And the bees in winter, these especially he loved, picturing how, as his own house stood drafty in the snow, the insects were gathered inside the hives in dense winter clusters, keeping each other warm. For years, now, they had made him honey and more honey, never stopping to notice when he took away a full honey super and replaced it with an empty one. There had always been some mites to deal with, but lately it had gotten so much worse, and he found himself lying awake at night picturing tracheal mites boring invisible holes through his windpipe, and varroa mites sucking his blood.

By day, he did what he could do. Crisco and sugar in the brood chambers for the tracheal mites. It seemed too simple, a home remedy, but it was supposed to disorient them and slow them down. Menthol crystals, he tried those too, and peppermint plants near his hives—a few people in the Beekeepers' Association swore it worked. For the varroas, Apistan Strips between the frames. Terramycin mixed with powdered sugar for the foulbroods. Most of his remedies he administered in two brief, hopeful seasons before and after the honey flow. Once he started drawing honey, he had to let things be, since medicating would contaminate the yield. He mixed and doctored, worried and tended, and still, over the past winter, he had lost eight of his twenty hives.

But if he couldn't save his bees, he could catch a thief. As he went about his chores the day after the honey went missing, he meant to keep an eye on the table but kept getting caught up in other things—his editor calling to say that the compost book illustrator would be faxing him questions, a tear in the wire of the garden fence, a faucet to fix, hives he needed to inspect. The air was humid and cloudy, the sullen weather of July, and he found himself edgy and impatient. "I was thinking maybe next we'd go for *Let Me Show You How to Build a Deck*," his editor said on the phone, and Burl thought, Oh Christ, but said, "Hmmm, that's an idea," and knew he'd have to do it because his savings were running out and you couldn't live on milk and honey.

That evening, he walked through the dusk toward the table. Drawing close, he counted six jars. He'd put out three more earlier in the day; that meant one was gone. He shook the cash box and heard not only the dry, papery sound of dollar bills, but also the clanking of change. Flicking the dials on the padlock, he opened the box. Four dollars—three bills and a dollar's worth of coins. Not the right amount for one jar of honey. His sign said three dollars. Once in a rare while, people left more, feeling, he supposed, that they were getting too big a bargain, or sometimes they had no change and left a five, counting it as credit for next time. Mostly, though, people around here lived by the book: leave three bucks, take a jar. So either this was one person who had overpaid, or else the honey thief had returned, throwing in a jangle of change as partial recompense. The mystery of it all was beginning to please him—a small adventure, a peculiar kind of game. He took the padlock off the box and left the cash inside.

As darkness thickened all around him and the mosquitoes circled near, he stood on the ground he had grown up on every summer, the air, the trees, the table almost as familiar to him, by now, as his own skin. He thought he might sense someone in the background, maybe off among the trees—or was it just his own desire?

He wanted a visitor; he realized it clearly. Someone to talk to, neither dog nor insect. He wondered when Alice would show up again and climb into his bed, when he would undo her braid and draw her to him, hip to hip. Probably not until Thanksgiving, when she'd brace herself to come with Meg and join her family for the meal. Or maybe not at all; one of these days she would start seeing someone again—*really* seeing, she'd explain, the way she had when she'd met Doug. Burl thought, as he often did in moments like this, about getting a job in town, something that would put him more among people. But what about his bees? And what about his book projects, which he complained about but actually enjoyed, how he could make *anything* (his editor knew it), then show the world how to follow in his steps? What about being able to go to the pond in the middle of the day, the deep, filtered solitude of swimming underwater, how much he loved being alone except when he didn't, except when it got to be too much?

Finally the mosquitoes defeated him and he went inside to check his e-mail. A bee question, this time, from a guy he knew in Oneonta, who was just starting out. A joke from his old friend Randy about a genie and a twelve-inch pianist. Nothing from Alice. He answered the bee question, fired off a joke to Randy, and spent the rest of the evening typing up a list of small improvements he hoped to make on his scaled-down, sorry excuse for a farm—the twelve chickens, one rooster and a goose, the cow, orchard and vegetable patch—modest versions of the farm his grandparents had run and which he longed for still, the cows spectral now in the vast barn, slow-turning their heads as a boy walked by.

At least, he often told himself, at least he hadn't sold the land to the developers who were creeping out this way. Instead, he'd spent two-thirds of his inheritance from the Philly side of his family to pay off his cousins for their shares of the place. For a while he had sat around cooking up grand plans—a cooperative farm, sustainable agriculture, or a commercial beekeeping operation, maybe even migratory hives that he'd load into a semitruck and drive across the country, following the bloom. Or an ostrich farm. He liked how odd they looked, somewhere between bird and beast, and they were supposed to be the new, low-fat red meat. Sometimes when he let his thoughts wander far enough, he'd had a farming and business partner who was also a mate. Alice, if he was honest with himself; he'd had Alice.

But Alice had moved to Colorado, gone to medical school, gotten married, had Meg, gotten divorced. Stayed. He had let most of the fields get overrun with cat briar and bittersweet and started only as many hives as he could manage as a serious hobby, on his own. He wrote his *Let Me Show You* books—*Let Me Show You How to Build a Stone Wall; Let Me Show You How to Compost; Let Me Show You How to Teach Your Dog to Laugh at Your Lame Jokes.* So maybe sometimes he got a little bitter, but only now and then. Day by day he was fine here, day by day he had a life, and why should he expect it to unfold like some kind of rosy dream?

4

Eva prayed. In the morning when she woke, at night before she went to sleep. Lying in bed, her hands clasped under her chin like she'd seen in pictures, she prayed to the Jesus on the wall, who was skinny and the color of old silverware, his body pinned to a brown cross. She didn't speak out loud. At night she was afraid her mother would hear her, and in the morning her voice rang too loud in the empty house. She prayed for the obvious things—that they would move back to New York, that Charu would answer her letter, that she and her mother would stop fighting and go back to how they were before.

But she also confessed. She knew how it worked, sort of, re-membered it from long ago, when her grandmother, her father's mother, would come babysit and sneak her away to a giant church. She remembered a smell like smoke and cinnamon, re-membered a wooden house like a playhouse inside the church, how her grandmother would tell her to wait outside. There was a father in there; you told him how you'd been bad and he forgave you. Each time they went, Eva hoped she would be allowed in so she could see this father and hear how her grandmother had been bad. Instead, she sat waiting outside the little house, watching the stooped shoulders and shuffling walks of the old ladies and wishing she could go outside. After her grandmother came out, they always kneeled together on a low bench and prayed.

Pray to the father, her grandmother used to tell her, or was it *pray for your father*, or was it both? Kneeling on the velvet bench, Eva would try to call up the faces of her own father and the fathers of her friends, but the praying always made her feel queasy, though she couldn't say why. Her grandmother told her that the church should be their secret, and each time, as they rode home on the bus, she snapped open her purse and gave Eva a soft dollar bill.

After Eva's father died when she was six, her grandmother almost never came to see her anymore, sending cards on her birthday instead, and checks, which Miriam put into a college fund, and pictures of saints and Jesus Christ. A few years later, Eva found another church to visit, right on her block. The Cathedral of the Holy Virgin Protection, it was called, and all you had to do was march up the stone steps, ring the bell and wait. After a while, Dimitri would come to the door, his eyes watery as if he had been sleeping. He never asked what she was doing there, or where her mother was. He let her in. The first day she rang, he showed her a big room like the one in the other church, except here there were no chairs or benches, just candles struggling to stay lit. She touched the cold side of a stone tub, wrote her name in the fur of a velvet curtain, looked up at a big cross with a skull carved into its base, and below it, letters in a language she couldn't read.

He took her downstairs, then, to where everything was old and dirty and cats ran wild, their turds littering the halls. Pushing aside a sheet hanging from the ceiling, he led her to where he did his work, which was to paint pictures of saints with stiff clothing, long fingers and sad eyes with no eyelashes. After that, she would come back sometimes and watch him paint, or he'd let her help mix the colors. Maybe add some eyelashes, she suggested once. Maybe make him wink.

She never told her mother; it was another of her secrets. She knew Miriam wouldn't like her being there, not with a strange man, not in the basement of a church. Eva asked Dimitri nothing about his life, and he asked her nothing about hers. One day he cupped her chin in his hands, searched her eyes and told her she could give up the burden of her pain to Jesus. She backed away, then. I'm Jewish, she thought but didn't say. After that she didn't go see him for a few weeks. When finally she rang the bell again, he let her in and spoke only of colors and cats.

But now, in her empty room with its brown cross and no one to tell her what to do, Eva found she had plenty to say to Jesus— sins to tell him, but also explanations. Her mother asked *why, Eva, why?*, but Eva couldn't explain the taut, swollen feeling that came over her, how she found herself needing to take something not for what it was, exactly, but for what it might prevent, visions she couldn't stop—her mother shoved by a crowd onto the sub-way tracks, her mother's bones poking through her skin, a truck heading for her mother on the street. She couldn't tell Miriam about such things, but Jesus was already dead so nothing could surprise him now.

She told him how she'd be standing in front of something—a roll of ribbon, a paperweight, a bracelet—and before she could stop it, the thought would arrive and she'd fall into it, through it, and the only way to stop the falling was to close her fingers around the hard, real surface of the thing. The objects she took were always different, but the thought was always more or less the same: her mother hurt, her mother dead, her mother hurt and dead. Somehow, taking the thing could kill the thought, and there was the real world again, crisp and clear; there was Eva— a girl with a mother, a girl—even better—who had saved her mother's life.

Jesus hung there day after day, never speaking. Was it because he knew she was half Jewish, or because he, like Santa or the tooth fairy, was only a superstition? After her father died, they had stopped celebrating Christmas but they still lit Hanukkah candles, *baruch atah Adonai*—Eva knew the words but not what they meant. Every Hanukkah now, as they stood over the faded candles, Eva wished for a Christmas with brothers and sisters, red-nosed reindeer, heaps of presents, leaping elves and blinking lights. The Christians had Jesus, Mary, Santa, so many *people*, but the Jews, as far as she could tell, were like Eva and her mother, only children, with just a few songs, just a wooden top to spin, and her mother never remembered what the letters meant.

In New York, Eva had banged on the floor to Charu each evening, stomping twice and waiting for an answer—tap-tap. Good night. Now, in her new room, she spoke to Jesus, going so far as to stand on her bed and kiss the wall beneath his feet. She knew she needed rituals, knew, too, that her mother wouldn't like what she was doing. Look, she sometimes imagined saying to Miriam, whose face would stiffen at the sight of Eva talking to the cross. Together, Jesus and Eva might cast a spell over her mother. "Our Father," they would chant, and they'd remind Miriam of how there was a saint named Francis. Eva had a little card of him, Saint Francis of Assisi, his hands and shoulders covered with birds. Made brave by Jesus, Eva would push. *Is he in heaven, my father?* You know I don't believe in that, Miriam would say. *But is he?* Her mother would get mean, then, sharp and short. What is it with you, Eva? Do you really have to ask the same thing a thousand times?

Days, now, she rode her bike. Her mother liked this. Look how strong and brown you're getting, she kept saying, and Eva rolled her eyes or shrugged. Mostly she rode because there was no one to play with and the TV still didn't work in the blue house. Mrs. Flynn said they needed to call the cable people but Eva's mother wouldn't do it. In the olden days, she said, people read books and talked and went outside, instead of staring at the tube. But Eva *did* read, and she would have talked if there'd been anyone to talk to, just like (she almost said it aloud) the fucking olden days. She missed sitting with Charu and Ratha watching the talk shows, which were always full of long-lost people shrieking *ohmygod* when they came on stage. Sometimes Charu and Eva did it, too, hugging and jumping up and down in front of the TV—*ohmygodohmygod I can't believe it's you!*—until Ratha told them to be quiet or they'd wake the baby up.

Now Eva rode her bike because she couldn't stand to sit in the house and listen to Mrs. Flynn sigh or snore or wonder what was happening on her soap, and because she knew there had to be kids somewhere and she might run into them. She rode, too, so she could see the honey and hives, which she had come to think of as her own private project. She thought of it as going to work— got to go arrange the bottles, check on my bees—the way she and Charu had played store, forcing Charu's little brothers to be the customers. The place was always a mess, the jars out of order, the table covered with leaves, sticks and bugs. Eva lined up the bottles in patterns and wiped their glass clean on her shirt.

And what of it if, one morning, the panic closed round her, making her fingers reach, and she took a few bottles, wedged them inside the metal rack on her bike and fled? Back home, she wheeled her bike into the shed, put the honey in her helmet, held the helmet against her stomach and went inside, slipping right past Mrs. Flynn up to her room. There she hid the honey in the far corner of her closet, inside the sleeves of a purple sweatshirt she had suddenly outgrown. She didn't return the next day, or the next. She sat inside and got Mrs. Flynn to make her chocolate chip cookies, which she ate until she thought she would be sick.

Three days after she stole the honey, Eva had nearly forgotten what she'd done. She had that sort of memory; some things stayed with her forever, others sailed right through her mind. So when she started riding the old route again, it wasn't to go drop six dollars through the slot of the blue box or revisit the scene of her crime. She felt happy that day. It was sunny out, finally, and she'd found a letter from Charu in the mailbox—and with it, in a smaller, sealed envelope, a letter from Ratha for her mother (Eva couldn't make out anything, even when she held it to the light). Also, though she would never have admitted it, she did find some pleasure in knowing the roads around their house, in passing things that felt, by now, familiar: a field where a house was being built; a group of cows behind a fence, ELECTRIC, DO NOT TOUCH; a sign that said DEER CROSSING, though she had never seen a deer there and didn't understand how they would know to cross the street at this one place.

So much to do, she thought as she rode, talking to the kids who would help run her shop, which was on Second Street and called BeeWitched and sold honey she got from the hives on her roof. She arrived at the table ready for a mess, only to find that the jars were still in neat pairs just as she had left them, except now there were four more. And something else was different. It was the money box—its lock was gone. Eva picked up the box and listened to the change. She looked up the driveway but saw no one, so she opened the lid and counted. Nine dollar bills, plus coins. Money didn't tempt her, too flimsy and dirty, too ordinary, each bill the same. She closed the box and set it down.

"May I help you?" she asked, moving behind the table and stretching out her hand. "Only the best, I get it from up there." She pointed toward the pine trees. "It'll make your throat feel better. I'm not sure, let me check." She scooped a steaming loaf of bread out of the air. "Five dollars," she said. "It's still warm."

It wasn't until she got near the hives that she sensed somebody watching her. She was standing on the edge of the field observing the thick, shifting flurry of the bees when she felt her body tense and moved reflexively into the cover of the woods. Was it a burglar, come to rob her store? Or something real—a bear, a murderer, a maniac with a gun? She stood unmoving, staring out.

She had on a green shirt and black cutoffs and hoped she blended, like a soldier, with the trees.

Then she smelled smoke. Run, she told herself. The hives, the trees, her hair, everything would burn. Or was she just imagining the smell? She heard a cough, as clear as anything, and saw, coming from behind a hive, a tall, faceless figure emerging from a cloud of smoke. Turning to run, she stumbled on a root and hit the ground hard, landing on her chest.

"Unh," she grunted as her breath left her and the strap of her helmet bit into her chin.

"Hello?" she heard a voice call.

She lay gasping for air, not moving, but the voice found her anyway; she heard its footsteps coming close. She would just lie there, that was what she'd do. She'd shut her eyes and eventually the man with no face would go away.

"Are you hurt?" the voice asked. "That was quite a fall."

Slowly, she turned, expecting to see a face without features, a vision from a dream. But standing above her, holding back a branch, was a tall, freckled man with a red beard and a regular face. She sat up and adjusted her helmet.

"Are you all right?" he asked.

Eva nodded. He reached out a hand, but she got up herself, brushing dirt and pine needles from her knees. The man was staring down at her.

"I wasn't expecting guests," he said, "or I'd have set up a tea party."

"That's okay," she mumbled.

"I don't think I know you. Where're you from?" he asked.

She had an urge to say *I fell down a rabbit hole* and see if he got it. "New York," she said softly, then added "City" in a louder voice, which for some reason made him laugh.

"Yeah?" He was whispering now, too. "Did you get off at the wrong subway stop?"

Eva shook her head, irritated, and looked down at her leg. Inside, it was throbbing; outside it looked like it always had.

"I hope you didn't twist your ankle," the man said, sounding nicer. "Try walking, just one small step, to put some weight on it."

Eva stepped forward and felt, almost to her dismay, no pain. "I'm all right."

"Good. So you're . . . you're from New York City? Are you visiting relatives?"

"I came with my mother."

"To see the Finger Lakes? Is your mother—" He looked around, "here, too?"

Strange man, stranger, have a candy, little girl. "She's right down the road," she told him. "We were bike riding. She has a new job here, but today she didn't have to go. I think it's—I forget exactly—it's some kind of day off at her work."

The man looked around. "Really? Not out here. The bees never take a day off. What's your mother do?"

"She's a paralegal."

"Oh." He nodded. "We need those. The bees are known for being litigious."

Cut it out, Eva felt like saying. Stop using big words and talking like everything is a joke only you get. She would go, just turn and leave, except what if this man had a daughter, the one she'd been imagining for days? "Do you have any kids?" she asked and saw how he looked surprised that it was she, suddenly, who was questioning him.

"Kids?" he said. "No. When I was around your age I had a couple of goat kids that I took care of. Do you?"

"Me?" She scowled. "I'm not old enough."

"I meant goat, not human kids, but I guess you wouldn't, not in the city. Some people in New York have carrier pigeons. Did you ever see that? They keep them in hutches on the roof."

"No," she said and turned to go, but not before she asked him over her shoulder, "but do you have other pets, I mean, like now?"

"I have a dog, Lissa. I think she's off hunting mice. And a cow, some chickens, an old goose. And the bees, of course."

He started walking and she followed him, staying a few steps behind until they were out of the woods and standing in the field. Eva looked toward the hives and saw, coming from one of them, a trail of smoke.

"That's on fire!" she said. "I knew I smelled something—"

He nodded. "It's my smoker. The smoke calms down the bees."

Eva squinted. "Really? Why?"

"The theory is that they think their house is on fire, so they fill up with honey so they'll have enough energy while they're away from home, and then they're so full that it's hard for them to bend into a stinging position." He rubbed his beard. "I think of it as the 'lazy glutton' theory. Anyway, I'm probably boring you—you know all this already, right?"

Suddenly Eva could see where this was going. He knew she had taken his honey; he would set her on fire or let his bees kill her with their stings. "I've got to go," she told him.

"Yes," he said. "Your mother's probably wondering where you are."

He put on the hat he'd been carrying, pulled a pale yellow net down to cover his face, and slid his hands into a pair of gloves that he retrieved from somewhere in the grass. Still she stood there, her helmet on her head. Still she didn't leave. Maybe he wasn't a man without a face after all, just a man in a funny hat.

"What are you going to do?" she asked.

"I'm giving them medicine. I was in the middle of it when—"

"Are they sick?"

He nodded, his face barely visible beneath the gauzy fabric. She felt better, somehow, now that she couldn't see his eyes.

"Some of them are sick," he said, "and others might get sick if I'm not careful."

"Does it taste bad?"

"No. Sometimes I give them worse stuff, but not at this time of year. This tastes sweet, like candy." He paused. "Or honey."

She could feel him looking at her. She dropped her gaze and looked away.

"I'm going over to that open hive," he said, "and it's not the high point of the bees' day, so if you're planning to stick around, you'll need to go way over by that bush and definitely not come toward me *at all*. They don't like dark clothing, and they don't like people who aren't used to them. You don't want to get stung."

She nodded, thinking, But they do know me. I visit them. She went to the bush and stood watching while he walked over to a short stack of boxes, puffed more smoke into the air, and started spooning something out of a bowl and putting it inside. From where she stood, she could see specks rising, landing on the net over his face, covering the sides of the hive. The bees' sound, too, reached her, a drawn-out, rising whine. The man had on pants and a long-sleeved shirt, but maybe bees couldn't sting through clothes, or maybe they liked him since he took care of them.

He set down the smoker and started putting boxes on top of one another until the stack was the same height as the others. Surrounded by a haze of smoke and bees, he looked shimmery and out of focus, about to melt. Finally, he gestured for her to follow him and walked away from the hives and over to the edge of the field, disappearing through the pine trees near the road.

Eva could, she knew, go running past him, get on her bike and go home. That was what her mother would want: a strange man, dangerous, blah-blah. But he didn't actually *seem* dangerous, just strange, and for days she'd been waiting to cross paths with anyone at all. And if he knew she'd stolen the honey? How could he prove it? And if he'd seen her do it? I've been watching the store, she could say. I was keeping it nice. Anyway, I was going to pay you back.

She went through the field and the trees, past the table, up the driveway. By the time she caught up, he had taken off his hat and gloves.

"Do you want to see something?" he asked, so Eva followed

him behind the house to another beehive, this one shorter than the hives in the field. This time, he didn't put on his hat or fill the air with smoke. This time, he simply lifted the lid and Eva felt no fear, almost as if she knew beforehand that nothing would rise up from inside.

The man pointed. Eva leaned. The hive was smeared with something brown and dark, like burned, syrupy clumps of popcorn. She took a step back: It was bees, hundreds and hundreds of them, and then she looked down and realized that the ground in front of the hive was also covered with bees, and that the crispy sound she had been hearing was the noise of them crunching underfoot.

They were dead, all of them. She had never seen so many dead things in one place. She didn't know what to make of it, knew only that it made her want to weep and that she'd never show it. She looked up, keeping her eyes steady. Why was he making her look at this? She had wanted to see bees making honey; instead he had brought her here.

"The whole hive got wiped out," he said. "They work and work—each of them makes only a teaspoon of honey in her life— but these ones got sick and didn't even get the chance. A teaspoon of honey for a whole life's work. What do you think of that?"

Then she knew he knew. She shook her head.

"In summer," he said, "I don't think they even sleep."

"I'm sorry," said Eva softly, and when he looked confused, she added, "I mean that they're sick. That they died."

"Thank you. Me, too."

"I've got to go," she said again, her voice too close to tears.

"Okay. Nice meeting you," said the man. "By the way, I'm Burl."

"Hi." She tightened the strap on her bike helmet.

He smiled a little. "Hi. So do you have a name, or are you a nameless fairy of the woods?"

"A fairy."

"I thought so. Your bike is by the table, right? There should be eight jars there, doing some kind of crazy line dance, plus a sample jar. If anything seems out of the ordinary, would you let me know?"

And then Eva was running, feeling him watching her, laughing at her maybe, and she didn't stop to count the jars, just picked up her bike and was off, pedaling through the heat. As she rode, she pictured the bees all around her, the ones who hadn't died. They were swarming after her, hovering in front of her, calling *a teaspoon*, calling *thief*! "I'm sorry," she told them, her voice lost among the buzzing. "I'm sorry," Eva said again. "I didn't know."

5

Once upon a time, Miriam had been a woman who loved touch. That was how she thought about it now—once upon a time, back then, over there, in another life that opened up in front of her like a house in a dream, filled with endless, surprising doorways, room after room: job, lover, food, drink, conversation, sleep, pregnancy, marriage, baby. It had all seemed remarkably easy, effortless almost, at first. Happiness had resided for her, in those days, in the trailing of fingers—first the lengths of Francis's body, his fingers coaxing her, then Eva with her early infant hungers, her hands grasping, her mouth rooting for milk, her folds which Miriam powdered and kept clean.

Who would have predicted that she would like it all so much? Before them, she hadn't thought she was that sort of person. She had liked aloneness, a good book, her desk drawers ordered, her desires never gaping, more like twinges or slow leaks. With her mother cheering her on, she had concentrated on her studies.

Education, not a man, is the surest path in life, her schoolteacher mother had said, and Miriam had nodded and wondered if her mother thought she wasn't pretty enough to find a man. For the first few years of college, she had done well and planned to apply to law school. The order and logic of the law appealed to her, but more than that, she knew it would make her mother proud. Every once in a while, a less familiar part of her surfaced—on her trip to Mexico, or smoking pot with college friends, or dancing at a summer block party, her hips swishing, her head flung back, a hunger rising up in her for—what? Skin, maybe, or was it distances, the world rushing by to sweep her up. Mostly, though, she was working hard, planning for a future that was sane and safe. What she hadn't planned on was her mother's death, was her own slow tumble into a grief that somehow felt anything but new. The year her mother got sick, her grades took a dive, and by the time her mother died, none of it seemed to mean much anymore—ambition, striving, law school, planning a life. Something lay down inside her, all muscles gone slack.

After college, she found an apartment uptown with Sarah and got a job as a paralegal—just for now, she told herself, but already the future wasn't something she was reaching for, not like Sarah, who was already in medical school, bent late over anatomy books with her new boyfriend, their bodies awake with multiple kinds of desire. Miriam went to work, came home, cooked dinner, often, for Sarah and her boyfriend. She took care of the household finances, visited her mother's senile great-aunt Lily at her nursing home in Queens, rented old movies, and went on the occasional uninspired date. Underneath it all, she was waiting for something—a sea change, a signal. Even farther underneath, she was coiled with a sharp, childlike anger. Because how could they have—her father abandoning her for Israel when she was ten, her mother dying—when all she had done, all she had really ever done, was be a good girl?

Then she met Francis. They had met one day in the pottery store. . . .

But how to tell their story—to herself, to Eva? Miriam tried to keep it clear and accurate, but often, over the years, she found herself embellishing a little, brightening the colors. Or worse, she found herself forgetting. Had he been wearing green the day they met? Had it been raining out, or snowing? *Raining*, Eva would remind her. *Right, Mom? It was raining and you went into the store to look at a sugar bowl and you were all wet and he gave you a cup of tea.* They had met in his parents' store uptown, yes, among jars of gourmet olive oil, strings of garlic, rows of Italian pottery— mugs and plates hand-painted with birds and leaves, pitchers shaped like fish and roosters with gaping mouths. In those days, Miriam occasionally bought inexpensive presents for herself; she had seen a sugar bowl in the window, its colors so bright she thought they might cheer her up. She was drenched, her hair plastered to her head. She had a perfectly serviceable sugar bowl at home, her mother's, and this one was ridiculously overpriced. She picked it up, turned it over. Put it down. Picked it up.

From the back of the tiny store, somebody spoke, but she couldn't make out the words. She turned toward the man behind the counter. "Excuse me?"

"Go away," he answered.

Miriam's laugh came out high and nervous. "I'm sorry—are you closed?"

"No, no." His laughter creased the corners of his eyes. "Rain rain, go away, not you. I'm working black magic with my chants."

A few minutes later, as she leaned over another piece of pottery, he appeared at her side with a mug of tea. "Here. For insulting you by mistake."

Taking the cup from him, she had registered his long fingers, the springy black curls on his head, his mouth, which played on the edge of a smile. "Oh," she said. "Thanks, you didn't have—"

But already he was gone, back behind the counter, bent over a newspaper. She hadn't bought the sugar bowl that day. Too expensive, she thought, but the next week on her lunch break she went back to look at it again. To look at him again, for already (how fast the mind, how fast the heart moves, knowing nothing at all), she had held him in the arms of her thoughts; they had filled the sugar bowl; she had tasted the salt of his skin, so different from the salt of her own boring, daily tears, from the slow-seeping grief that she couldn't seem to stem, eighteen months gone by, already, since her mother's death.

She went back, sure he wouldn't remember her, but he did, and they chatted—his parents' export business; the town called Deruta where the ceramics were made. Was he from Italy? His parents were. His gaze on her, taking her in, her own eyes suddenly self-conscious, dropping down. Was she Italian, too? No. He gave her more tea and it might have seemed, on the surface, as if he were wooing her, but Miriam knew, looking back, that it was not so; *she* had returned there—so unlike her—and placed herself in his path.

She stayed for nearly an hour, watching as he unpacked pottery from clear green bubble paper, wiped it with a flannel rag and placed each piece carefully on the shelf. He showed her a mug with a yellow, blowing serpent on its side—the wind, he said— and replicas of sixteenth-century pharmacy and spice jars marked *salvia, timo, lauro, malva.* He showed her a bowl painted with pomegranates—*melagrana*—an Italian symbol of friendship, the fruit split to show its blood red seeds. As her lunch break reached its end, she felt words climbing up her throat and so she asked him: Coffee, sometime, maybe? I mean, to repay . . . since you . . .

He looked surprised but not displeased. "Oh," he said. "Sure, let's—umm, how's Thursday for you?"

"Thursday? Okay, great, at . . . ?"

"I don't get off until seven. We could get a bite to eat."

Dinner. She asked him for coffee, he turned it into dinner. At the time, walking back to the office trying not to smile, she thought she was drawn by the gentleness of his hands unpacking pottery, by the tea he made for her. Later she would wonder. Go *away.* His first words to her. Or no, she was wrong. His first words were so soft she couldn't hear them: *Rain rain.*

And then?

Then, I don't know, I guess we started to do things together sometimes. We'd go to the movies, or we'd take walks in the park, and I was surprised because he'd grown up in the city but he knew the names of all the trees and birds.

And he took you to the zoo.

Right, he took me to the Central Park Zoo where we saw monkeys and deer, and as we were leaving, we saw a woman outside who was all dressed in fur and sitting under a bush in the cold, and he knelt right down and spoke to her, and I saw how kind he was.

How kind and (this part of the story not for Eva, not even for herself, except in her most limp, unguarded moment, after a glass of wine, or as the Ativan spirited her to sleep) how *compelled,* kneeling by this woman who looked almost like an animal, her hair matted, her skin filthy, her old fur coat covered with dead leaves. He gave her five dollars. Are you hanging in there, Molly, he asked, and she nodded yes. Then Francis pet her; that was the strangest part. He reached out his hand and stroked her arm as if she were an animal in the petting zoo, or as if she were a friend, or a lover. Miriam had watched his long fingers stroking and felt her own skin sing, surprising her, and the woman in fur was talking gibberish, a long stream of unconnected words, but Francis nodded as if he understood.

"Who is she?" Miriam had asked when they were out of earshot.

"Molly. She lives in the park. I see her on my walks."

"What's wrong with her?"

Francis shrugged. "She thinks the squirrels are her children."

"Does she have a doctor? Does she get help?"

"She's all right, I think. She manages."

"But what does she eat? Is there a shelter where she sleeps?"

"She sleeps inside a tree, snuggled with her little gray babies," he said, and then he put his arm around Miriam's shoulder, his cold knuckles grazing her cheek. Snuggled with her little gray babies. She had loved how he said it, the words surprising coming from a man, even as she'd known they weren't true.

And then?

You know, Eva. I've told you before. We spent some more time together and we . . . well, I guess you could say we fell in love.

That afternoon, they went back to his apartment in the East Village and made love for the first time. He unbuttoned her shirt, unwrapped her, opened her, this man she had met in a shop two weeks before. He told her she was pretty and she thought no I'm not, but later she caught a glimpse of her flushed skin, tousled hair, bright eyes in the bathroom mirror and thought he might be right. Who are you, she had wondered about him, because he wasn't like anyone she'd ever known, hardly asked her anything about her job, her family, didn't seem to care who she was except as she breathed against his chest, except as she existed, another human being, in his arms. Miriam had been used to answering questions—what do you do, how do you like it? Such moments always made her panic, convinced, before she opened her mouth, that she would disappoint. Sometimes she had slept with the few men she'd dated, but her mind had always hung far above her body, quizzical and alert.

The studio apartment where Francis lived was dark and cluttered, the blinds half drawn, a mattress on the floor, books in piles everywhere. In one corner was an easel; in another, an electric keyboard. She had expected, somehow, an apartment like the store, filled with braids of garlic and jars of olives, painted pottery and yellow stucco walls. This was more like a burrow—flickering tongue, blinking eye, interlocked bone, salt sea. Lying in his arms after (another surprise) she came, she found her face damp and realized that for the first time in months, she was not crying for her mother. For herself, she was crying—for how carefully alone she was, for how badly she wanted to enter the world of the living. Here was a man whose breath she could feel rise and fall, a man who made things, the traces everywhere. A vivid, lively man who seemed to want to touch her wooden self. And here she was, dissolving. Silently, he licked her tears away.

Collect yourself, Miriam remembered thinking. She got up, buttoned and zipped herself into her clothes, parted two slats in the blinds and felt the world as a startling, overbright place. She went home, then, took a shower and scrubbed the strangeness from her skin. Probably, she thought as the water poured over her, I'll never see him again. There was something slippery about him—in the silences between his laughter, in moments when she could tell that his mind had swerved away. No doubt he slid easily in and out of bed with women far prettier and more successful than she; he'd had a stash of condoms within easy reach. But that night she called him, and when nobody answered, not even a machine, she took the subway back to his apartment, startled by both her hunger and her bravery. She climbed the five flights and knocked. He opened the door and let her in.

"I tried calling." She was still breathless from the climb. "I guess . . . I mean, that was really nice, earlier. I kind of—" She rolled her eyes. "Now I feel stupid—I just . . . I guess I missed you. I . . ." She shrugged, wishing she hadn't come.

He didn't say he had missed her too, or that he'd been out on an errand when she called. He didn't gather her up or say come in. He stood, maybe about to smile, maybe just staring at her, absorbing her tumble of words. And it was she who moved toward him, propelled less by desire, suddenly, than by a brief, untoward fear that he would disappear before her eyes. She touched his face, drew him toward her, felt him slowly rise beneath her hands.

"Good Catholic boys don't usually do it twice in one day," he said afterward, combing his fingers through her hair.

"Are you a good Catholic boy?"

"Clearly not. Are you a good Catholic girl?"

She laughed. "Me? No, I'm not religious. I'm Jewish—by birth, I mean."

He pulled away to look at her harder. "Oh, that makes sense."

"It does? Why?"

"You have that . . . oh, I don't know . . ."

"No, what?"

"A certain sadness, maybe. I'm overgeneralizing, aren't I? I'm stereotyping. But they say Italians love food and music, and well, they do, anyhow *I* do, and so do all my relatives, you know what I mean? Or maybe you don't know—I'm sorry—I'm blabbing on here. Tell me to shut up."

Miriam had, in fact, been annoyed, but had said nothing. My mother died, she half wanted to tell him, but did her sadness begin there or had she carried it forever, a hibernating snake inside her genes? She didn't think, anyway, that she came across as a sad person, but then again, she'd been crying in front of him just that afternoon.

"My sadness isn't a religion," she told Francis.

He had looked over her shoulder at something she couldn't see. "It's not?" he said. "Sometimes I think mine is."

Later, she would wonder what he meant by this. She would wonder, too, if the woman in the park made it through the winter, but she never told Eva that. The Squirrel Lady, Eva called her, and over the years she became sleeker, softer, less tattered. *The Squirrel Lady. My father pet her and you saw how kind he was.*

6

The girl kept coming back. He'd be out by the side of the house measuring the space for a deck he didn't want so he could take step-by-step photos of it to give the illustrator for the *Let Me Show You How to Build a Deck* book, and he'd look up to see her standing fifteen yards away, watching. Or he'd walk down to add jars to the table and there she'd be, lurking about. Someone bought a jar, she'd announce almost proudly. A man with a baseball cap. An old lady in a truck. And part of Burl would want to send her home, but another part remembered how, as a boy, he'd hang around this table for hours hoping for some other kids to show up, or for a pat on the head from a grown-up, or an invitation to ride with the mailman on his loop. He had liked his official duty, even as he knew his grandmother was inventing a job to keep him occupied.

This girl, this Eva (finally, on perhaps the fourth visit, she had told him her name) was a mystery to him, her mere presence a force field of mixed signals, glowers and dark stares which turned, without warning, into smiles. Or she'd twirl a lock of hair around her finger and fire off a barrage of questions: What's that? What're you doing now? How come the cow is lying down? Mostly, she wanted to know about the bees. How do they eat? How do they make the honey? What's a honey super? How come they don't sting you? How do they know which hive is theirs? Will the rest of them get sick?

At first he was a little suspicious. This kid was, after all (he was ninety-nine percent sure), the one who had made off with his honey. There was something not quite right about her—too old for her age, or was it too young, as if she were, in fact, the fairy of the woods he had dubbed her that first day. And her hands—always moving, fidgeting with her hair or the dirty string bracelets on her wrist, picking at bug bites on her arms. At times, the fierce way she watched him set him on edge, some kind of *wanting* radiating from her, though what it was she wanted, he didn't know. Other times, she just seemed like a garden-variety bored kid, and who was he to pass up a chance to talk about his bees?

He told her that the big wooden boxes on the top part of the hive were called honey supers and explained how the queen was kept out of them by a device called a queen excluder, which forced her to lay her eggs down below. He told her how the bees picked one honey source and drew from it until it was all used up, so that some honey came from apple blossoms, some from linden, clover, peach, or squash, each source resulting in a different tint and taste. He told her about the queen bee and the workers, how most of the bees inside each hive were female, how there were nurse, guard, field and house bees, and the task each bee performed depended on its age. Eva listened, nodded, asked more questions: What's a queen excluder? What's a nurse bee do? Can I see the queen?

One morning, as he sat on the lawn greasing freezer paper for the mite detectors, he told her about the mites. Most people didn't want to hear about it, made uneasy by the thought of a world under seige in ways invisible to the human eye. Or maybe that was giving them too much credit. Probably they were thinking about the price of gas grills at the mall. Alice, when she visited, tried to be interested in the bees, but she quickly grew impatient. Those precious bees of yours, she'd say almost bitterly. Your *raison d'être*, your bee cause. Eva, though, seemed genuinely interested, so he dove right in and told her that last year, in 1998, the cultivated honey population was down eighty percent in New York State, and that since 1995, New England had lost nine-tenths of its honeybees to Asian mites.

"Well at least," she said philosophically, "there are lots of other bugs."

He groaned. "How can you say that? Did you know that one-third of your diet relies on honeybees? Who do you expect to pollinate your tomatoes and apples, your pears, garlic and squash, your—"

"I don't like squash," she interrupted, parting the grass to look between the blades. "I don't know. Maybe a machine?"

He told her that bees from a single hive could visit over a hundred thousand flowers per day, spreading pollen without doing damage to the blooms.

"Wow," said Eva, then looked at him skeptically. "How do you know?"

"Scientific studies. Scientists like to gather statistics the way the *Apis mellifera* likes to gather nectar."

"Apis what?"

"*Apis mellifera*. 'Common honeybee' in Latin."

"*Apis mellifera*," she repeated. "*Apis mellifera*. And what else?"

He told her that the bees fed the newborn Zeus with honey, that the Egyptians embalmed their pharaohs in honey, that some honey could kill you or make you see visions.

"Visions of what?" Eva asked.

"I don't know. It's never happened to me."

"Who'd it happen to?"

"Supposedly to the people of ancient Greece, when they ate honey made from rhododendron flowers."

She looked around. "Have you got those flowers here?"

"No." He gathered together his mite detectors, put the lid on the Crisco and stood. "I have work to do inside now. You'd better head home."

"I wish I knew," Eva said as she got up, "what those visions were."

One day, as he was out in the field trying to pry off a stuck honey super, he had the prickly sense of a human presence nearby and looked over to see her standing among the pines. "Stay there," he yelled. The bees were anxious, darting at his hat and veil; he wasn't wearing the bee suit and had already been stung a few times. The super was stuck fast, and although Burl kept loosening the edges, it wasn't budging, and sweat had started trickling down his back.

This gathering of honey was one of his favorite things, even when it made his muscles ache, even when he got stung. He loved how heavy the supers were, loved the vibrating but manageable haze of danger, so that often he didn't put on the bee suit and tried instead to radiate a calm, slow-moving, taming presence. Sometimes, as he lifted the brick, pried off the top and looked inside, he flung his mind elsewhere—to ancient Greece, or to Nepal where, for generations, the honey gatherers had scaled high cliffs, coaxing honeycomb as big as themselves into baskets, which they lowered down on ropes. Burl had read that they recited bee-calming mantras to the giant black bees, and he had seen pictures of the nearly naked men clinging to rope ladders, so small beside the stretch of rock, like insects themselves, the landscape setting them in scale. Sometimes he went so far as to pretend he was on a cliff in Nepal, or he thought his way to ancient Egypt, where he scooped lime blossom honey from tree hollows, or ancient Athens, where he made hives from grooved clay pots.

These were, for him, times of intense and rapt aloneness, like swimming underwater at the pond in the far field behind his house. Not loneliness, not feeling himself as separate in the world. He was, here, part of the world, but skinless, boundless, traveling inside the hive as he leaned over it, bending time and space. His father, of course, thought he was a coward, unable to handle the demands of the real world—Burl might, after all, have made partner by now: *That boy has a mind like a steel trap.* And later: *He thinks he can change the world by sticking his head in a haystack.* Even at the nursing home, the "assisted living" home, Burl was sure his father kept at it, his words formal, his tone full of bile: *Did I mention that I put my son through college and law school so he could learn how to shovel excrement?*

If his mother had been alive fourteen years ago, when his grandmother died and he decided to move back here, she might have understood his choices a little better—this was, after all, her place, too. Her parents had thought she'd done so well, marrying the wealthy lawyer from the city, but what about her sadness, low-level and constant as white noise, and the drinks she mixed to numb it, and the waxy, lipsticked tightness of her smile? *That* was cowardice, as far as Burl was concerned, the way she used to do his father's bidding, jump at his commands. Only in illness, only in final, all-out exhaustion, did that false, unhappy smile leave her face, and what was left, after so many years, was not the playful, generous, pretty woman who used to make up stories for her son, but a shrill, bitter person bent with need. *I told you, I need chamomile tea,* she would tell her husband in a petulant voice, her hands fluttering in the air, the tables finally turned. *No, nothing makes me comfortable—bring me that foul thing, quick—I have to go!*

In the end, it was leaving that saved Burl—moving out of the city and coming back to the farm, where he found ways to pump all he had been fleeing from his blood. In Philadelphia, he hadn't been an athlete. Like his mother, he had spent a lot of time reading; he had studied hard and developed an ironic, dodging social style that won him many acquaintances and few friends. Always, he'd a sense of something being *off*, made more complicated by the fact that he knew he was, in the scheme of things, lucky, possessing brains, money and passable good looks. He wasn't a hippie, wasn't a hiker, farmer, or back-to-the-lander. When he first arrived, he was twenty-eight years old and had no vision of any kind. He came because he had, in the past, been less unhappy here than elsewhere, and because—by now he could admit it—he knew his father would think it was a terrible idea.

Slowly, though, as the months, then the years went by, he had found himself to be someone who loved motion. He swam, chopped wood, ran through the trees with his first dog until blood throbbed in his temples and the world blurred. Exercise, exorcise—they were almost the same word—but what began as a way to drum out anger turned, after a time, into a simple, necessary pleasure, feeling his muscles stretch, his heart quicken, his skin release sweat. He made some friends in town, dated women here and there, got ten chickens and began dreaming of all the things he would do with the farm. When he was thirty-one, Alice came back for Thanksgiving and they slept together the way they had as teenagers. At Christmas they did it again. The next spring he went to bee school at the university extension service, cleaned off his grandmother's old equipment and started a hive. That August he extracted his first honey and watched as it poured, slow medicine, into clean glass jars.

So while he didn't mind Eva's dropping by, he wasn't so keen on her hovering near the hives. That day, his mind was not on her. He was sweating, working and daydreaming, listening to the bees; this hive, at least, seemed populated and healthy. Afterward, he would realize that she must have been edging toward him for a good five minutes, from the moment he had told her to stay back. She must have decided, right then, to disobey, because when he did look up again, she was standing much too close, only a few feet away, her hands clamped over her ears.

Burl wedged the hive tool deep between two supers and felt—
finally—the top one give. But he couldn't take it off, not with
her so close. "Damn," he said. Hadn't she heard him? He left the
super in place and moved away from the hive, waving for Eva to
follow.

"Go on," he told her when they were standing side by side.
"Into the woods, like I told you before. No, on second thought,
go all the way to the table." She didn't move, staring at him, and
he glared at her as best he could through the veil. "Go."

The veil always turned things pleasantly milky and vague, but
as he walked toward the table, he took it off and saw the world
with all its hard edges. Up ahead, Eva was already fiddling with
the jars.

"What was that all about?" he asked, half trying to put on the
voice of a scolding teacher but sounding, instead, as frustrated
as he felt. "I told you not to come over when I have an open
hive."

She wouldn't look at him.

"When I tell you to stay back," he said, "I mean it. Do you
get that?"

She nodded.

"Do you understand why?"

"Because—" Eva's voice was singsong. "Every bee has a stinger,
and when they're mad, they sting you and the barb gets stuck in
you and puts out van . . . vannim—"

"Venom." She was reciting his bee lectures back to him, her
tone mocking and sure until she stumbled on the word.

"Yes," she said. "And then . . ." She rubbed her elbow. "Then
the sting hurts but not so much, really. Actually I don't think it's
so bad."

He looked at her arm. "Were you just stung?"

"No." She sounded almost disappointed.

"But you could have been," he told her. "I was about to lift
the whole super off. You would have been a few feet away with
no suit or anything."

She toyed with a jar. "I just want to see inside. Can I maybe wear your hat?"

"And what would I wear?"

She shrugged. "Don't they sort of know you, like pets?"

"No," he said. "Of course not. They're not pets—they're never pets, not like dogs or cats. They're wild—cultivated, yes, but always feral in the end. They won't grow to love you, that's for sure. It's their hive, their home, you're entering. Of course they'll sting."

He heard himself growing agitated, pedantic, using words she probably didn't know. He didn't even believe what he was saying; he did feel, on some level, that his bees knew him. There was an old English custom of turning the hives away from the beekeeper's funeral procession so that the bees wouldn't swarm from grief. Whenever Burl thought of that, he found it moving. So why had he said the thing about the bees not loving? As soon as it left his mouth, he heard how it sounded cruel.

Eva, though, seemed unfazed. "We could make another hat out of something—like maybe part of a screen. That might work, don't you think?"

He found himself admiring her tenacity, even as it baffled him. Didn't she have dolls to play with, or music to listen to, or computer games to play—whatever kids her age did for fun? "A hat isn't enough," he explained. "I couldn't let you near them unless you were covered from head to toe. You could be allergic, for all I know."

"I'm not. I've been stung before. It hardly even hurt."

"In Manhattan?"

She raised her eyebrows. "We have bees. It was in Central Park. They . . . I remember they put a popsicle on it, instead of ice, I guess."

"Really? And more bees didn't come flocking, for the sugar?"

"No. Please can I see them?"

"I might be able to rustle up another bee suit. Would you be extremely careful?"

"Yes."

"And do everything I told you?"

Eva made an X motion over her chest, and for a moment he thought she was making the sign of the cross. "Cross my heart," she said. "Hope to die."

"How would your mother feel about it?"

"Fine."

"Why don't you call her, just to check? You can use the phone in the house."

"She's not there . . . they're doing—I guess they have a trial today."

She met his eyes steadily, and Burl felt a stab of anger; he, too, had been a lying child. "Look," he said, "don't make things up, all right? How can I trust you with the bees if you make things up?"

At first he thought she might turn and run away; she pursed her lips and peered darkly down the road. But then she glanced at his bee hat, which he had let fall to the ground. "I just know it'd be okay with her," she said. "I've told her all about the bees. She said she thought it'd be great if I learned how to be a bee-keeper, as long as I was careful. In New York I did stuff much more dangerous than this."

"Like what?"

"Like . . . I took the subway and busses alone and stayed home after school by myself." She looked up at him, flirtatious almost, her finger toying with her hair. "Oh yeah, and I sold crack and I had a couple guns and—"

"See," he said, "you can't go two seconds without lying." But he was smiling, couldn't resist her brightness, her elusive play. Anyway, where *had* she come from? He had no idea. The other day, as he dropped off honey at the health food store, he had noticed a slight woman with wavy brown hair who had somehow reminded him of Eva—in the shape of her face, maybe, or her intent expression as she read a label, or the way she wiped her hair off her brow. He had almost wanted to ask her if she was

Eva's mother, but the question would have seemed too odd. Now an image came to him—Eva as a grown woman sitting across from a man in a restaurant, raising her eyebrows and laughing at a sidelong joke she'd just made that her date wasn't sure he understood.

"All right," he said. "We'll look in the barn for my grandmother's bee suit and cover you from head to toe. It'll be too big for you, but not by much. She was tiny. She—" He stopped short, unable to put her into words.

"What?" Eva asked.

"Oh I don't know. You would have liked her—she loved her bees. When she got older, she stopped wearing the suit. She used to let them sting her. She claimed it helped her rheumatism. But I don't think they did sting her much."

"Maybe I can tame them," Eva said. "I know they wouldn't be my pets, but maybe they'd recognize me? I don't mind if I get stung a little."

"You're getting ahead of yourself," he said, and part of him was wondering if he'd be stuck with her every day and should he try to call her mother and what was the deal, the way this kid was left to wander by herself? But another part was imagining Eva with her arms outstretched like the bee nymph Melissa (she had learned how to ferment honey into mead; he had named Lissa after her). Eva fit the part, so small and quick, so reaching. As they walked to the barn, he pictured the bees making their homes in the intricate alleys of her curls.

7

How quickly they had moved. Later, Miriam would be reminded of a flipcard book Eva had brought home once from a birthday party; you flipped the pages from front to back and a man in a bowler hat jumped on a unicycle, juggled some balls, fell off the cycle, hopped back on, went for a ride, fell and made a final, solemn bow. Or you could flip the book in the other direction, and then the man hurried backward with the same solemn dog-gedness, defying gravity and the forward march of time. Except who was to say that time, or books, always moved from left to right? She remembered the Passover Haggadah of her early child-hood, how much she had loved turning the pages from back to front in search of the four questions. Who was to say, except perhaps in hindsight, that she and Francis had moved *too* fast? Sometimes she tried to imagine other ways it might have gone: they could have waited a year to move in, gotten to know each other better. Or waited longer to have a baby, made more money first. Or she might have met Francis when her mother was still alive, or . . .

But each chain fell apart so quickly, the facts too intransigent—her mother dead, the baby they'd had so quickly, not just any child, but Eva; Francis not just any man, but Francis—together they had shut their eyes and leaped. What would it look like, she wondered, in a flipbook shuffling backward—the two of them holding hands in a black-and-white photograph, springing up in a reverse arc to land on a firm, steep place? But no, the facts again—gravity, for instance. And it wasn't so firm, the place she'd come from—her muddy, slogging, self-serious little life.

Francis put words together in quick, sparkling runs and made her laugh. He seemed to know something about everything, unlike Miriam's father who had known—or thought he'd known—everything about a few things: Israel, the Jews, the proper way to live a life. Even after her father had left for Israel, her childhood had taken place in a slim, small space: This is the way to set the table; these are the hours for studying; your eyes are bigger than your stomach, sweetheart—please don't take more than you can eat. Francis painted, played jazz piano, kept books for the store, shoveled down food, spoke English and Italian with equal ease. He built things—bookcases and countertops, display racks for the mugs. His intelligence amazed her, how quick and fluid it was, how ready to change shape. In certain moods he'd speak to anybody—on the street, in the subway. Like the Ancient Mariner, whose verses he liked to recite, he fixed them with his glittering eye. He would, she thought at first, fix *her*. Repair her. She wanted to think so. With his hands he soothed her; with his voice he instructed, charmed and entertained. At first they were (she was sure of it, flipping backward or forward) happy—blessed, even. Who wouldn't move ahead with such a life?

But why so fast, her mother would have asked. The problem was that, looking back, she couldn't quite remember how things had gone. She knew some of the swiftness had to do, as things tended to in New York, with housing. Francis had a friend who was vacating the Second Street apartment. Rent stabilized, two tiny bedrooms, a small eat-in kitchen, sloping hardwood floors. An eat-in kitchen! Who could say no to that, who would stop to think? She and Sarah had been growing apart anyway, and Miriam was tired of having to clear the kitchen table of textbooks on disease and wait for Sarah's boyfriend to finish showering so she could take her turn. Here, her own man, actual, substantial, in the flesh. She realized she had never quite expected to find one, had never even really looked. "We," she kept saying, the pronoun clumsy and exciting on her tongue. "We're going to dinner. We might go see a movie after." "Have fun," Sarah would answer, as if it were the most normal thing in the world.

Had she and Francis discussed moving in? They must have, but she couldn't remember. Four months after they met, she moved her things, most of which had been her mother's: a tall, scarred dresser; a maple kitchen table with four chairs; a rocking chair; a Russian nesting doll; cast-iron frying pans; a carved box filled with necklaces she couldn't yet bring herself to wear. She nailed her mother's mezuzah slantwise by the front door—in memory, she told Francis, but really she was half hoping it would bring them luck. Francis moved his mattress, keyboard, easel, books. He strengthened the loose legs on the chairs and built high bookshelves along one wall, put up kitchen shelves and a cabinet in the bathroom, made a ledge over the radiator in the living room.

She watched as, all around her, places to hold things kept cropping up. "Why didn't you ever build anything in your old place," she asked, wanting him to say something out of an old movie—*without you I was nothing, because I didn't have you*—but he only shrugged. They painted the bathroom a deep apricot with glossy, black trim. Miriam made curtains for its high window from a silk kimono she had picked up secondhand. She found an armchair on the street and covered it with a throw, and over that, a crocheted afghan from her Grandma Rose. Each day after work, she wanted only to hurry home to the apartment. Francis brought back chipped Italian pottery from the shop and built a blue shelf for it. Miriam had always loved that pottery, long before she met him; now she could turn and see it, intricate and foreign, on her wall. She was twenty-four, Francis thirty. They were old enough to be doing this but still it felt a bit unreal to her, like playing house.

At the time, she probably would have said she knew him. She knew the basic facts, anyway: his parents' two shops, how his mother ran the one on the East Side and Francis managed the one on the West Side. She knew that his father was in Italy, taking care of the export side of the business.

"But they're still married, right?" she asked Francis once. They were sprawled on the futon couch on a cloudy Sunday morning, each at one end, their feet entwined.

He raised his eyebrows. "Till death do them part."

"So he's coming back?"

"Apparently. Don't place any bets."

"What's he like?"

"My father? I don't know. Just a regular guy. A little out to lunch sometimes, but it's not really his fault."

"What do you mean?"

"My mother ..." He cleared his throat. "Let's just say I wouldn't want to be married to her."

Miriam laughed. "That's a relief. But is she—I mean, what's so difficult about her?"

"*She* is."

"But specifically."

"Specifically? The package deal. Her self."

He started cracking his knuckles, though he knew she hated the sound. Miriam reached out to stop him but he was too far away. "Really?" she said. "But you talk to her so much, and you work for her, isn't it sort of—"

"She's my mother," he said flatly.

"What about your sister? Where is she, again?"

He swung his legs around and sat up. "In Italy, too. She married

64

an Italian. You know that—I already told you. What is this, twenty questions? I just woke up."

"Sorry." Miriam sat, too. "I'm a paralegal. I'm trained to do research."

"Well I wasn't at the scene of the crime."

"What crime?"

"Whatever crime you're researching."

She slid closer to him and touched his shoulder. "No crime. I just . . . I want to know you better, that's all."

"Not through research," he said sharply, and she took her hand away. "It's an American obsession," said Francis. "This . . . this *muckraking* of people's childhoods. Every time you turn on the TV, somebody's blathering about how their mother screwed the mailman in front of them when they were three. That's not how you get to know someone. You live with them, every day, you just . . . live. Haven't you read your *Tao Te Ching?*"

She fought the temptation to lie. "No," she said, then added, more quietly, "I wasn't muckraking. That's not what I was doing."

Francis nodded. "All right, I'm sorry. I know. It's just—how about . . . I'll . . . I could show you a picture of them or something. I don't mean to be a jerk."

In the photo, his sister Ginny was small and elfin, with big eyes and dark hair cropped close to her head. His father, standing next to her, was the only one smiling at the camera, his features cruder than Francis's and less striking, though he looked jovial and kind. Then there was his mother. Miriam took the picture from him. Such a strong face she had, too long and angular to be called pretty, but with a kind of beauty to it, a tense, insistent dignity. She was staring at the camera, or maybe at the person behind it, with something of Francis in the power of her gaze. Her hair was pulled tightly back; her clothes were elegant: a fitted gray suit jacket, red scarf and long, narrow black skirt.

"God." Miriam returned the photo to Francis, who let it drop into a manilla envelope. "Is that what she really looks like?"

"More or less."

"She's so fashionable. What was the occasion?"

He shrugged. "Nothing special. She dresses like that all the time."

"You must think I'm a frump."

"No. My mother thinks every day is her own exclusive date with Jesus Christ."

"Are there any of you as a boy or teenager?"

"I'm starving," he announced abruptly, as if he hadn't heard. "I'll go get bagels and the paper."

But then he just sat there, the envelope pressed up against his chest. Watching him, she felt an almost painful tenderness for all the muffled parts of people, all the far, far parts. He had never asked to see her family photographs; if he did, she knew she'd be resistant, too. What would she show him? Not the overdressed, pale baby wedged between her parents in a photo booth, not the picture of her mother in her last month of life, her skin gray, her wig slightly askew. Not, certainly, the mousy ten-year-old girl smiling too hard for her father, her kneesocks sagging, her hand raised in a stiff, old-fashioned wave. *Next year in Jerusalem, bye-bye.*

Francis stood. "Poppyseed?"

She didn't look up. "I don't care."

"Come with me?" His voice was kind; his hand stretched toward her.

How could she not? She reached.

Almost every evening, his mother called, sometimes twice. *Is Francesco there? This is his mother*, she said formally if Miriam answered. Never *Hello Miriam*, but then Francis hadn't taken her home to meet his parents yet. Slowly, he said when she asked why. Because I'm Jewish? Because . . . lots of things—we're living together, it's been so fast, my father's still in Italy. . . . As he talked on the phone, Miriam would watch him lean into the receiver and listen to his mouth pour forth a stream of foreignness. The phone calls always felt secret and intimate to her, a rapid rise and fall of Italian. *Mamma*, she could hear, or *sí sí*, or *no*, or *prego*, but nothing she could make sense of; even the tone was impossible for her to read. Francis sometimes sounded impatient, but maybe it was just the way the language fell.

One day after work, as he talked to his mother on the phone, she reached into an old marmalade jar and pulled out a half-smoked, wrinkled joint that she had left there among the dusty pennies, paper clips and rubber bands. Every now and then she liked to get stoned after a long day; it eased the pounding in her head and loosened her stiff neck. She lit the joint, sucked in the sweet, rough smoke and leaned back against the countertop, shutting her eyes as she inhaled. When she opened them, she found Francis staring at her, the phone back on its stand.

"What are you doing?"

"Hmm?" She exhaled and coughed. "Just getting high. You want some?"

He shook his head hard. "I didn't know you did that."

"What?"

"Got high."

She took another, smaller toke. "Oh, hardly ever. I've had this for ages—it was Sarah's. It's probably not even good anymore." She held the joint out, but Francis waved it away.

"No," he said. "I lost enough brain cells in college and the smell makes me sick, I—" He looked agitated, almost panicked. "Do you think you could . . ."

Surprised, she stubbed out the joint in the sink. Francis opened the window and leaned his head into the street. Watching him tipped over that way, she had an urge to grab hold of his beltloop to anchor him. Finally he drew himself back in and started fanning the air.

"I didn't know you were so squeaky clean," Miriam told him.

"I'm not. It's just that . . . I had a bad thing with pot once, I sort of—" He walked into the living room and she followed.

"So do you still like me?" He turned, suddenly, to face her.

"What? Because you don't smoke pot?"

Francis shrugged. "And I lost some brain cells."

"I like the brain cells you have left."

"All three of them?"

"All four."

"I hate to break it to you, baby. All three."

And Francis, what did he see in Miriam? One day she asked him. They had been living in the apartment for over a month. Each weeknight they came home, changed into shorts and T-shirts and lay on the floor in front of the fan, eating cheap take-out with plastic forks.

"What do I see in you?" he said. "Don't know. Come here."

She slid over to him on the floor and he cupped her chin, lowered her jaw and tried to peer inside her mouth.

"I see . . . mangled Pad Thai."

She jerked her head away. "Let me swallow. Come on, be serious."

"I see . . . a filling or two. A nice tongue and teeth."

"Okay, okay, but what do you see if you look, you know, more abstractly?"

"Um . . . tastebuds. Did you know some people have many more than others? Actually we all taste things differently—I read an article. It looks like you have a lot."

She hit his shoulder. "In me. As a person."

"I'm not sure I like this game. Why do you want to know?"

Because, she might have said, because I don't quite believe this, the whole thing—that you want me, that you know me, that we know each other, that I, Miriam, am the genuine object of your desires. But she didn't say that, couldn't quite. He might have answered: You're right, we don't know each other, hardly at all. Or: I see little in you. Or: Your ordinariness is a nice change—I'll stay here for a while, then move on.

"It's how the game goes," she said instead.

He liked, he told her, how she talked to herself in the shower,

68

how she noticed things, how she had come back to the store a second time and asked him out. And this, he said, resting his hands on the place where her hips flared out from her waist.

"What else?" She knew she was fishing but couldn't help it.

"This." His finger stroked her earlobe.

"My ear?"

"Your lissome, lickable, luscious, labile lobe. Why? Don't you like mine?"

She fingered it; it was, in fact, remarkably soft, like the rosy tip of his penis. "Yes."

"And what else?" he asked.

"About you? I like . . . I like your creativity, how you're always making things."

He snorted. "How I'm always dabbling, making little pieces of shit, music turds, paint turds, you mean? You like *that*?"

"What are you talking about? It's not shit."

Francis lowered his chin, put on a deep radio voice: "*By day he worked balancing books and dusting knickknacks in his parents' overpriced store. But by night, by night his true talents came out and he sat on the pot and shit out little works of art, experimenting with different styles—diarrhea, stony little turds, long thin ones . . .*"

"Stop." She shuddered. She didn't like him like this. "Why are you so hard on yourself?"

He shrugged. "Truth is a strict taskmaster. Who said that?"

"Is it from the *Tao Te Ching*?"

"No."

"Marx? Buddha? I don't know."

He kissed her on the forehead. "I said that! *Moi*. Will you fan me with lotus leaves and rub my belly?"

"I might."

"Even if I make shit? Even if I *am* shit?"

"Maybe." Rubbing a slow circle on his stomach, she felt a flicker of desire and let her hand travel down his thigh.

"That's what I like about you," he said.

"What?"

"You're not afraid of shit."

I am, she should have told him. She was: afraid of chaos, of mess, of death, of unclenching, of letting go. Of shit, even, literally; it made her gag, she didn't know how she'd ever change a diaper. But Francis, was she afraid of him? No, because first of all, she didn't believe him when he talked like that, was sure it was all shiny surface, all swift words. And how could she be afraid of someone whose stomach she was nuzzling now, whose hands were rocking her, whose baby (she wasn't at all sure; her period was late, her breasts ached but she hadn't done the test yet) might be starting to take shape?

And so, by keeping silent, she had lied to him. What if she had spoken then and allowed him to see her more clearly? Or listened harder to the things he tried to tell her, instead of glossing over, passing by? Later she would think about it, but that, again, was hindsight. The next day she peed into a plastic strip. Two pink stripes. Eva. The first few cells.

8

In the warm, wide barn where dust floated visible in the air, Eva prepared to meet the bees. Three days had passed since Burl had promised to show her the inside of a hive. First there was Saturday, when she and her mother drove to a big discount store to get bathing suits and stuff for the house, and then to a lake where Miriam thought Eva might get a swimming lesson and meet other kids. The lake had been nice but there were no lessons and the kids all hung around in groups. What was Eva supposed to do, walk over and say, "Hi, I have no friends"? At one point, she had waded in above her waist and her mother had called out to her—Careful, Eva, don't go too deep!—so then the whole world knew she couldn't swim. On Sunday they had driven into town to get the paper and sit in a cafe. Just like in the city, Eva had eaten a bagel and drawn on the Sunday *New York Times*, putting eyeglasses, tattoos and mustaches onto the models in the ads, then adding animals, kids and cartoon bubbles filled with words. As she sat there covering a model's white dress with dots, she had almost wanted to tell her mother about the bees, offer to show them to her even, explaining all the things she'd learned. But her mother was so suspicious lately, so nervous and ready to get mad. You'll get stung, she might say. Or: Who is this beekeeper and why aren't you home with Mrs. Flynn? Or even (worst of all): Bees? You want to show me bees?

Now, in the barn, Burl asked her nothing, just told her what to do: Step over here, one leg in, that's right, good, now the other—it's a little big, we'll roll up the extra once it's on. The bee suit was made of stained white cloth and smelled old like the barn and sweet like honey. In the city, Eva had learned to be careful, walking fast past alleys and keeping her gaze flat and straight ahead when boys or men called out to her—Yo, baby doll, hey, *chica!*—or even muttering "Fuck off, loser" in her most scornful voice. Now, though, here she was somehow, alone in a barn while a grown man knelt fiddling with her cuffs. She knew her mother wouldn't like it, but she didn't care; she trusted him, she just did. Maybe it was stupid, but she trusted that he wanted what he said he wanted—to cover her so she wouldn't get stung, to show her his bees. That was all, except how to explain the shiver of excitement, or was it fear, passing from her stomach to her chest?

Burl's grandmother, he told her as she stood there, had worn this suit for years. For an instant she saw a body rotting in the dirt; then she blinked the thought away. She had come prepared, done everything he had told her. She wore pale cotton pants, white kneesocks, her high tops, a long-sleeved pale yellow shirt which she thought, with her black hair, made her look a little like a bee. For once, that morning, she had given Mrs. Flynn something to do, asking her to put her hair into two thick braids and pin the escaping curls to her head. She wasn't sure that Mrs. Flynn bought her stories about I'm-going-to-see-my-new-friend-Lissa, but the old lady didn't seem to care what Eva did, as long as she didn't stay away too long.

"So you asked your mom and she said it was all right?" Burl crouched at her feet, winding string around her ankles so the bees couldn't get inside.

Eva nodded. She didn't know if he believed her either. Even when he talked like a grown-up, he sounded, somehow, as if he might be kidding. Also, he told her things, like they were friends: This is the hay chute I used to slide down. This is where my grandmother nicked my height into the wood. Here's an old honey extractor I need to fix. Listening, Eva felt the thick past of the place everywhere, like something she could cup inside her hands.

Before he got out the bee suit, he had stood her against the wall, cut a notch in the wood and carved her name alongside it with a knife, a few inches from the column where his own growth had been marked by his grandparents, year by year. See, he had told her. At eleven, I was just a little taller than you are now. Eva had tried to picture him as shorter, younger and without a beard—a red-haired, sunburned boy. Watching him bear down on the straight edges of the "E," she had remembered the height chart inside her closet door in New York. Most of her was there still: Eva 2, 4, 9. The mark on the barn wall looked too high to her, too grown, floating by itself as if she'd only ever been eleven.

He zipped and snapped the bee suit up to her chin, cuffed the sleeves until her hands appeared, and wrapped twine around her wrists. Inside the suit, she started to sweat.

She squirmed. "It's really hot in this thing."

"Wait until you put on the hat—it turns into a sauna. You don't faint from the heat, do you?"

She didn't bother to answer. Burl put two fingers in his mouth and let out a piercing whistle, and Lissa appeared at his side.

"Ready guys?" He jerked his chin toward outside. "Oh wait a second—I might as well put on a suit, too."

"I'm broiling," Eva said. "I'm melting in here."

"Go."

And then she was running, feeling the bee suit bulky on her

legs, seeing Lissa wheel around and follow her. Outside, she stopped, threw her head back and filled her lungs. The air was like a present, clear and cool.

Near the hives, she held out first one arm, then the other, and he gave her his grandmother's long canvas gloves, which were only slightly too big. Then the bee hat. A veil, he had called it the week before, and although she had seen his own hat and should have known, she had pictured herself dressing up as a lacy queen bee bride, all white froth and gauzy frill. This thing was made of yellow and black nylon and looked more like a construction worker's hat, or like the bag onions came in. He lowered it over her head and looped more string around her, wrapping her up like a package. Hotter and hotter, Eva felt, but now (the shiver in her stomach come and gone) safer and safer, too—from the bees, yes, but also in a bigger way, for though she couldn't have put it into words, she felt like an infant being swaddled in yards of sweet-smelling fabric, close-fitting as a cocoon. Suddenly she was sleepy and wanted to plop down in the grass and watch the sky through the scrim of veil.

"All right," said Burl, and she looked up and saw that he, too, had put on a bee hat and long leather gloves. "I'll take off the honey supers, and then we'll go into the hive bodies and make sure everything's in working order. They haven't been flying in and out much so I want to take a look. Sound okay?"

"Yes." Her voice seemed small and muffled to her. Inside the hat, she could feel the close heat of her own breath.

He knocked on the top of her hat. "Everything all right in there?"

Eva nodded.

"If you get stung through the fabric—it's unlikely but it could happen—just walk away slowly. Remember, this is their house we're breaking into, so they might get pi—they might be irritated."

"Pissed." Eva pointed at the hive. "I don't think I can reach."

"Oh." He looked her up and down. "True. It'll be shorter than this because I'm taking a few supers off, but I'll get you something anyway."

He found a cinder block in the grass and brought it over to the side of the hive. In the air all around her, she could see bees coming and going. He had told her how they went off to the flowers, filled their stomachs with nectar, got pollen on their legs and came back to show the other bees where to go. But he was right—this hive didn't have nearly as many bees coming in and out as its neighbors did. Now she was about to see inside, but what if he lifted the lid and the bees, like in that other hive, were lying crisp and dead? She wanted to see the whole family inside—nurses, cleaners, guard bees, babies, a whole bunch of sisters (and Eva without even one), plus the drones. And the queen—especially the queen. Eva pictured her wearing a crown made from flowers, sitting proudly, everbody's mother, while the other bees fanned her with their wings.

What she saw, when finally Burl managed to remove the top boxes and pry the lid off one of the boxes farther down, was a mess. Bees everywhere—in the air in front of her, crawling on her veil inches from her eyes, covering the box like a piece of moving velvet. Eva had envisioned something much neater—little nurse bees in one corner, dropping things into the babies' mouths, bees dragging garbage out, a queen in the center keeping watch. This was more like being dizzy, like a fever, more motion than she had ever seen in one place, even in the city. Watching, she felt as if something had gone wrong with her eyes, brown spots appearing out of nowhere, movement she couldn't make sense of, and then the sound—a rising, falling metallic whine, airplanes diving in and swooping off, the noise so close, so full and *everywhere* that it seemed to live in her own head.

"You okay?" Burl was asking her, and she nodded, but was she okay, she wasn't sure. Something felt wrong inside her, all *buzzing*, and the bee suit was suffocating and how were you supposed to tell anything from anything in here? This was their home? Why hadn't Burl told her it would be like this? I am, she thought, I am about to faint. She shut her eyes and took a long, deep breath. When she opened them again, he was handing her a metal stick with an L-shaped hook on each end.

"I want to take a look at some frames. You can help me," he said, and she realized that he had probably been talking to her the whole time.

Like a good girl, like a grown-up, like someone not hot, tired and disappointed, Eva took the tool. With her mother she would have cried out now, torn the hat off, stormed away. Even when she was only sort of mad, she did that, threw tantrums and then felt bad about it. But Burl was different from her mother, didn't expect her to be a spoiled brat, hardly knew her. And here he was, puffing smoke at the bees, leaning over them, asking her to help. She stood on tiptoes and leaned forward. He wedged the end of his own hive tool beneath a piece of wood at the top of the hive.

"Like this," he said. "You do it on the other side and we'll lift the frame out."

Eva moved the tool toward the bees, then took it back. "I can't. They're in the way."

He bent across and brushed a few bees away with his gloved hand. There were dead bees among the live ones, Eva noticed— on the edges where he'd taken the lid off, in the middle where two bees were trying to drag a dead one away. One bee lay on its back with liquid oozing out of it. She steeled herself, then wedged the tool in and felt it catch on an edge of wood.

"Now straighten it up and pull. That's great," said Burl.

And then together they were lifting, something was rising, a piece of the hive, fat with some kind of growth and covered with more bees. Burl grabbed it from the top and held it up.

"Look," he said. "A full honey frame. Isn't that beautiful? Take a look at that."

*   *   *

Together, then, they worked, she helping to pull out more frames, he looking at them, nodding, putting them back, stopping to add more puffs of smoke. As Eva helped him, something in her calmed a little, even though the air was even thicker now with bees—flying toward them and away. Maybe, she thought, the smoke was working on her, too, relaxing her the way it calmed the bees.

"Damn," Burl said finally. "It is—it's honey-bound. I should have checked it sooner. They've been making a lot of noise."

He told her how there had to be room for air to move through the hive so it didn't get too stuffy, and so the bees could evaporate the nectar and make it into honey. Eva remembered a word for that—cross-ventilation. *We're lucky we have cross-ventilation*, her mother used to say when she complained about the heat. They needed, Burl explained, to take out some full frames and replace them with empty ones so air could get through, and so the queen would have room to lay her eggs. She remembered walking around the farmhouse with her mother and Kate before they took it, so many empty rooms where people had lived, where Kate, a long time ago, had been a girl.

"Okay," Burl said when they finished. "Good work. Do you want to see a few things before we close up the hive?"

He showed her the honey cells—capped and uncapped—and the nectar cells, and the dark, sticky stuff called propolis. He showed her the brood cells, poking a toothpick down into one of the holes and pulling out a slimy white and purple glob. *This* was a baby bee? It looked a lot like snot. He pulled something tiny and red off the brood and showed it to her.

"Bingo, on the first try," he said. "They love the drone brood. Witness the root of all evil, the ferocious varroa mite."

"Kill it!" Eva cried.

He looked down at his finger. "After long and careful deliberation, the presiding judge has ordered an execution, Mighty Mite."

"I didn't mean . . ." She shook her head. "You said it's messing them up, right?"

"It is." He squashed the mite between two fingers. "This one mite can only do so much damage, but yes, we've got ourselves a real problem and I appreciate that you understand the gravity of the situation. I've been doing an experiment with them, feeding them wintergreen oil mixed with sugar and Crisco. That's what I was giving them the other week, remember? A guy I know swears by it, but my mites might not go for it, the little bastards."

"Where's the baby bee the mite was sitting on?"

"At that stage it's called a pupa, larva little earlier," said Burl. "It wasn't a baby bee, not yet. Actually 'baby bee' is sort of a misnomer, since they start working the second they come out— no prolonged childhood for these folks. This one came to an abrupt end, but there are plenty more, look."

She tried to fold her mind around that: To get hold of the mite that was killing the bee, you needed to kill the bee. It didn't seem to bother Burl, just as he didn't seem to notice the bees he kept killing as he moved things around. She had thought he loved his bees, but now he seemed more like a careless giant, wrecking everything with his huge, gloved hands.

"Death," he was saying, "is an everyday event in the bee world, but then what's new? Every time we lift a frame out, a couple hundred bees don't make it. And did you know that bees always die when they sting? The stinger pulls the abdomen out with it. Except for the queen—her stinger is retractable, so she doesn't die." He pulled on his veil. "*Retractable*, in case you didn't know, means capable of being withdrawn."

The Queen. Eva fastened on the word. "Can we see the queen? Maybe if she's okay, that'll be a good sign."

"It is." He sounded impressed. "It would be. But she's probably down below. We've left her some nice room, but we've also shaken things up. I think we've done enough damage for today."

"But maybe we should just check on her, down below?"

Burl put one lid on the hive, then another, then the brick. "Not today. I don't want to disturb them anymore. Aren't you ready to get out of that suit?"

"But another day?"

"Walk over into the woods." He handed her a paintbrush. "And brush yourself off." He puffed some smoke in her direction. "I'll come in a minute and help you out of the suit."

Eva took a few steps. "But another day, can I see her?"

"You," he said, "are one persistent girl. Sure, another day, the princess can meet the queen."

"Thanks." She ran the paintbrush over her arm, liking its fat blond bristles. "How'd you know I was a princess?"

"It's in your bearing. What's your lineage?"

"My what?"

"From what line of royalty does your family descend? You know, like Scottish lords and ladies, or Masai kings."

"Oh. My, my fa—. . . one side is Italian kings and the other is, um, Jewish queens. From Russia, I think. I forget."

How was she supposed to know, her mother's mother dead before she was even born, her grandfather alive in Florida, but they never saw him, though he sent money around her birthday, and once, a backpack with Minnie Mouse ears, which Miriam thought was tacky and Eva pretended not to like. Her other grandfather, her father's father, lived somewhere in Italy. Her father's mother, as far as Eva knew, still lived in New York City but never came over anymore. Eva reminded her too much of Francis—that was what Miriam said. That grandmother sent pink cards with *Happy Birthday Granddaughter* in silver script, and checks, and pictures of Jesus Christ. Eva was the only kid she knew who got sent presents from two grandparents she never saw. In fourth grade, when her class was told to make a family tree, she had given herself a sister named Carrie, an aunt named Nancy Drew. She had made leaves of tinfoil and a popsicle stick trunk with hard spaghetti roots. *Good work!* her teacher had written. *Fancy tree!*

"So where does your dad live now?" Burl asked.

Eva rapped her knuckles on the brush's wooden handle. Where was her mother—hurt, safe, hurt? "Can I call my mother before I go?"

"No problem." He lifted the veil off his head and looked down at her. "Why do you want to see the queen so much?"

She had the queasy feeling, then, that he could see through her veil, through her skin, into all her messy thoughts.

"I mean," he said, "wouldn't a lot of kids be bored by this?"

"No." Suddenly Eva wanted to be riding, to feel the air rush by. She handed him the brush and turned to go. "Everybody wants to see the queen."

9

You're not, he said when she told him. Miriam had done one home test, then another, squatting in the bathroom in the early evening, Francis still not home yet, the light coming in dusky purple so that she'd turned on the lamp above the mirror to make sure she wasn't seeing things. Oh my god, she had muttered when she first saw the pink double line. A deep, uncomprehending surprise, except how could that be, because on some level she had known for a few days—her period late, her breasts swollen, a watery, unfamiliar feeling in her limbs.

They had been careful at first, used condoms. Are you, you know, okay, she had asked him after the first month. Yes, he had answered. Me too, Miriam had said, and the next day she went to the clinic and got a new diaphragm. They had used it—mostly. Except for some times she could hardly keep track of, dream states almost, when she would half wake in the middle of the night and realize she was tangled in him; he was stroking her, silently, with a steady, concentrated touch.

The space between Miriam and the diaphragm was not, at those moments, more than twelve inches—she could picture it snug in its case—but how blinding the light would be if she turned it on to find the gel, how much easier it was to welcome him inside her, just for a sleep-stretched second, maybe two. Because actually this was her favorite kind of sex, like being slightly drunk in a dark room, rising from dreams to skin, taking a breath, sinking back again. There were no words here, no carefulness, no stiffening at the way that touch, when she was more awake, could bring her to the slicing edge of grief. This was pure floating, blurring, the diaphragm a bland moon far off on the horizon, ever present but easy to ignore. And something else—an impulse so dim that she herself barely knew that it was there. Tempting fate, was it? An easy ticket to a life with a more substantial, even a more demanding, shape? *It just happened,* she might say, and then she could sit back and let her body deliver her to a whole new place.

You're not, he said when she told him. As she'd sat waiting for him to come home, she had visited both abortion clinics and baby stores in her mind, picturing her body flushed clean, its old, knowable self, then trying to imagine it turned into a busy factory: fingernails, eyelashes, a pink tongue, and Miriam a mother, but where was her own mother to tell her what to do?

No, he said, and she said yes, according to the home tests she was, but she'd get a blood test to be sure.

Francis shook his head almost angrily, and she realized she hadn't given this part any thought. Her own body, she had focused on, looking hard inside herself, but now he was staring at her with an expression she couldn't pinpoint. Fear flip-flopped in her stomach and for a second she thought, though she knew it wasn't possible, that she felt something move.

"Jesus." He blew air out his mouth, a long, deflating hiss. "I can't believe—" He turned, walked to the window, turned again. "We," he said, "are idiots. Listen, I can't, I should've . . ."

His voice broke off then. He stood dully, his hands hanging at his sides. Can't what, Miriam wanted to ask. Can't believe it, can't handle it, should have used a condom, should have known? Suddenly she wanted to comfort him, or perhaps herself.

"It's okay," she said calmly. "It'll be all right. We need to figure out what to do, that's all."

He looked up at her, his gaze, once again, unreadable. It's still me, she would have liked to say. The same flat stomach, the same dip where my waist comes in from my hips. But already, she knew, things were shifting, her hipbones starting to melt, her bones moving apart to make room for something new. And was it the same Francis? As she stood across the room from him, she wasn't sure. How far away he looked, yet oddly distinct at the same time, like a stranger she had met on the street, taken home and burdened with this news. For a moment she realized she had no idea who he was, then he came into focus again.

"I need—Listen, Mim, I'm going to take a little walk," he said. And when she didn't answer, he simply turned and left.

Miriam sat on the bedroom floor, rocking. Her hands, she noticed, kept finding their way to her abdomen; she wedged them underneath her thighs. She would just get rid of it; that was what she'd do. She was too young to have a baby, and sure, she thought she loved Francis, but what did she know, really, and wasn't it wrong to bring a child into the world in such a haphazard, careless way? Friends of hers had gotten abortions; it would hurt, she knew that, but not unbearably, more like a bad rush of cramps, and it served her right for not being more careful. A clump of cells would be inside her, then not. She would be distracted for a week or two, and later in her life, when she had—but would she?—a few planned kids, she might look back and wonder what this one would have been like. She could handle that. How big could her sadness be for something she'd never known?

What she couldn't handle was Francis as a stranger, out pacing the city now, moving away from her, thinking thoughts she couldn't read. No, not that—not finding herself alone again, not after she'd taken the headlong step of linking her life with his. That was what mattered. I'll take care of it, she'd tell him when he got back. Oh Mim, I'll go with you, he'd say. And afterward, when she was back to her same old self, he would rub her shoulders and make her tea.

By the time Francis returned, she had managed, in some fitful, sidelong way, to fall asleep.

"Hey."

She heard him speak from a great distance and tried to rouse herself. "What're . . . where'd you go?"

"Just around, wandering." He patted her shoulder through the covers. "You okay?"

Awake now, remembering, she shook her head. "I don't know. I think so, I guess—"

"You really took me by surprise," he said. "I'm not ready for this, Mim. There are things . . ." He sat down. In the dark, she could feel him reaching for words. "I'm kind of a fuckup," he said finally. "I mean, actually you have no idea."

"Me, too." Suddenly Miriam felt light-headed, almost giddy. "I'm kind of a fuckup, too. I put up a good front, but it doesn't matter, I've decided—"

"No. No, you're not. You're not a fuckup, I know your mother dying was really hard for you, but—"

She sat up and put her hand on his arm. "Please will you listen to me for a second? I'll . . ." She had thought it would be easy to say: *I'll get an abortion*—such simple words. She tried again. "I won't have . . ."

And then, again, he was gone from her, across the room. She watched as he tripped over a pile of clothes and caught his balance. "I can't be responsible for that," he said.

"What do you mean?"

His words, now, came out staccato and swift. "Once a Catholic, always a Catholic, is that what I mean? I don't know, I guess—" He sat down on the bed, his back to her. "Whatever you do, don't do it for me, okay, and don't expect . . . I can't . . . you just need to do what you want, and I'll try, okay, whatever happens, but you've got to understand that, Christ, I'm not the most—"

"Me neither," she interrupted, not sure what either of them meant.

Francis turned to her, reached for her hand. "I can't even believe . . . this might sound crazy, but I can't even believe it *worked*, you know? Somehow I figured after all the dope I'd smoked, all the things I've—I mean, do you think it'd even be healthy, be okay?"

Ten flesh and bone fingers, she pictured. Ten actual toes, the stub of an umbilical cord where they cut it from her. Eyelashes and fingernails. Girl. Boy. Girl. "Don't," she said, and then he was in bed with her, she was in his arms, crying the unruly, impossible sobs of a child.

"Shhh," he kept saying, "shhhh, stop," but Miriam couldn't stop, gasping, reaching out to pull him closer. How had she come to this, ever the careful one, her mother's good, neat girl? She herself had been born of long trying; it had taken her parents years to conceive. Her bedroom, she knew, had been overready with its rocking chair and tinkly Russian music box, waiting like a room in a museum. Her parents had been married five, maybe six years by the time Miriam was born. *That* was planning, everything in place, and yet where had it gotten them? Maybe it had worn them out, trying so hard, or perhaps her father had been disappointed by her, expecting a miracle after all that time.

Stay here, be a good girl, I'll be back or else you'll come to me, he had told her when he left. Patiently, solemnly, she had waited, memorizing the postcard places—Western Wall, Red Sea—and writing to him at his kibbutz in her best script. But of course he had never come back, not for more than a few weeks at a time, and eventually Israel had turned into Florida, where he found a rich second wife, built a kidney-shaped pool, and sent her Hanukkah presents from this, his second Promised Land. "Forget about him," her mother had told her bluntly when she was a teenager. "He was trouble from the start, sweetie—a lot of big ideas but inside he has a kind of . . . emptiness, you know? He could never stick with anything for long." Listening, Miriam had thought she did know, maybe too well. Because didn't she have it, too, that emptiness? Wouldn't that explain why she had always felt as if life—the secret heart of life—was not for her to have? Over the years she had assumed she had inherited her mother's reluctant womb, her father's distant nature, but here she was in a new world, a rash, close place of multiplying cells.

"We don't need to decide right this second," Francis told her after she managed to stop crying.

"Yes we do," she said. "If we're going to—if it's coming out, I need to do it right away, I can't just let it keep—"

"You're right, maybe it would be better. I don't know if I'm father material, I have a hard enough time running my own life."

"Me, too," she told him, but she didn't really mean it. Running her life was not her problem, never had been; her problem was *living* her life, staying deep inside it, feeling as if it had a shape, a steady course. You're so gifted, she remembered her mother saying before she died. You could be anything you want; what do you want to be? Miriam had said maybe a professor or maybe a lawyer. But what had she really wanted? To please her mother, mostly, not to disappoint. And then her mother had died, leaving her in what was, in some ways, her most comfortable state—waiting for nothing, good or bad, to happen, wanting nothing much at all. Only now she kept seeing a black-haired baby—swelling her belly, strapped to her front. She would take it to the store. Francis would come from behind the counter and grab its toes, speak to it in Italian, show it off to customers.

"I think you'd be a good father," she told him.

"Really? Why?"

"Because, I don't know . . . you're a good person."

"Me? You think? What if I have you completely fooled?"

"What, you mean you're a con man?"

"A wan man, a gone man," he said. "A lawn man."

"So we'll move to the suburbs and you can water it."

"Or maybe a faun man. The kid might have hooves. Even in this neighborhood that would draw some stares."

"Please," she said. "We need to talk about this."

"Okay, okay." He sat up in bed. "I'd *like* to be a great father, you know, but shit, I'd like to be a great artist or furniture designer or the leader of a small nation, and actually, I sell mugs. We really kind of just met, you know. We don't know each other that well. People are . . ." He shook his head, silent for a time. When he spoke again, it was in a deep British television voice: *"People, ladies and gentleman, are complex."*

"I think you know me pretty well," Miriam said. "I don't know you? Really? At all?"

"No," he said. "Yes and no." He brushed his palm against her stomach, smoothing circles. "Biblically, you know me, don't you? You have carnal knowledge of me—we're begetting and begatting. What a thought, huh? Right in here." He lowered his ear to her belly. "Anybody home?"

"Do you think it's a boy or girl?" she asked quietly.

"It's nothing yet, Mim." His voice was far away now, muffled by the sheets; she couldn't keep up with him. "It's a glob of mucus—"

"But it's male or female, it's already determined. You're the one who just talked to it." She pulled away. "Stop talking to it, then. I can have one later, after I go to law school or something, right? Otherwise I'll be resentful that I didn't have time to get my life together and the kid will be messed up." She wiped her eyes on the hem of the sheet and blew into the tissue he handed her. "Or maybe not, maybe we should just go ahead—I mean, we were careless, right, we must have sort of . . ." She lifted the sheet and looked at her stomach. "Maybe I'll have a miscarriage. Or I could fall down the stairs."

"No," he said. "Fall asleep, that's all. Tomorrow it'll be clearer. Turn over—I'll rub your back."

"You should sleep, too."

"I'm not tired. Go on, turn over."

His hands on her back were like twin irons, smoothing her out. He leaned close to her ear. "Thanks, Mim."

"For what?"

"For saying I'm good, that I'd be good. You almost make me believe it."

You *are* good, she meant to say, but already he was singing: *Ninna-nanna, ninna-oh, questo bimbo a chi lo do?*—a song his mother must have sung to him.

That night, Francis stroked her back, sang her to sleep, comforted her long and well. Like a lover or a husband. Like a father (somebody's, not hers); she *could* see it if she let herself, the games he would play, the way he could coax a smile from a stone. She wasn't, it turned out, wrong about that part. My flying angel, he would call Eva two years later as he lay on the floor and balanced her on his upturned feet. My flying devil, monkey, fish. Down, he lowered her, then up, up and down again, until Eva hovered just above his face. Miriam would stand on the sidelines, a little left out, watching how enthralled Eva was when Francis played with her like this, how deeply (for there were no other words for it) in love with him she was. Close, he made her fly, then away. Close, away again. Flight and contact, his long fingers holding her—the finding, the losing, of a kindred spirit in the world.

10

"I'm moving back to New York," Eva announced.

"You're what?" Burl asked as if he hadn't heard; in fact, her words had simply taken him by surprise. He looked at her hunched across from him at his kitchen table. It was still morning but already hot, the old fan on the countertop struggling through a medium that seemed thicker and less hospitable than air. An hour earlier, as he was getting ready to extract, Eva had arrived at his door in a glowering, sullen mood, his mail in her arms. I'll help, she had told him, and so he had shown her how to tip the honey frame over the metal bowl and scrape the caps off the honeycomb with the uncapping knife. She had caught on right away and worked quietly and swiftly, but the air had felt fraught in the kitchen, and he had found himself wishing she would chatter, laugh or tell a joke. Now she looked up and dropped the knife onto the table, where it spun and then lay still.

"You're moving?" he repeated, realizing how sorry he would be to see her go. "Why? Is your mother's job not working out?"

"*I'm* going. Like I wanted to all along."

Her father—of course; she must be going back to her father. The one time Burl had asked her about him, she had ignored the question, and he had wondered if her father had run off before she was born, or if maybe he had died. But probably, he saw now, she had a father waiting for her in Manhattan, or even Italy. Italian kings, she had said last week—kidding, he assumed, but still he pictured a romantic figure, tall, handsome, irresponsible, a bon vivant with his daughter's wild hair. Maybe a drunk, or foreign diplomat, or the owner of an Italian restaurant in New York. He probably contacted Eva only sporadically, sending her expensive gifts and promises of trips to Rome. Or maybe there had been a custody battle and the mother had fled with Eva, kidnapping her, even, thinking no one would find them out here.

"Will you live with your father?" he asked, hoping to get her to say more.

She shook her head.

"But your mother's not coming? Really?"

Eva shrugged. "She can move to Mars for all I care."

"So what's your plan then? Where will you live?"

Reaching into the bowl in front of her, she scooped up a gooey handful of wax cappings, balling it in her fist. She squeezed and the wax spurted out between her fingers. "Can I do more now?" she asked. "I'm all done with these."

"Not yet." He had covered the table with newspaper and could see that her hands were inky from the paper, wet from the bowl of water, mucking up his wax. "We need to run the frames we've done through the machine before we start more, or we'll have too big a mess. And actually, I'd prefer that you didn't get those cappings dirty with your hands. It's the purest, best wax of all— I sell it to a guy who makes candles and ornaments from it."

Eva threw the clump into the bowl. "*Actually I'd prefer. . .* how come you don't just say *cut it out, stop it*? You're like my

90

mother—she pretended it was both of our ideas to move to this place because I saw the town on the map. *'Eva found this place, we're moving to this wonderful place Eva found.'* Except I *hate* it here, just like I knew I would. She knew it, too—it's why she didn't ask me. *Actually I'd pre—*"

"Whoa," he interrupted. "Fine, then. Cut it out, stop it." He tried to echo her voice so she could see how petulant she sounded, but the words came out in a ridiculous falsetto.

She glanced up at him, suppressing a laugh, he thought. Then she plunged her hands into the bowl again and met his eyes for a long, challenging moment. Clearly she was picking a fight, but he wasn't her mother, wasn't her father or even her babysitter, and in truth it wasn't a big deal if she mucked up the wax; it had to be melted down in any case. Still, he locked eyes with her, staring. She got to him, somehow; he had noticed it before. Her moods soaked into the air. Her stubbornness turned him childish and made his own rise up. For a long minute, he didn't speak or drop his gaze.

Finally she lifted her hands from the bowl. "Do people really have hives in New York City?"

Burl nodded. "Sure. They get them all over their bodies, from the pollution." He stopped and looked at her. "That was a joke, Eva. To cheer you up."

She gave him a weak smile.

"No, actually," he said, "I've read about people who keep bees in the city. There have to be enough blooms around, and the neighbors have to not mind. I guess you're planning on living alone? Does your mother know you're leaving?"

"My mother? She wouldn't notice. She's never home. She just expects me to sit there all day with that fat old Mrs. Flynn."

"Andrea Flynn?" Burl reached over to her side of the table and picked up the bowl of wax, then stood and put it on top of the fridge, hoping she wouldn't notice.

"I saw that." Eva grimaced. "You know Mrs. Flynn?"

He sat down again. "I've known her for years, if it's the same

Mrs. Flynn. Andrea. She went to church with my grandparents. Her husband died last year." And her son was killed in Vietnam, he started to say, but stopped himself. "Is she babysitting you or something? You never told me that."

Eva snorted. "She just sleeps all day. And she smells."

He had a jabbing, guilty urge to protect Andrea Flynn, whom he remembered as a well-meaning, sluggish woman who had brought cookies to his grandmother in her last days, when she was too feeble to eat. After Russ Flynn died, Burl had meant to offer to help with groceries or yardwork. He helped out two of the other local widows—bright, funny women who asked him in for coffee, called him "son," and made spunky jokes about their shrinking lives. But something about Andrea Flynn—her pale, broad face, her almost bovine slowness—had made her all too easy to forget.

"Why don't you give her a break?" he said. "She's old. She lost her husband."

And then Eva was standing, slamming her hand down on the table, making the frames rattle and shake. "I don't give a *fuck* about that! See, I don't *talk* like a stupid baby. I hate it here, I hate all of you! I don't care what she lost—I don't even know her! Why can't everybody just leave me alone?"

Her face was flushed, her whole body clenched, and then, as he sat staring at her, something else took over, her eyes spilling tears, her breath coming quick and shallow now, her chest heaving, shuddering with sobs. Oh shit, he thought. What did he know about crying, furious little girls, about this flood coming at him in his kitchen, which made him want to cover his ears, shut his eyes and back out his own door? Watching her, he felt as if he were witnessing a scene from a movie—the possessed child, the bad seed. The word *fuck* coming from her mouth had sounded grim and poisonous, too old for her, and on some level he wouldn't have been surprised if she had grabbed the uncapping knife and started hacking at his kitchen table—or at him. This was all too much. Family was one thing; you were born into it, you managed the best you could, but why should he have to put up with this from some kid he barely knew?

But then he looked at her hands, curled tightly at her sides, and at her face, which was contorted with a strangely adult-looking pain, and for a second he found himself wanting to comfort her. Only no, because that was another bad movie—the remote farmhouse, the single, middle-aged man reaching toward the sobbing, prepubescent girl in the faded tank top, her pretty shoulders gleaming in the light.

In the end, he had no time to do anything, because as he groped for something inoffensive to say (Would you like a glass of water? Do you want to talk about it? *Shit.*), Eva turned and fled the house.

Alone in his kitchen, surrounded by the heady, familiar smells of wax and honey, Burl loaded the frames into the extractor and waited, as the machine vibrated and whirred, for the honey to come through. Eva had wanted to see this, but he had no idea if she'd be back and he couldn't wait all day. He had orders to fill—three cases to deliver to the health food store, eight jars each for the B&B's, a case to Carole DeVaux, who was hosting a family reunion and wanted to give honey as party favors. "For My Sweet Family," she had said she would write on the labels, and he had wondered if she meant it. At one point, during a lull in the work, he thought about looking for Eva. Maybe as an adult, it was his job to see she made it home all right. But what about her mother, who didn't seem to keep track of her? And what about the fact that, though he couldn't quite admit it, she had bruised him with her words? He, who did not make friends easily, had considered her a sort of friend, and he had been generous and patient with her, teaching her about the things he cared most about in the world. Now she was spitting insults at him, cursing him for no good reason, feeding him fibs about moving away.

So let her go, let her cry. Other people suffered, too; eventually she'd figure that out. Other kids moved, and had babysitters, disagreements with their mothers, times when things didn't go their way. As a boy, he would have never thrown a fit like hers. Grow up, he wanted to tell her. He could picture her narrow shoulders squared, the proud, even arrogant tilt of her chin. I am, she would answer. I am. I already have.

Anyway, he had the orders to fill, and the work absorbed him, and an hour passed, then another, without him going outside. With his grandmother's pinking shears, he cut a new cheesecloth strainer to catch the bits of wax and wings that came through the extractor with the honey. He lifted and moved buckets, filled jars, scooped wax from the extractor, uncapped and loaded more frames. When he had filled a dozen jars, he skimmed off the bubbles and wiped the outsides clean. Finally, when his hands were too webbed with honey to be of much use, he stood at the kitchen sink and scrubbed the stickiness away.

This, the honey flow, was Burl's favorite time; each year he waited months for it, trying to be patient, like the bees. He loved the whole thing, from start to finish: putting in the bee escapes; feeling the weight of the supers when he lifted them; seeing the way the frames, when you pulled them from a healthy hive, were full of food. He kept expecting the novelty of it to wear off, but so far it hadn't. He loved the smell in the kitchen, and the wax (why had he been so stingy with Eva?) which his grandmother used to let him mold into sculptures.

I hate it here, Eva had said, but this was the place where, for weeks at a time, he managed not to return to the memory of his father's tight-lipped rages, his father's large hands reaching out to cuff his ears when he lost his house keys, or filled his pockets with dead bugs, or picked, as a teenager, at his acned skin, or came home smelling of dope. The nail-chewing, silent disappointment of his mother, the long dinners where his father made him stammer through his day (*F-f-f-un? What's "fun" mean, Burleigh Edward? Can't you do better than that?*). Burl had hated all of it; he, too, had hated, but so quietly, backing farther and farther away. And slowly, by removing himself and coming to this place, he had worked a kind of transformation, turning that hatred into something approaching love.

But love for what? For his grandparents, his dog, the land, Alice, the bees. For some dead people, insects, an occasional, casual lay? But Alice wasn't a casual lay, he cared about her, he loved her. Maybe he did.

"You're talking to yourself again, Bozo," he said out loud. It was one of the hazards of living alone, these exchanges that had, oddly, all the qualities of real conversation—jokes and rebuttals, anger, hurt feelings, surprise. It was like talking to Lissa, who seemed, with her moist gaze and cocked head, to be always on the verge of speech herself.

Around midafternoon, he drove over to Matthew Hartz's, where he kept a couple hives, and left a jar of honey wedged behind the screen door. In Matthew's orchard, both hives looked all right. He took a full super off and replaced it with an empty one. He didn't bother to wear the bee suit and got stung twice on his arm, as if the bees could sense his lousy mood. If anything, though, the stings made him feel better. There was a pleasure and pain in being stung, something like sex—the heat of it, the burn, the way his body wouldn't let him turn away.

Driving home, he slowed down by Andrea Flynn's but didn't have it in him to stop and see if he could help around the house. It was only after he was a mile down the road that he remembered that Andrea Flynn was at Eva's—the old Coulter house—baby-sitting. He could stop by, offer Andrea a hand, check on Eva. Last summer, a few months after Pete Coulter died, Burl had driven up the driveway to find the place a mess—the porch floor buckled, the blue paint peeling, the garden merging with the field. Somebody had left a heap of trash by the side of the house: garbage bags, a rusty walker, a porcelain doll that he had picked up, thinking maybe Meg would like it, then tossed away when he saw that it had no arms.

The first time he'd asked Eva where she lived, she'd been

evasive—down the road, over (a wave at the horizon) there. Once he'd figured it out, though, she wanted to know everything —who the Coulters were; how may kids they'd had; how, why, when and where they had died. Pete Coulter, Burl told her, died in the hospital of old age, a few years after his wife. How could you tell a kid that the old man's heart had stopped in the upstairs bathtub where she, no doubt, took baths? Now Burl drove past the drive-way but did not turn. A deep weariness had come over him, though about what, exactly, he couldn't say.

By the time he got home, the sun had managed to come out, so he walked up to the small pond in the far field behind the house, stripped naked and dove into the cool water. There, finally, he let himself relax, diving down, feeling the water cut past his face and along his sides, then swimming up to float on his back, his body green with slime. And down again, this time all the way to the bottom, where he skimmed the pond floor and scooped up fistfuls of silt. He dove and tumbled, kicked and splashed, opened his eyes underwater to see what he could see. Here at the pond he felt ageless, not forty-two, as he was, nor ten, as he often felt himself to be. He was an animal, a muskrat with a coat of slicked-back fur, an otter darting at a flash of fish.

It was late afternoon by the time he went into the barn to stack wood. It bothered him to have such a big barn with so little inside it so he'd begun making a long, low woodpile along the south wall from wood he had cut with a handsaw and hauled to the barn. He was bent over, pulling out the largest logs from a pile of split wood, when he heard a cough and turned to find Eva standing a few feet away. She must, he saw, have just climbed down from lying in the hay—her hair was spiked with it and stalks clung to her clothes.

"Oh," he said. "You're still here? I assumed you'd gone home. I didn't see your bike."

"I hide it in the bushes. I lost the key to my lock."

Relax, Burl was tempted to tell her. This is the country—

you're the only thief around. She scratched her arm, yawned and stretched, so casual, as if she hadn't been screaming at him just hours before.

"I guess I fell asleep," she said. "What time is it?"

He held out his bare wrist. "Don't know. Afternoon, late-ish. Did you wake up on a better side of the bed?"

"Of the hay? I guess so. It smells good but it's itchy."

He nodded, remembering his own naps out here—the careening, drunken flies, the smell of manure rising, sweet and grassy, from the stalls. Other things, too: smoking pot and cigarettes though he knew he could burn down the place; fumbling with the clasp on Alice's bra until she grew impatient and unhooked it herself. And another girl—from England, visiting somebody, he forgot who. Katie, maybe, or was it Caroline, so many years ago by now. She had made him laugh without intending to, she, too, growing impatient with his awkwardness: *Can't we please take our knickers off?*

"I used to nap out here," he told Eva.

"When you were my age?"

"And older, and younger."

She picked at the hay on her shirt. "When you were a baby? Did they leave you here by yourself?"

"Not as a baby, I don't think," he said. "But as a small boy, yes."

Eva nodded. "Um, I wanted to say . . . I mean, I'm sorry I yelled at you, before."

"Thank you. I appreciate that."

"I mean, it's not your fault."

"What's not?"

She shrugged. "Everything. My dumb life."

Burl held back a smile. "Come on, Eva—you're young, you have your health, you don't have to work for a living yet. Your days are your own. You might look back on this time and realize that life was pretty good."

She gave him a withering look.

"Sorry." He realized how pompous and smug he sounded. "Do you really think your life is dumb?"

She leaned against the barn wall and fingered an old, dusty bridle.

"Sometimes I wonder," she said. "I mean, like, what if I'd been born someone else?"

"That's an interesting thought. Like who?"

"Maybe a girl with tons of brothers and sisters, and pets, and lots of money. And . . . and . . ." She let the bridle drop. "I don't know."

He knew what she meant; if it wasn't one thing, it was another. He had always wanted not money, which he'd had, but a different kind of ease—being able to speak up for what you believed in, doing work out in the world, not feeling its bumps so badly that you kept running back to your hole. To lobby for environmental legislation, or be a real commercial beekeeper, or even just a guy with a wife and a few kids. Courage—that was what he wanted, the regular, daily, unheroic sort that so many people around him seemed to have. An end to mites. An ability to forgive, to weather storms. He wanted durability and elasticity, strength. Eva seemed to have those qualities, though what did he know about her, about anybody? He wanted compound eyes that, like the bees', could see many things at once, not just sights but perspectives, habits of thought, lost traces—a dog's or a father's, a grandmother's or a bee's.

"So you really want to go back to the city?" he asked.

She sat down on the barn floor and stroked Lissa's head. "My mother won't let me, not without her."

"I guess she likes it here."

"Maybe a little. Mostly she wants to punish me."

"For what?"

She started fiddling with Lissa's ears. Burl stretched his neck, sore from all the lifting. Up above, swallows were darting in and out of the rafters, quick and slim as bats. He reached for a log and started stacking again.

"Nothing," Eva said finally. "I can't wait till I'm not a kid anymore. *I* should punish *her.*"

He hefted a log onto the pile. "Why, what'd she do?"

"Lots of stuff. She used to read my diary—she still would, except I hide it better now. She doesn't even know I found out but I put pieces of my hair in it—that works really well—and the next time I looked, they were gone. And she goes through things in my room and comes in and just stares at me when she thinks I'm sleeping. I hate that. Actually—" she lowered her voice, "sometimes I think something's wrong with her, like she's going a little nuts."

"Maybe the move has been hard for her, too," he suggested. "Have you asked her?"

"'Fine fine fine.' That's what she'd say. She . . ." Eva paused. "She doesn't—well, like, okay, once in my diary I wrote, *hi Mom I know you're reading this so just tell me and I promise I won't get mad.*"

Burl smiled. "And?"

"Nothing. It doesn't matter. She never tells me anything and now we're in a big fight again. She didn't even say she was sorry before she went to work." She made a dismissive puffing sound. "Can I help make some more honey? Just for a couple minutes?"

"I'm afraid it's all done. Once it's uncapped it can't sit around."

"Then can we look for the queen?"

He hesitated, afraid to refuse and unleash her wrath again, or send her into tears. But it was late in the day and her urgency exhausted him. He wanted a chance to read the paper and check his e-mail, no more scenes. "Not today," he said. "Next week I'm going to re-queen a hive. I ordered a new queen this morning. How about you help with that, as soon as she arrives?"

Eva stood and dusted herself off. "Do you promise?"

"Cross my eye," he said. "Stick a needle in my heart."

"Shake." She thrust out her hand.

He reached and was startled by the firmness of her grasp; he could have been shaking hands with a grown man except that her palm was so small.

She was almost outside when she stopped and asked the question he was beginning, by now, to expect: "Can I please call my mother before I go?"

The way the light fell in the doorway, he could only see her outline, and suddenly she seemed her age again, or even younger, the tense, waiting figure of a child. If he squinted and got rid of her tumble of hair, she could have been him at ten or eleven; he could have been his grandfather, who could still walk then and spent long hours working in this barn, though his hands trembled and his shoulders twitched. Burl used to hover, running his fingers along the oily teeth of farm equipment or hanging over the edge of a stall where an animal stood chewing hay or peeing in a heavy, satisfying stream. Sometimes his grandfather would talk about the weather, or the past, or the weather in the past. More often he worked in silence, setting Burl before a milk cow with a tin of balm or giving him a round brush and letting him figure out, without instructions, how to work circles on a horse's flank and make the dust rise up.

"The door is open. Help yourself," Burl said.

11

Can I please call my mother before I go, she had asked, and of course Burl had said yes because it sounded like a simple question. But now the secretary was saying sorry, hon, your mom's left for the day, now Eva was hanging up the phone and having to tell herself to stop because here it was, starting up again, the ache in her gums and jaw and behind her eyes, the pressure swelling up inside her skull.

So she ran. Out the screen door, past the barn where he was stacking wood, down the driveway to where her bike lay hidden in the brush. She knocked twice for luck on the stem of a bush, grabbed her bike and took off down the road, pedaling as fast as her legs would go because no, hon, your mom just left, the phone call messing her up all over again, forcing her back to her same old games: Got to get home before a truck hits, before something happens, her palms damp against the rubber grips of her handlebars, her earlier anger curdled now, turned to sour fear—*please*

please let her be okay. Nononono as she rode toward the blue house, rounding bends that had become, already, almost too familiar, like a maze she'd been stuck in before.

And now, as she got closer to the house, the thoughts were coming on so fast she couldn't stop them—gears grinding, a thud against her mother's chest, a leg all by itself. Her mother's leg. She had seen it on the front page of the newspaper the week before, in Israel after a bombing by some group called the Millenniumists—a schoolgirl's leg so clean and perfect in its white kneesock that it looked like it had fallen off a doll. In five months there'd be a whole new century, the nines losing their legs, the zeros holes you could fall into, a girl on her own in the year 2000, an orphan girl—*in another century, my parents lived.* The world would turn old, Eva would turn twelve. At twelve you hardly needed a mother anyway, except she did, she still did, *let her let her be okay.* Her breath came raspy now as she bumped up the driveway: *I'm sorr—*

Then relief like a parachute opening wide, white and floaty in her head. The car parked neatly, safely, by the house. Her mother waiting on the porch, lifting her arm and waving. Eva waved back and went to put her bike inside the shed. Already she was making up her story, how she'd spent the afternoon at her new friend Lissa's at the farm down the road. They'd made butter, or sewn a quilt or done some other farmy thing. She knew her mother would believe her because Eva was an excellent liar and told her exactly what she wanted to hear. A friend, that's great, I knew you'd find one, Miriam had said the first time Eva told her about Lissa. And then, a little jealously: You've always been so good at that.

"Eva? Where are you? Where've you been?" her mother called, but Eva didn't answer.

For a long minute she stood catching her breath in the dark shed, feeling her heartbeat slow, letting her mother wait. Finally, when her heart was no longer hammering in her ears, she tried to make her face look blank and regular and stepped outside. She didn't need to say she was sorry; her mother would be happy to forget about the fight. Hi, she could say. Hi Mom. Like that. It would be plenty. It would be enough.

12

How was I born again?

You know, Eva. At noon, at Saint Vincent's Hospital.

In time for lunch. And it happened really fast?

I was only in labor for four hours. You were a Curious George, like now.

And you knew I'd be a girl, right?

I didn't really know—I had a feeling. I could have been wrong.

Did it hurt to have me? On TV they scream.

It must have hurt, I know it did, but then there you were and I forgot everything. Supposedly that happens to women after having a baby. You get a kind of amnesia.

A what?

Amnesia—when you forget big chunks of things.

So you forgot what it was like to have me?

No, I remember a lot of it, it's just that the actual physical pain is

*hard to recapture, which is fine with me. It happened so fast and then
there you were, looking up at me.*

Did I smile?

No, you were too little. Later you smiled.

Did I cry?

*Yes, but that's a good thing. They spank you to make sure you can
breathe. You know, silly girl—I've told you this before.*

But could I? I could breathe okay?

Perfectly.

And my father was there too?

He watched you be born.

And then what?

*Then . . . they cleaned you off. And he cried, too, he was so happy
to see you.*

*And after, you took me home and there was a picture he made of
a cricket and a sunflower holding a baby and you showed me and I
just stopped crying?*

See, you know the whole story. You should be telling it to me.

I was too little. I can't remember.

But you remember what I've told you. And you've seen pictures.

But that baby doesn't look like me.

What Miriam did not tell:

How, though Eva did stop crying for an instant when they
held her in front of the picture, she quickly started up again. How
much she cried during those first few months. The doctor said she
seemed fine, some babies were simply colicky, nothing to worry
about, just ride it out. But Miriam did worry. Eva was small, barely
six pounds, and her belly button was herniated, creating a bruised
knob that made it look as if she had been wrenched from the
womb, and her scalp was peeling in white flakes. There were
names for all of this—cradle cap, colic, hernia—but still, Miriam
found it frightening and would look down at Eva as she lay
sprawled across her lap and wonder how such a creature could
weather the jolts of the world.

Other things she did not tell Eva when she asked (she is six, she is eight, ten, her body curved toward her mother like nothing so much as a question mark). How, during those first few months, Francis slept less and less, Miriam more and more, and Eva slept in brief, deep spurts, then woke and howled out her need. She never told Eva how *agitated* a newborn she was, all twitching legs and high, reedy wails. Miriam, in contrast, was tired all the time, as if her every ounce of energy had been piped into the squirming body of this child. For the first week or so, the occasional visitor tromped up the stairs with stuffed animals and hooded towels. Sarah came with bags of deli food, and though she cooed at Eva, Miriam read relief in her eyes that her own life hadn't yet taken this turn. I'll come next week and bring more food, Sarah said. You don't have to, Miriam told her. I *want* to, said Sarah. You'll do the same for me. The visitors brought onesies, snugglies, rompers, receiving blankets—so many new words to learn; it wore Miriam out. She would chat for ten minutes, then feel her eyelids droop.

A baby nurse came for three hours a day. Lady Competence, Francis called her, and with her expert hands and firm voice she reminded Miriam of her own mother, who would have known exactly how to sponge-bathe Eva, clean her umbilical stub, get her to burp. Even Francis's mother warmed up a little, coming by with an elegant Italian baby sweater set and a tiny cross on a gold chain which Francis fastened round Eva's neck, then unclasped as soon as Flavia left. In the midst of it all, Miriam lay fighting sleep, fingering her pouchy stomach and trying to make Eva nurse for more than ten seconds at a time. *Soothe* was the word that kept running through her mind: *I want to soothe you, just let me soothe you.* And stuck inside her throat, her own sharp infant wail: *Me, soothe me!* Sleep was her blanket, her escape, and she gave into it again and again, leaving Eva in more capable hands. Everyone, it seemed to her during those early months, was better with this baby than she was, and sometimes, as she drifted into sleep, she found herself thinking she had made a terrible mistake.

* * *

The more she slept, the more Francis stayed awake. How lucky, she thought at first, and she marveled to her friends at how tireless he was. After the first few weeks he took over two of the night-time feedings, using breast milk she had pumped during the day. He was remarkably, unusually good with the baby, grasping her firmly and talking to her as if they were old friends. In his arms, Eva seemed almost to change shape, becoming less fragile, less otherworldly. And he could get her to stop crying. Miriam thought maybe it was his jiggling, the way he danced around the apartment with her, swooping and swaying, chortling and singing. Miriam couldn't do that—for one, she was too sore and sleepy, but also she was afraid the baby would break. Francis treated Eva as if she were an extension of his body, whereas Miriam kept having to remind herself that this creature had come from inside her and had moved into their apartment for good.

After the first week, Francis went back to work, and it was during those times, with him at the store all day, that Miriam often felt Eva to be truly inconsolable—a fiery, breathing package of fury and discomfort. Rub her stomach, said the book. Rub her back. Give her water to drink. Rock her. Try music or a pacifier. Try nursing. Turn on a fan or vacuum cleaner. Hum, sing, relax. Miriam tried everything except relaxing, and sometimes Eva settled down and they collapsed together, napping on the futon couch, the rise and fall of the baby's breath a reassuring pattern under her hand. But these were the rare moments; more often nothing worked, and it would be morning still, a long, relentless day stretching ahead, Eva's cries vibrating through the apartment like an alarm.

One afternoon Miriam heard knocks through the crying and opened the door to find a very pregnant woman in a pale green sari.

"Excuse me, I'm Ratha," the woman said. "From downstairs— we just moved in. I could try something, to—you know—help the baby settle down."

Miriam nodded, immensely grateful to this stranger, whom she trusted out of desperation, and because her voice was calm. She handed Eva over and stood watching as Ratha laid her on a blanket on the couch, folded her arms over her chest and swaddled her in a tight cocoon. In less than a minute, Eva slept.

"Oh," Miriam said, "oh, thank you." She felt like weeping. "That's amazing. I'm really sorry she's been bothering you."

Ratha shrugged. "She has too much room, that's all. They want to feel cozy, like in here." She patted her own protruding stomach.

"When are you due?"

"A week or so now. Soon you'll be hearing mine."

"Is it your first?"

"Oh yes."

"So how did you know how—"

"I'm the eldest. Of five. All of them are back home." Ratha flicked her wrist toward the window. "In India."

"It must be hard," Miriam said. "To be so far from home."

"Sometimes. We're managing, though."

"You don't find New York too difficult?"

Ratha shook her head. "We're lucky to have found this apartment, and I think my husband will study hard and do well. And maybe I can go back to school eventually. I was getting a business degree." She dropped her eyes, suddenly awkward. "Well, you've got a pretty baby, with strong lungs. I have food cooking, I'd better go."

"Wait—" Miriam said, then was embarrassed by the urgency in her voice. "I'm sorry. Could you—would you mind showing me how you wrapped her?"

Ratha waddled over to the couch and picked up a big stuffed rabbit with a cardboard tag still attached to its ear. Watching her turn sideways so she wouldn't have to reach over her stomach, Miriam remembered the full, mysterious weight of being pregnant and found herself wishing that she could spirit Eva back inside her, curled and peaceful. "Good, another blanket," Ratha was saying, placing the rabbit on top of it and arranging its limbs.

"Like this," she was saying, and Miriam thought, *yes, like this,* and again (would it happen forever?), she heard her mother's voice.

At the other end of the couch, Eva slept, her brow smooth, her lips puckered; even in sleep, she seemed to be yearning toward a breast. "Then like this, you see, tuck it in here, nice and tight." And although Miriam wanted to watch, wanted to be a good mother and keep her baby from crying, she found that she couldn't concentrate, her limbs too heavy, Ratha's hands too quick for her, the instructions rising and falling like a lullaby.

Slowly, Eva's days in the world turned into weeks, then months, and Miriam started to wake up a little, as if both she and Eva were coming into the world for the first time. Slowly, too, things started to get better. Eva's skin turned from mottled to clear, her scalp stopped peeling, her hernia grew smaller day by day. She became an expert nurser, latching on ferociously and stroking Miriam's breast in feathery circles with her hand. "There," Miriam would whisper. "There, see, isn't that good," so relieved that she was able to do something for this creature, filling her with food. And the more Eva nursed, of course, the bigger she got, so that soon she actually looked less like a dispossessed, skinny, breakable old man, and more like the baby on the diaper package, plump and padded. Her eyes began to focus more, and she cried less and less with every day, watching the light as it filtered through the curtains and turning her head at the sound of her mother's voice.

You were so friendly that people stopped us on the street to talk to you.

You smiled early, at around two months.

You loved music. Your father played the guitar for you and made up songs. You and Charu used to dance to them. She was a beautiful dancer even then.

What songs? Sing me one.

I don't know—not real songs. He made them up.

But like what?

Like . . . oh, I don't know. Funny songs, with your name, like . . . "Eve, Eve, my heart is on your sleeve." Something like that.

And what else?

Nothing else. Where's your jacket? We need to hurry or the laundromat will close.

When Eva was three months old, Miriam had to go back to work. The timing seemed unfair, to have to leave at precisely the moment that she was falling in love with Eva—with the sounds she made in sleep, with her burrowing body and alert eyes, with the tightness of her grasp. It seemed strange, especially since it took months to happen, but it *felt* like being in love—her attention was that narrow, that focused. She wanted the bulk of Eva in her arms where she could stroke her limbs and smell the soapy, slightly sour smell of her scalp. She sat for long minutes staring at Eva's face, trying to picture her at four, or ten, or twenty. "Hi, I'm Eva," she'd say sometimes to the air. "Maybe—let me check with my mom."

The happier Miriam got, the calmer Eva grew, or was it the other way around, the baby somehow drawing her mother toward her, wordlessly saying *come here*? Or maybe it was Ratha who turned Eva into a happy child. Charu was born a month after Eva, and by the time Miriam went back to work, Ratha had offered to babysit, taking on the two infants as easily if they were pet birds. Go, she'd say to Miriam in the morning, reaching for Eva. Go, you'll be late for work. Miriam would kiss Eva and leave, but part of her always lagged behind. The subway, the sidewalk, the stairs, the hall—all these were now lines leading toward Eva or away from her, longer than they used to be, stretched tight as wire. Walking home from the subway at night, Miriam would feel her breasts start to leak and her stride quicken, so that if there hadn't been people crowding her on every side, she might have broken into a run.

And Francis, amidst all this—where was he? Later she had to

ask herself. He was there. Yes, certainly; he was present. He was so good with Eva, so energetic. Inventive and charming. Sweet. But where was *he?* Working hard at the store with a new fervor; trying to convince his parents to open a branch in SoHo; drawing plans for an elaborate display window—a real olive tree filled with live doves and hung with plates, mugs and white lights. For Eva, he said. Everything was for Eva: the tree, the shop, his hard work. Miriam's mother had been like that, too. For you, she always said, leaving Miriam feeling both lucky and oppressed. For Eva, and Francis walked her up and down the narrow hall, sang to her, told her stories even when she was too young to understand. *Once there was a very small baby who lived in a very big city . . . and the baby slayed the dragon . . . and the baby wiggled across the Brooklyn Bridge to find biscotti for her dad.* On and on, the stories went, traveling the globe. Even in bed, with Eva sleeping, Francis wasn't tired. Almost every night he turned to Miriam and wanted to make love, or at least to tip her nipple toward him and taste her milk, and it wasn't exactly that she didn't desire him, but she was distracted, two places at once, and she had so little time. I have to sleep, sweetie, not now, I have—And waking later to find him gone from bed, but how was the baby and was she still breathing? "Francis," Miriam would call out, thinking, Eva, is she okay?

She was distracted, or worse? Unseeing, maybe, in the way of a person in love, her vision narrowed to the point of blindness. Or maybe not, maybe it wasn't her fault, perhaps anybody would have been fooled, because on the surface things seemed fine—better than fine, even, a whole new life, an unexpected gift. Except for . . . except for what? At the time, she noticed only that he had bursts of irritation at her slowness or sleepiness, or because she forgot to turn on the answering machine when she went out. He had never spent much time on the phone, hadn't even had a machine in his old place, but after Eva was born, he stayed up late and called people, friends Miriam hadn't heard of.

"So guess what—I'm a father," she heard him say once as she lay in the bedroom with a pillow clamped over her ear. "I know, it's unbelievable . . ."

"Who was that?" Miriam asked sleepily when he came in.

"What? Oh, Stephen, a friend from college. I haven't talked to him in years. He's a professor now at some branch of Penn State. He used to be a real stoner. Professor Deacon. I have to say, it kind of freaked me out. He said he got interested in classics and—"

"What time is it?" she interrupted, turning over. "Isn't it really late? Didn't you wake him up?"

Francis was bent over by the foot of the bed, half-lit by the streetlights from outside. "What'd we do with that child development book, the big paperback?"

"I don't know. It's the middle of the night. Come to bed."

"She'll be hungry soon, I figured I'd just wait up."

"But you have to work tomorrow, I don't understand how you're not totally exhau—"

"Let me just turn on the light. I swear it was right here, the big orange book, you know which one, I just need . . ."

Though she dove back under the pillow and shut her eyes, her eyelids burned from the glare of the overhead light and she could hear him rummaging through books.

"Where is it?" he said finally. "Where the fuck did that book go?"

Miriam roused herself and sat up, her eyes tearing. Francis had toppled a stack of books and was sitting naked on the floor with his legs splayed out. He was reaching in front of him, behind him, under the bed, shoving books aside, his hands a blur. Inside her, something clicked, a small waking of confusion, a sense that the man sitting before her was a stranger. A flutter of fear, then it was gone.

"What are you doing?" she asked. "You'll wake Eva. We'll find it in the morning. Come to bed."

"I need it now," Francis said, but he stood and shut the light off, startling her again with the sudden change. "I've got to look something up."

"In the morning. Please." She lay back down.

And then Eva's cry came, and Miriam felt her breasts grow hot.

"Coming, *bambina*," he called. "Hold on . . ."

"I can nurse her," Miriam said. "I'm awake now."

But he must not have heard her, or he must have chosen not to listen. A minute passed, then two. She lay waiting, her head aching, her breasts engorged with milk. But he didn't bring Eva in to her and she was too tired to call again. Finally she hugged the pillow to her face and slept.

He used to buy presents for you.

Like what?

Toys, mostly. Some of them you still have, like that wooden lamp with Humpty-Dumpty on it, you know? The one on the bathroom shelf.

Oh yeah, he made that for me.

No, actually he bought it for you.

You told me he made it.

He could have made it—he made you lots of other presents—but not that lamp.

But you told me he made it.

I didn't, Eva.

You did so. You said: Did you know your father made that lamp for you and painted on your name?

No, no, I didn't say that, or if I did, I was mistaken. Or maybe, I don't know, maybe he bought the lamp and painted the name on. It was a long time ago. It's certainly not worth arguing about. Tell me about school.

So did he paint my name on it?

Jesus, Eva, it was ten years ago, okay? I don't remember anymore.

*   *   *

When Eva was around four months old, Francis began to bring home baby things. Not just the normal supplies—diapers, Balmex, baby wipes—but bigger, more elaborate purchases: a brand-new, battery-operated swing with a built-in music box; a bright, flowered bumper for her crib, though it already had a plain yellow one; a ringleted doll, bigger than Eva and dressed like a skater, with a muff and fur-rimmed hood. Before the birth, Miriam had combed the city for bargains. The crib, changing table and high chair had all come from secondhand stores, and Eva's stroller and bouncy seat were from a discount baby place on the Upper West Side. When her mother died, Miriam had inherited twenty thousand dollars—her mother's life savings—and put it in a treasury note fund, determined not to spend it, her only cushion, her safety net. Like her mother, she was a coupon-cutter, a bargain hunter. She shopped the sales and almost never bought anything at full price. Now she would come home from work and find some bulky new package in the living room, or she'd open Eva's closet to find a violet party dress, starched and prim, not the sort of thing she would have thought Francis would pick out, or was it just that she didn't like it herself?

Inklings, then, nervous tremors, too small to add up to much. He was spending unwisely. He wasn't planning ahead. He was on some sort of odd, off-kilter lark. But side by side, relief and even admiration, for how could she fault him for being generous to Eva, and her own childhood had been so pinched and frugal, the money so carefully meted out, especially after her father left. When she told Francis that she was worried they were over-spending, he said the store was doing great, his parents had given him a raise. And when she brought it up again, a few weeks later, as the purchases grew more and more elaborate, he told her not to worry, he had sold some stocks.

"Stocks? What stocks?"

They were sitting in the living room while Francis finished setting up an elaborate plaything he had bought for Eva—an arched, wooden contraption hung with dangling mirrors, hand-painted acrobats, monkeys and clowns. Tied to a clown's leg was the price tag: $99.99.

"Some investments my parents got for me a while ago."

"Oh, I didn't know they . . ." She looked at him. "Really? Shouldn't we put it in a fund for her, or use it to pay Ratha? We're not exactly drowning in money."

Francis put Eva on her back under the arch and batted a clown over her head. "Don't worry, you worry too much. Your mama is a worrywart," he said to Eva, then began to sing it in a bluesy tune: *"Your ma-ma-ma is a worrywart, don't you worry, baby, don't you cry . . ."*

I'm not, Miriam tried to interrupt, but he wasn't listening, bent over Eva, who was staring up at him, rapt.

"Oh she worries in the day and she worries in the night and she worries on the ground and she worries while in flight—"

"Francis," Miriam cut in, unduly wounded, close to tears. "Don't tell her that. I'm not, I don't."

About that, at least, she had been right. She didn't worry, not enough, or not about the right things. Later, she would see how she should have worried more, louder, faster. Because while Francis stayed up all night jiggling Eva, and brought her home gifts, putting slot A into hole B, C into D until the toy took shape, things were coming apart inside his head.

13

One morning after they had been in the country for a little over a month, Eva woke with her limbs stiff and her mind crackling, the kind of sudden waking where she knew her dreams had taken her somewhere she didn't want to go but couldn't remember where. No lying in bed for her then, no drifting in and out of sleep. She got up, walked barefoot down the hall, leaned in (her mom still asleep, it must be really early) and felt herself wanting to burrow in next to the warm, quiet hump that was her mother breathing under covers. But no—Eva was too old, too itchy for that—so she went slowly back to her room and grabbed her book, a story about clones and aliens, from where it lay open on the floor.

So she didn't hear her mother get up. She really didn't. Already she had fallen deep inside her book. Later she realized that she must have gone into the bathroom, but she couldn't even remember walking down the hall.

"I told you, I need to shower." Miriam's voice came through the bathroom door, and Eva swam up, up out of the book to find herself sitting on the toilet.

"Just a sec," she called, reaching over to lock the door and sitting down again. In her book, a spaceship was taking off, and anyway Eva hated how rushed her mother was in the morning, how she ran around in her slip while the iron warmed, dabbing lipstick on her mouth and smoothing her hair into a silver fish barrette that Eva had bought her at a street fair in New York. No time for breakfast, no time for talking, even though Miriam had said that life in the country would be slower—we'll have time, finally, to hear ourselves think. But why should Eva want to hear herself think while her mother got in the car and drove away? *It's getting better at work. I met some interesting people today, from the newspaper office across the hall. One of them has kids around your age. Maybe sometime we could have a little housewarming party? What do you think?* Okay, Mom. Sure. Her voice sarcastic—a word she loved—and meanwhile it was just Eva and her soggy cereal, Eva and Mrs. Flynn, Eva and a TV that didn't work.

"Sweetie, it's after eight. I really have to shower. Can't you please hurry, or finish up downstairs?"

"I told you—I'm *going*."

Turning another page, the lie so easy for her; it was, after all, her own private matter, until finally Miriam starting banging. "I am telling you to let—me—in!"

But Eva wouldn't, couldn't let her in; she was blasting off, up into the sky, and *all* of it was disappearing—the move, the too-long days, the guard with his hand on her neck—all of it, she was lifting off, up, except she couldn't, her insides felt so clogged—she couldn't go, even if she tried, and then somehow she was crying, sitting there with her knees jutting out, her underpants around her ankles. She covered her mouth to hide the sound but still a croaking noise came out.

"Eva, what is it?" said her mother through the door. "Are you okay? Now I'm getting worried. What's wrong? What happened?"

And what *was* wrong; what *had* happened? She didn't know—
it just rose up in her lately, a bottomless, nameless something
that coated her mouth and made her stomach burn. When it
came over her, she had an urge to lower her head, ball her fists
and hurl herself against Miriam until she shoved back, hard, and
sent Eva sprawling to the floor. There they'd be, then, she and
her mother, looking at each other, maybe crying, maybe laughing.
There.

The day before, Eva had found three new hairs on her body,
down below, poking through her skin like wires. She had read
books about girls who actually wanted all that—bras and periods
and boobs—but the whole thing made her sick and what she
really wanted was to be a baby again, strapped to someone's back,
smiling at strangers on the street. She had plucked the hairs, her
eyes stinging at the pain, but she knew it didn't matter, they'd
be back. Later that day, after Mrs. Flynn left and before her
mother got home, she had gone into Miriam's bedroom and rum-
maged through her drawers, looking for—what? Her mother's diary, maybe, if she even kept one. *Today I read Eva's diary. Today
I watched Eva sleep.* In the nightstand by the bed, she had found
a magazine called *Country Living*, a few paperback books, a vial
of pills, some eye cream which she smeared on her elbow, a re-
laxation tape—breathe in, now let it go—that Miriam used to
help her sleep. Then she had gone further, picking up the books,
shaking them out. Some papers had fluttered out—bills, it looked
like, one with a sticky note attached: CALL VISA. There was a
blank card with sheep on the front, a coupon for an oil change
and, there—the letter from Ratha. As Eva pulled it from its envelope, she realized it was what she had been looking for all along.

*Mahesh and I are getting along a little better, I think—I'll tell
you more on the phone. Anyway, I signed up for the course.
Charu's dance recital is on August 22. Maybe you can come? I
hope Eva is doing well. I'm sure the counselor was right about*

her. Please try to believe this. We will come visit as soon as we can.

Now, as Eva started to get up, a hot coil uncurled in her belly. "Leave me alone!" she screamed, sitting back down to a surprising, hot rush of diarrhea. What is it, her mother kept asking through the door, but meanwhile she was checking her watch, brushing her hair, getting ready to leave; Eva could hear the staticky swish of the brush.

Slowly, she wiped herself and flushed, then stood and washed her hands, still breathing through her mouth because her own smell made her sick. Her face in the mirror looked back at her, swollen and ugly, a girl she wouldn't want to know.

"Eva," her mother was saying. "I'll get you some Kaopectate, or whatever you need. It's in the closet there, just open up."

"I don't need it. I'm fine," she answered, and her voice surprised her because, in fact, it sounded fine.

"All right, then, please let me in."

She opened the door and saw her mother all ready to go in crinkly black pants and a pale green blouse, green glass earrings dangling from her ears.

"Are you okay?" Miriam asked. "If you're really sick, I can call in, I—"

"No, actually I was faking."

"You know that's not what I meant. I meant is it serious, does your tummy hurt?"

Her mother leaned closer, as if she thought she could see right through Eva's clothes and skin to what lay inside. Eva shielded her stomach with her hands. "I just had a little . . ." She rolled her eyes. "I'm fine, okay? I'm not sick."

"Why don't you take two teaspoons of Kaopectate to be safe? It's the mildest—"

"I said I'm fine. Fine. In English that means okay. Not sick."

"All right, good. Great, Eva, great. I'm glad you're fine. I don't understand what's gotten into you, I just—" Miriam looked at her watch. "I have to go, I can't lose this job. I got dressed—I don't have time to shower now." She slipped past, pushed the window open and took her toothbrush from the counter. Eva turned the hot water on, stood squarely in front of the sink and began, for the second time, to scrub her hands.

"For godsake." Her mother let out an unhappy little laugh. "You don't want me to get fired in the first month, do you? You can't *do* this to me in the morning—we talked about this last week. Would you just let me brush my teeth?"

But no, Eva couldn't let her, wouldn't, because in fact she wasn't fine, her stomach hurt, and her teeth, bones and brain, and in a few minutes Mrs. Flynn would roll up and get paid to sleep, and Miriam, speeding down the highway in a car she could barely drive, would get hit by a truck, and Eva would go to the funeral knowing that if only she had kept her mother home a little longer, or had let her go a little earlier, everything would have been all right.

"Can't I please come with you?" she begged, as she did every third or fourth day. She turned the hot water off and made room. "You could just drop me in town."

"All day? You know it's too long for you to be wandering around alone. If you're sick, get back in bed and I'll stay home and take care of you. If you're not, you need to stay here with Mrs. Flynn."

Eva slammed down the lid of the toilet and sat down. Her mother was afraid of her stealing from the stores in town, though she'd never say so. She was afraid that Eva would take something, get caught, and be sent by juvenile court to a home for delinquent girls, where she'd shoot up drugs and end up as a crazy homeless lady with no teeth. "There but for the grace of God goes every one of us," Miriam said once after they walked by a woman like that (*but I thought you didn't believe in God*).

"I understand." Miriam turned on the cold. "You're bored and lonely—I would be too, but it's temporary, I promise. School starts in less than a month and you'll make lots of friends. What about that girl down the road? Elisha. Is that her name?"

"Lissa. I told you before."

"Whah bough huh?"

Toothpaste dripped from the corner of her mother's mouth; Eva had to look away. Lissa's a *dog*, she almost confessed, but that would prove she was a liar in addition to being a thief. "She's busy today," she said instead, going even further. "She has to go to the doctor. Something's wrong with her back."

Miriam rinsed, wiped her mouth with a towel and pulled the skin below her eye down with one finger, crayoning brown eyeliner along the inside edge. "That's too bad. I hope she's all right." She started the other eye. "Is your stomach really okay?"

Eva nodded, watching her mother watch her in the mirror.

"Good. Shit, I'm really late." Miriam turned and pecked her on the top of her head. "Okay, 'bye, baby. Mrs. Flynn will be here any minute. I love you. I'll call about more camps today. 'Bye."

It wasn't until her mother was at the bottom of the stairs, almost out the door, that Eva stood, and then she was rushing down the hallway to the top stair, words flying out her mouth. "You *won't* call!" she yelled down. "It's too late for camp and you never call! You promise and promise and never do anything! I *hate* you, you leave me here like a stupid pet, it's no fair, it's—" The words all stuck in snot and spit, in hot, rising tears, and there was her mother turning at the bottom of the staircase, so far away, so dressed and pretty and late.

"Eva, please—not now. I called a few different places, I told you that. One was full and the other didn't seem right, but I'll try again." Her voice was so even and controlled that it made Eva want to hurl herself down the stairs and land in a limp pile at her feet. "I'm asking you not to start this now, to try . . ." Then her voice snagged, and something in Eva leaned forward and back at the same time: Was her *mother* about to cry?

"We both need—we really need to calm down," said Miriam. "This is a big change and it isn't easy for me, either. I've started a whole new job—it's very stressful for me with the driving and . . . and trying to figure out how to manage everything at work and get you settled, but I'm doing it because I, I just thought it'd be good for you—for both of us, of course, but for you in particular, so when you *scream* at me like this, don't you see how you, how I just can't . . ." She put her hand over her mouth and made a breathless, gasping sound.

Don't cry, Eva thought, her own eyes growing hot. Just don't.

"I know this whole thing is hard for you," her mother said more calmly. "But I'm exhausted, I hardly slept at all last night and I need you to try to think a little about me, too."

But Eva did think about her—all the time, way too much. From where she stood, she could see her mother take a deep breath, could almost hear her counting backward to herself like a spaceship about to launch: three, two, one, a belch of smoke, then gone. If only her mother would *talk* to her, would settle down on the stairs, take off her shoes and let her real face show. What would she say? I'm sorry. But why would she say she was sorry when it was Eva who'd had a fit?

"I—have—to—go—to—work," Miriam explained. "To earn—"

"I know that," said Eva loudly. "All you ever talk about is money. You think I don't know?"

"Then you need to understand. I'd like nothing better than to spend—"

"Well I wouldn't—I hate you! Didn't you hear me the first time? Are you deaf or something? What's *wrong* with you?"

She turned, ran down the hall and flung herself, sobbing, onto her bed. She cried for the day that stretched ahead of her, for the night that lay behind her, for the way that everything—her friends, her mother, even her own dreams at night—felt just out of her grasp. Curled in a ball, she cried extra loud for her mother's benefit until her throat burned and her rib cage felt like it would split. Finally she stopped and turned over onto her back. She wanted her mother to come upstairs and say she was sorry, or at least say that she'd come home early so they could go out to dinner, or make cookies, or take another walk behind the house, where darkness would come quickly and Eva would be allowed to be scared of the dark, to be scared. Come on, goose, Miriam might say. Let's blow off work and go for a drive. Or: Let's surprise Charu and Ratha and make an overnight trip to the city, what do you say?

Instead, Eva heard the car door open and shut, heard the car start up and go down the driveway, spitting out the pebbles in its path. Her mother was giving up on her; they didn't even really like each other anymore. When Eva was six, or even eight or ten, she had fit right up against her mother. Spooning, Miriam had called it. You're my perfect girl, she'd say. What would I do without you? And she would rock Eva as if she were a baby still, though Eva was too big and her legs dangled down. For a little while, there—Eva couldn't remember how long—her mother didn't have to go to work and Eva didn't have to go to school. They made cookies and read stories, went to the zoo, cried, both of them together, though Miriam cried more, and Eva stroked her mother's cheeks and hair and whispered shhhh. And all Miriam's friends seemed to understand that Eva had an ache in her fingernails and teeth and the roots of her hair that might never go away because *my father died*—she said it often, to her teachers when she went back to school, to her friends—three little words and peoples' faces grew soft, or sometimes scared. It had been true and not true; she hadn't quite understood, then, what "died" was, knew only how funny the world felt without her father in it, and how her mother squeezed her hard, sometimes too hard, and let her sleep where he had slept, in the queen bed, which Eva had thought must be from Queens, like her mother was.

For an hour, maybe, after her mother drove away, she lay in her room. At one point Mrs. Flynn came in downstairs and called out. "I'm sleeping," Eva called back, and then she actually did go to sleep, pulling the quilt on top of her, its weight a comfort like the lead X-ray apron at the dentist's office, whose even heaviness she loved. Finally she got up and peeled her nightshirt off. It was a hot, cloudy day, her skin already sticky. She put on a tank top and shorts and went downstairs. Mrs. Flynn was sleeping, too, stretched on the plaid couch in the living room, *People* magazine open at her side.

"This is so dumb," Eva said. "I'm going out."

Mrs. Flynn turned as if she might wake up, then settled more deeply into the couch.

Eva raised her voice. "I just wanted to let you know that I'm going into town to get drunk and steal some earrings."

It might have been funny if there'd been someone to hear it. She pictured her new friend Lissa laughing, tossing her blond hair. Or Charu, who was more real than anybody, impossible to invent. Charu's hair was black and slippery-shiny, with a little red from the henna her mother put on it, mixing the green powder with a raw egg, coffee grounds and a squeeze of lemon juice. A few times, Ratha had done Eva's hair, too. Now Eva tried to remember the smell—sweetness and spice, clay and dirt, Ratha gathering up her hair and rubbing the paste into her head. "Actually I'm going to Lissa's," Eva said, and saw in her mind the real Lissa—her black nose, the gray-pink insides of her ears.

"And to Burl's," she added. Her only real friend around here, but she knew better than to tell her mother about him. Eva knew more and more things, these days, that she didn't tell her mother—about the bees, for one, and gardening and mites. Not to mention her talks with Jesus, the hairs on her body, her nipples, which were starting to chafe against the insides of her shirts. The honey in her closet. Her diary, which was hidden away like the queen bee.

Her father, Francis DiLeone, had liked insects. It was one of the things she remembered about him. He had liked insects, birds, the chimps in the zoo. His name meant "of the lion." Her name, Eva DiLeone Baruch, meant Eva of the Lion Blessed, because *baruch* meant blessed in Hebrew. When she was born, her last name had been the same as her father's; her middle name had been her mother's last name, and they had picked Eva after her mother's mother, Evelyn, who was dead. But after Eva's father died, her mother wrote away somewhere and had the name switched around so that Baruch came last—*so people know we're a team.* In Eva's baby book, it was the old way, Eva Baruch Di-Leone. When she was younger, this had confused her, as if the book was about a slightly different girl, or a world with a slightly different order.

Her father used to take her to Central Park and teach her the names of things. Most of it she had forgotten—tree names, bird names, her father's face except for how it looked in pictures or came to her in pieces, a loud, short laugh at something funny she had said, a head thrown back, the dark tunnels of his nose. Other bits surfaced in her mind now and then: the fuzz of her mitten against his leather glove; his palms cupping her knees when he held her on his shoulders; getting home late one time, her mother mad. She remembered (or was it from her old *Desert Creatures* picture book?) a big lizard in a cardboard box. One day he brought it home for her; then it was gone.

My father died, she used to say, but now she almost never brought it up. It had happened too long ago and didn't make her sad anymore, at least not in any way she could explain. Lots of kids only had a mother, anyway—it wasn't a big deal. For some reason, though, last winter she had stood in the basement of the church on Second Street and told Dimitri as he fed the cats: *When I was six, my father had a heart attack and died.* He had nodded like he wasn't surprised and told her that her father was still with her, that God took the bodies of the dead but let their souls return in different forms. Yeah, right, she had thought at the time, but now, as she went to the shed to get her bike, it crossed her mind that maybe her father was returning in the form of a bee, the way Jesus had come back after he died.

But no, because Jesus hadn't really come back—not if you were

Jewish. Jesus was an extraordinarily kind but regular man; this was what Miriam said once when Eva asked. An extraordinarily kind man and some people wanted to believe he was the son of God. Anyway, hope worked better if you hoped for tiny things. Eva would hope small—that there'd be a letter from Charu, that she'd see a deer in a field, that today would be the day she'd see the queen.

14

When did it begin? Afterward—right after and much later—people kept asking Miriam, as if she held the key. In truth, her hands were empty, more than empty—knotted, terrified. When did it begin? She didn't know. As a student she had hung posters on her walls with pale blue putty, pressing firmly with her thumb but knowing that eventually, gradually, in a movement invisible to the eye, the putty would lose its grip, the poster would slide softly to the floor. It was like that, what happened to Francis. This day or that day, she might have ventured. August tenth, September nineteenth, October first. Or the hour of his birth, or the night of his conception, or the moment of his parents' births or conceptions, the trouble lying buried in their genes. Or sometime in the years before Miriam knew him, or during the many hours of their life together when he was awake and she was sound asleep. Please, she wanted to beg her questioners. She had known him for less than two years—had known him, she was realizing, hardly at all.

One day in early September, Francis came home with five bottles of orange antiseptic soap, the liquid kind you pumped into your palm. A bottle for the kitchen, he said, plus one for the bathroom, one for Ratha downstairs, two to save. Eva was five months old, fat and healthy.

"We don't need to wash before we touch her anymore," Miriam told him. "The book says just for the first month."

"I read a different book." He was already at the sink. "And we live in a filthy city. Come, wash your hands"—his voice so commanding that her skin suddenly felt coated with grime.

Was this the beginning? Maybe. Probably not. She didn't know. Possibly things started to fall apart the day he brought home covers for the electric outlets, though Eva couldn't crawl yet, and a baby gate, though they had no stairs. Or was it the moment that Miriam stood in the laundromat emptying out his pants pockets and found a plastic bag full of half-smoked joints in his jeans, though he'd told her he never got high? It was hard for her to say, especially because, on the surface, September of that year mostly seemed like a good month. The stifling August heatwave was finally over; the apartment was cooling down. Eva smiled constantly and was sleeping through the night. Miriam was back at work, tired and torn but managing. And Francis— Francis was happy, or at least he said he was. "I'm so happy," he kept announcing. "I never knew I could be this happy—let's have a thousand more kids!"

That was the month he stopped sleeping altogether, but Miriam wasn't witness to that, too often sound asleep herself. Later his doctor would ask her how many hours a night he had been sleeping, and she would find that she couldn't say. When she was awake, she saw how he planned and plotted, drew pictures for Eva and played his guitar, shopped and shopped, spending money she hadn't known they'd had. First he brought home toys, then air and water filters, a lead-detection kit, a plush carseat, though they had no car, a baby monitor, though their apartment was so small that it was impossible *not* to hear Eva when she cried. He started taping foam padding around the sharp corners of tables and bolting bookcases to the walls, and one day he came home with a strange fluorescent yellow seat contraption (for a boat? a bicycle?) called Baby-Hold-Me-Safe.

Inappropriate Safety Items. Later the doctor wrote it on the report and Miriam realized that she should have caught on sooner. At the time, though, many of his purchases seemed smart to her; she wished only that she had thought of them herself. What was wrong with her, that it hadn't occurred to her to check the paint, to filter the impurities from the air and water? Why hadn't she noticed the electrical outlets with their shocked faces, the chipped paint on the windowsills, the sheer drop from couch to floor? Before long, Eva would be crawling, cramming loose objects into her mouth. Statistically, Francis told her, babies choked most often on Barbie shoes, then on popped balloons, then dog food. They lived, he said—but somehow always so cheerfully—in a dangerous, dirty, overcrowded city, in a country burbling with toxic waste. Be more careful, she told herself sternly. The world (she had always known it; why was she somehow forgetting now?) is a very dangerous place.

Then the pamphlets. *Baby's Ear Infections; Baby's Upset Stomach; Sudden Infant Death Syndrome; Signs of Spinal Meningitis; How to Tell If Your Baby Has Hearing Loss.* He didn't show them to her. She found them folded small and tucked like talismans in the dark cranny between cushion and chair, in the flyleaf of an old Italian cookbook, in the pocket of his bathrobe. Her worry sprouted then, but for Eva, not for Francis—or at least these were the thoughts that rose, visible, to the surface of her mind. Did Eva have hearing loss? Would they come in one morning to find that she had stopped breathing in her crib? Miriam refolded the pamphlets along their creases and returned them to their hiding places. Would a more capable person, she had to ask herself later, would a better, a braver person have gathered the evidence, stacked it in a pile and asked the question she couldn't seem to ask, nor even quite think: *What's wrong?*

Miriam asked nothing. This wasn't difficult; Francis seemed so gleeful, so full of plans. For the new store in SoHo—he would put all the profits in a college fund for Eva. For a trip to Italy when Eva was a little older, so she could learn about her roots. For a book he had begun (waving a sheet of paper in front of her) on the history of Maiolica pottery. They could go to Deruta; he would interview his relatives there. Or maybe a children's book— yes, that would be even better. He had an old friend in publishing who had been bugging him to write one for years. He would illustrate it, too; it'd be about a kid who apprentices himself to his grandfather. Or *her*self. A girl. Eva. She can paint like Michelangelo; people come from miles around to watch. *Che pensi, piccola mia*, he asked her, and Eva made her birdlike trilling noise.

So much busy happiness in their apartment; it startled Miriam after so much quiet sadness, made her tiptoe, afraid of messing things up. Eva was becoming herself; already you could see her comic sense of timing, her stubborn will, the way her eyes swept around the room like searchlights, gathering. Her hands, too, were always in motion—squeezing, grasping, stroking. Each night Miriam arrived home hungry for her touch. She'd put on a jazz CD, draw the curtains, light a candle and arrange the baby on her lap to nurse. The city, the world, work, even Francis fell away, then. It was just Miriam and Eva, fastened to each other. Sometimes Francis was home already and wouldn't stop chattering, walking in front of the rocker, behind it, in front again, circling Eva as she fed. It got on Miriam's nerves, but she tried to be nice because the books all claimed that nursing made the father feel left out. Mmmm, she'd murmur, not exactly listening, too taken with the grunting noises Eva was making, with the dense, mysterious weight of her head.

One night she got home from work and stopped by Ratha's to pick up Eva. The door swung open the instant she knocked, as if Ratha had been standing waiting with Charu in her arms.

"Hi," Miriam said, reaching to touch Charu's cheek. Later, it all felt etched in her memory: the way Charu turned her face away, the smell of onions cooking, the purple-blue glow of the TV in the background, a car alarm going off outside somewhere, the baritone murmur of the evening news.

"Is she sleeping?" Miriam peered into the apartment.

Ratha hesitated, then looked at the ceiling. "No. A few minutes ago he . . ." She shook her head. "Francis already came for her."

"Oh, good. Is she still touching her ear? I hope she's not getting an infection."

"She's fine, Eva's fine. I didn't want . . . he was . . ." Again Ratha raised her eyes to the ceiling. "I'll talk to you later. Why don't you go upstairs?"

"Why? What happened? Did something happen?"

Ratha touched her arm. "Go now, please. Hurry. For Eva."

Miriam ran down the hall, up the stairs, *for Eva, for Eva*, punctuating her every step. And it was then, on her brief, rushed climb to the apartment, that a door in her mind swung partway open and she saw the events of the past months in a harsh new light. *For Eva*—it could only mean that she wasn't safe with him, that Francis might be hurting her—what else could Ratha mean? *Hurry*, and she was, she was hurrying, but she couldn't get in, her keys lost in the bottom of her purse, her mind flapping—impossible, unlikely, not Francis, no. *Find them*, she ordered herself, just as her fist closed around a key.

She opened the door to find Eva making spit bubbles in her bouncy seat, to find Francis on the couch with the cordless phone, talking as he jiggled the seat with his foot. She stood in the doorway, trying to absorb how ordinary they looked. When Francis glanced at her, she lifted her hand in a slight wave, then went into the bathroom, closed the toilet lid and sat down to catch her breath. *For Eva?* What was going on? It made no sense. Why would Ratha say something like that when Eva was obviously fine?

Francis was still talking on the phone—some kind of business call, it sounded like—when she came out, unstrapped Eva from her seat, and took her into the bedroom to nurse. He had bathed her. Her hair and eyelashes were wet, her forehead scrubbed; she smelled sweetly of lotion and soap. "You're fine, aren't you?" Miriam whispered. "You're just a hungry girl." Eva nursed for twenty minutes, then let her head go limp and fell asleep, so Miriam took her to her crib. When she came out, Francis was on the couch with a pen in his hand and the phonebook open on his lap.

"Hi." She leaned over to kiss him.

He jerked away. "Where have you been?"

"Right now? In the bedroom, nursing her. She fell asleep, I just put her down. Did something happen, Ratha seemed—"

"No, no—before, I mean—where were you before? You don't even get home from work in time, you don't even . . . you just leave her with that . . ." He slapped his palm down on the phonebook, and Miriam took a step back. So something *had* happened; he and Ratha must have had some sort of fight.

"I was a little late," she admitted. "There's a deposition tomorrow. They wanted me to stay even longer. But Ratha never minds, I pay her for the extra time, we've discussed—"

"Of course she doesn't mind!" He looked up, his eyes shining. "It's just what she wants, to get her hands on Eva for as long as possible, to infect her with all that, that *garbage*. I know what she's doing down there, I can hear it!"

"What? What can you hear? What are you talking about?"

"On the monitor. She's telling her filthy stories, from her fucking *Kama Sutra* or whatever, all the positions—in out, up down—and giving her infections, it's what you get hiring the first goddamn person who comes along without an interview or screening—you can't just dump her in a stranger's hands, my mother was right, we should've gone through Catholic Services and now

I've been calling every fucking place between here and . . ." He held up the phonebook, and Miriam saw that he had looked up Nanny Services and drawn thick blue X's through more than half the numbers.

"I don't understand," she said. "On the monitor? Ratha? What're you talking about—"

She didn't know what to say, or even think. Ratha had, over the past months, become her friend. On Saturday mornings, twice now, they had met for tea. Each morning when Miriam brought Eva down, Ratha opened the door first an inch, then two, and peeked through, calling, "I see somebody—I see you," until Eva crowed and reached. Ratha would never . . . no, it was impossible. Except that nothing was impossible, not if Miriam could stand in their apartment, a diaper draped over her shoulder, and hear Francis say such things. Because what did she know of Ratha, really? People could fool you, saying one thing, doing another, and yet you trusted them, you gave them your child, left her for hours, for days at a time, then accepted her back like a bundle of laundry, a packet of mail. A good day. A taste of applesauce. Two nice naps. And the baby? The baby, of course, was speechless. She couldn't say.

"Tell me again," Miriam said. "What did Ratha do? What did you hear? I just don't understand how you could hear her on the monitor, how—"

"I *told* you, dammit," Francis said impatiently, and even his voice sounded foreign to her—faster, sharper, almost obscene. "I'll just have to stay with her," he said, "until we find someone, or maybe for longer—you can't leave your kid and expect her to be all right, I mean the whole thing is completely out of control and I kept trying to stop it, every day for months and months, you know, but it just keeps *coming* at her, I mean, how dare you, how fucking *dare* you leave her with that Indian rat-assed bitch?"

As Miriam listened, something detached inside her. Something took small, careful, backward steps until, though she was standing a few feet in front of Francis, she felt herself float very far away. Eva, she kept thinking. Don't worry, I'm right here. Her whole body was poised for flight, and at the same time, she was watching Francis, *seeing* him for the first time in months—how feverish his eyes were, how thin and pale he looked, how his shirt was buttoned wrong, making him look lopsided. It wasn't Ratha; it was Francis. Why hadn't she noticed? He was hallucinating; he was sleep-deprived, or sick, or doing drugs. He was saying crazy, awful things he didn't mean. Because this wasn't him, it couldn't be. And then, somehow, she was flung back inside herself, right there next to him again, wanting to touch him, bathe him even, take a washcloth and wipe this violent, outside thing away.

"Francis," she said, and he looked up as if he was surprised to hear his name. "It's me, Miriam," she added stupidly, but he nodded as if he hadn't been sure. "What's wrong? Did you take something? Are you tripping? We can call a doctor. I'll call—" She was crying now, holding a lock of hair over her mouth. "What's wrong?" she asked again. "Are you okay?"

For a long instant he stared at her, and his eyes seemed full of sorrow. She took a step closer and reached out her arm.

"Don't!" he yelled, shielding his face. "Get away from me—your hands are filthy, even the tokens have it slime-balled on them, the banisters and barristers, fucking germ dogs pigeon shit, didn't you look inside that monitor? I'll kill her, I swear to god, I'll fucking strangle her, she's giving Eva chlamydia, which for your information is a hidden disease, she's putting her hand up her—"

"*Stop*," Miriam told him. "You don't know what you're saying, you're—" She pointed—toward Eva or Ratha, she didn't know. "Please," she said. "Please try to stop."

Francis squeezed his eyes shut and jerked his head back and forth. When he spoke again, his voice was quieter, murmuring a kind of chant: Okayokayokayokayokay.

"I don't—" Miriam faltered. "Listen, Francis, I have no idea what's happening, but you're . . ." She swallowed and tried again.

"You're scaring me, and you'll scare Eva, so you need to stop. For Eva. You need to stop for Eva? Okay? Can you do that?"

He nodded as if he understood. "Okayokayokay," he said, "so just relax and let me take care of it and find a new sitter for her, I just need to find one, I need to concentrate, that's all, just for a second just . . . just stop talking so loud so I can . . ." He leaned back over the phonebook. "Mary Jo Family Care ABC Nanny Warranty Shmarrenty, the Magic Helper, there's a zillion of these things, look at this, we live in the world's greatest city but you've got to know what you want or they'll screw you left to right, here it is—criminal background check CPR first-aid TB test drug test driving records support systems. See?" He held up the book again. "You have to do all that for Eva, I mean, she's the most unbelievable kid, we need to make sure she's—"

Miriam nodded. "I know, of course, I'll . . . why don't I go check on her?" She began backing toward Eva's room, needing the child in her arms, needing—what? To think straight, to not fall apart, the telephone, yes, to pick up the phone and call for help. But the phone was sitting on his lap.

"Don't forget to wash your hands with antiseptic soap!" Francis called, singsong, after her.

"I already did," she lied. "In the bathroom, when I got home."

"Do it again, you've touched things—you touched the filthy telephone and the video cameras, which are all . . . all—red but nobody can sterilize it, it's just . . ."

Walk, Miriam ordered herself. Toward Eva. And then, though her legs were wobbly, it was as if she had people propping her up, her mother on one side, Ratha on the other, holding her by the elbows, guiding her to Eva's room. I'm coming, she kept thinking. I'm coming, I'm almost—And then she had rounded the corner and there was Eva, asleep in her crib. Miriam lifted her out. "Shhh," she whispered as Eva resettled against her. "Shhh, you're all right," as if she was comforting her child, not herself.

Telephone, fire escape, front door. They needed to leave, of course. To go outside for help. But how could she trust herself to

135

climb with Eva out a window, down a steep iron ladder to a concrete sidewalk, and anyway, the fire escape was outside the living room, just like the front door was off of the living room. All right, then, walk down the hall, step past him, undo the locks. But with Eva? He'd never let her; in a second he'd be at her side, twisting Eva from her arms. With the heel of her shoe, she came down sharply on the floor—one, two, three, four times. A knock for each letter—H E L P—but would Ratha hear it, and if she did, would she understand?

"Leave a message?" she heard Francis saying in the living room. "Right, I need a goddamn nanny tomorrow and I don't care what she costs but she needs to be a healthy, certified virgin, and ... and totally a hundred percent disease-free, *capisce*, I happen to have invented the test—*this is only a test, I repeat, ladies and Gentiles*—I'm going to patent it, you might want it for your business, with autoclave test tubes and whatchamacallits—test-testicles, and this, this *girl* better have references from God himself and keep her fucking hands off my—" Then silence. "They hung up on me!" he called out after a few seconds. "How dare they..." And he switched into Italian, a long, fast, stream that Miriam couldn't understand.

She took off her shoes and tiptoed down the hall with Eva in her arms. When she reached the end, she looked around the corner. He had moved to the floor and was sitting over near the bathroom, facing the wall. He had taken off his shirt and was leaning into himself; she could see the sharp wings of his shoulder blades, the hard knobs of his backbone. Francis. This was the body, along with Eva's, that she knew best in the world—the smooth torso, the long fingers, the tiny scar above his right eyebrow from where he had fallen playing basketball as a boy. Yes, this was Francis, of course, but then not quite, because he looked too pale and raw now, too naked, as if he were sitting cross-legged in a field of snow.

He wasn't himself. She wanted to believe it, could almost hear the phrase coming from her mouth: *For a little while, he wasn't himself.* He was talking again, leaning over the phonebook. Miriam scanned the room but didn't see the phone, then noticed its antenna sticking out by his elbow. Though he was still speaking Italian, it sounded even more foreign now, a blurry jumble; here and there she could make out an English word. She edged toward the door but as she neared it, Francis swiveled around. He was cradling the phone in his lap, pressing its buttons, stroking it, speaking—his voice gentle, then agitated, then murmuring. As she stared, he turned the phone over and patted it three times. Then he spit into his hand and began, quite tenderly, to clean it with his spit.

How long that moment seemed as she stood watching—as if time, like Francis, was being tugged on and deformed by a muscular, unseen force. Later, when she thought back on that night, Miriam would be struck by how time was the most elastic, the most flexible of properties, a year in a minute, an hour in a second. Though less than an hour had passed since she'd come home, each second already stretched far and wide, changing the color of everything, swallowing both the future and the past.

She walked with Eva back to her room, not knowing what else to do. She sat down in the rocker. Rocked. She waited: for Francis to lose interest in the phone or come down from the drug trip she was beginning to hope he was on; for her dead mother to tell her what to do; for his mother to call, or Ratha, or Sarah. Call, she kept thinking. Ring or knock. Break in.

When a knock came on the door, she almost didn't respond, so sure it must be lodged inside her head. And then again— another knock. Eva started to whimper and Miriam got up with her and walked down the hall again. Francis was facing into the corner, talking to himself. She looked through the peephole and saw the blue front and silver badge of a police uniform. Had Francis committed a crime? Had he—*Calm down, they're here to help. Ratha must have called.*

"Hold on," she whispered. She unlocked the top lock, then

the bottom, slid the chain off and opened the door to two cops, as if she was in a 1950s detective film—one man tall and thin, the other short and broad. "I . . ." she whispered, pointing to Francis, who didn't seem to notice they were there. "He . . ."

The taller man spoke in a low voice. "Are you Mrs. DiLeone?"

She nodded. "I have a different last name, but yes, he's my—"

"You're married to him? Is he the father of this child?"

"Yes. Please, I don't understand what's happening, I need to know—"

"Could you step outside for a minute, ma'am?"

She looked back at Francis, then moved with Eva into the hall, leaving the door slightly ajar. The shorter policeman, she noticed, had his hand clamped firmly on his gun.

"Your downstairs neighbor called in," the tall man said. "She says there was some yelling and violent behavior and that your husband is, uh, mentally unstable, a danger to himself and others. Where there are children involved, our protocol is to get here as quickly as we can."

"Oh." Miriam was surprised, in the midst of everything, that the NYPD would take the time to answer such a call. "Yeah, I—I have no idea what happened, he just totally flipped out, he's saying crazy things, like he can hear voices and see things in the baby monitor—"

The tall policeman nodded. "Any illegal substances involved, to your knowledge, or excessive use of alcohol?"

"No, he says no, and he's never—I really don't think so, but a doctor would be able to tell, he really needs help, please—"

"Has he been committed before, ma'am?"

"What?"

"Committed, you know—to the hospital, the psychiatric ward. Either we bring him there so they can evaluate the situation, or we take him over to the precinct. Has he been abusive, hit or threatened you or—?" He pointed at Eva.

"No no, of course not, he'd never . . ." If she let them, she saw that they would drag Francis to jail and book him for child abuse.

But if she said everything was all right, they might turn and go away. Francis looked, after all, quite harmless, sitting in the corner by himself. "He's saying some crazy things," she told them. "But I'm sure it's because he—I mean, something must have happened, he needs medical help." She took a breath. "Could you just stay here while I try to convince him to go to the hospital?"

The shorter man reached around her and pushed open the door to the apartment. She heard Francis burst out. "Where the hell is Eva? Who *are* you? What the fuck did you do with my daughter? I'll kill anyone who touches that girl, I swear to god I'll blow your fucking brains out—"

"Francis—" Miriam stepped into the room, Eva suddenly wailing in her arms. "Francis, she's here. Look, I have her right here, I've got her. Shush, Eva, shhhh."

"Give her to me!" he yelled over Eva's howls. "Get away from my daughter, you goddamn prick police freaks, you wash your hands when you come in here in your cop costumes playing god, I'll take her, Mim, just give her to me!" He stood, reaching.

"Francis, no, she needs . . . her ear hurts, she has a bad infection. I have to nurse her, it's supposed to help."

The lie left her mouth as easily as if it had been waiting there forever, fully formed. She spotted a pacifier on top of the bookshelf and slid it into Eva's mouth.

"I'll do it," Francis said "I'll give her a bottle, just get these people out of here, staring at your naked tit like some kind of loosie-goosie strip show, get them away, you don't open the door to germ-bomb infiltrators, I could've told you before, come here, babe, come, just let me . . ."

He leaned forward, teetering a little, and the shorter policeman stepped forward, his hand still on his gun. "All right, that's enough—we need to get him to a hospital. Sir, we're going to take you to a doctor to get you some help."

Francis lunged toward him but stopped a few feet away, as if he had come up against a wall. "Don't you fucking touch me! Don't you dare touch me with your filthy hands, we have soap here, for strangers and friends, we have antiseptic, antibiotic soap—"

"We've all washed," Miriam found herself saying. "Look, Francis. See my hands? We're all extremely clean."

The rest happened swiftly, in a strange, fast-forward blur. Somehow Ratha's husband, Mahesh, appeared in the outside hall; somehow Eva was passed over to him and taken down the stairs when Francis wasn't looking. "Where is she?" he started screaming when he realized she was gone, and one of the cops said she'd been taken to the hospital for her ear infection—they could follow in the squad car to make sure she was all right. Miriam listened, nodded, did nothing to undo the lie. She got Francis a shirt and jacket and slid his socks and shoes onto his twitching feet. On and on he talked, about Eva, Jesus, saints, infections, Mexico, killer whales, sponges and germs. He talked like that all the way down the stairs and into the cruiser, and he kept talking as they drove through the city, and he was still babbling, faster and faster, as they went into the emergency room, where they were allowed to cut ahead because he was screaming again and came in flanked by cops. "Where is she?" he kept yelling, scanning the waiting room where other babies sat snug in other parents' arms. "Where is she? They take them and kill them—where the fuck did Eva go?"

And then Francis, too, was gone, guided through some swinging double doors. Miriam made her way to the restroom, kneeled by a toilet and vomited until she had nothing left inside. Then she washed her hands, ran a wet paper towel over her face and went to find a pay phone so she could find out if Eva, Ratha—if everyone but Francis—was all right.

15

And so it began. The doctors and nurses, the candy stripers, receptionists, social workers, interns and orderlies. The question-naires—long forms attached to clipboards embossed with the names of drugs in sky blue or shamrock green—the colors, some-body must have thought, of calm, or hope. The waiting, for hours at a time, among the city's sick and injured—people on crutches, children with bright gashes on their lips and foreheads, an old man calling *I been shot, I been shot,* though he clutched at nothing and there was no wound in sight. That first night, Miriam sat in the ER waiting room for hours, her breasts aching with milk. In this same hospital, Eva had been born five months earlier. Now nurses appeared and disappeared, calling out other people's names. Stretchers, wheelchairs and supply carts rolled by on rubber wheels; the swinging doors opened, swung shut, opened, shut again. The waiting room smelled of urine, of vomit, of bodies coming undone, but Miriam barely noticed, sitting upright, still in her work clothes, her hands laced together around her purse. Anything could have happened and not surprised her: a doctor appearing—*I'm sorry, but your husband passed away*—or Francis pushing the doors open, striding toward her with a wink: *Hey Mim, I'm fine now—let's get out of here.*

At some point in the middle of the night, a slim boy came out in a white coat, spoke her name and led her through the double doors. To Francis, she assumed, and so she looked for him, but the boy ushered her into a folding chair in the hallway, sat down next to her and said he needed to ask her some questions—he was having a hard time getting Francis's history. "Who are you?" she asked, and her own voice rang nasal and metallic, as if she were hearing it on a tape. The boy stuck out his hand. Dr. Avery. You're a doctor? He nodded. Yes—a second-year resident in psychiatry. Oh. She realized his hand was waiting there in front of her, suspended, so she shook it. What she really wanted was to roll up her sleeve, stick out her arm and have this doctor, if he was one, inject her with some clear, cold liquid that would bring the old world back.

"Where is he?" she asked.

He pointed down the hall.

"Could I go see him?"

"Let's do this first. He's very disoriented, delusional, actually, I'm afraid, going on about your daughter. The officer said he was doing it at home, too, which was why they—"

"Oh god," Miriam interrupted. "I forgot—he thinks Eva's here, in the hospital, the cop told him they took her in for an ear infection, they—we—I mean, I lied to him, I just . . . it was the only way to get him to . . . I need to tell him she's all right—"

The doctor raised his index finger to his mouth and she realized she had been talking too loud. "I know this is hard, Mrs. DiLeone, but just listen to me. We told him your daughter is fine but he's completely unable to absorb that right now. He claims she's a saint who's been kidnapped by the hospital staff to be used in scientific experiments." He looked straight at her, then, and she saw from his weary eyes and the bags under them that he was not a child. "Your husband is psychotic right now. He tried to attack a nurse and we had to put him in restraints. We've given him a sedative and should probably start him on an antipsychotic, but I'd like to get his history first, in case there are contraindications. Often the family can help fill in the blanks."

"What? I don't understand." She shook her head hard. "I mean, people don't just *turn* crazy overnight. He must have taken drugs, I found pot in his pocket the other week, maybe—"

"We did a drug screen. It came back clean."

"Then how . . . ?"

"That's what we need to figure out," said Dr. Avery. "That's why we need your help."

Questions, then, he asked her. The first ones were simple: Francis's date of birth, address, workplace, phone number, the names and ages of his parents and sister, of Eva, of herself. Like a dutiful schoolgirl, she answered. Good, yes, said the doctor, and he wrote her answers down. Then his questions got harder. Previous hospitalizations? Medical conditions? Allergies? Operations? Head trauma? Strokes? History of substance abuse in himself or his family? Relatives with a history of psychiatric difficulties, suicides or suicide attempts?

I don't know, she kept repeating, but to herself she was saying *breathe*; she was saying *focus on his shoes*, which were black and polished, the most solid thing she had seen in a long, long time. She was, she realized, supposed to know everything about Francis; he was, after all, her *husband*—the doctor kept using the word. We moved so fast, she wanted to tell him. We talked about so many things, but not this, not these. "I don't know," she repeated instead. "I guess he never said."

Finally the doctor finished, his notepad specked with tiny black question marks and scribbled words. "Is there someone you could call? His parents or sister? The more information we have, the better we can proceed."

"Maybe his mother. His sister and father are in Italy. I can try calling her, but she doesn't like me much—I'm not . . . We . . ." She shrugged. "It's a long story. But I could try."

"Good," said Dr. Avery. "When you finish, just ask the receptionist to page me."

As if on cue, his pager beeped, and he rose. Miriam stood, too, but as she straightened up, her stomach cramped and the hallway spun spidery black and gold. She groped for the chair, lowered herself down and shut her eyes. "I threw up earlier," she announced as her head began to clear, but when she looked for the doctor, he was gone.

At the pay phones, a line. She wanted to push through to the head of it—*It's an emergency, let me go!*—but then she remembered that in this, of all places, emergencies were the order of the day. Finally it was her turn. The phone at Flavia's rang and rang. Just when Miriam was ready to give up, Flavia answered, her voice crisp and formal.

Miriam tried hard to get the words out. At the hospital . . . no no, he's alive, of course . . . hearing things . . . the doctors . . . history . . . sick . . . no one is sure . . .

"What do you mean, he's sick?" asked Flavia. "I just saw him. He's too tired, that's all. He works too much, and with the baby up at night—"

"It's not the baby, it's Francis, the doctors say he's . . . he's very sick right now. He thinks—he's saying he hears saints talking in his head." As soon as the words left her mouth, she realized they were a mistake.

"Of course he does," said Flavia almost proudly. "For a long time he tried not to think about this and now it's coming too fast and so he becomes sick. He wants to raise his daughter Catholic—that's what's this is. He's afraid to tell you—"

"Did he tell you that?"

"He's my son. I know his mind."

"The doctor also asked," Miriam said, "about his parents, if anyone had ever had, you know—" *Psychiatric difficulties.* She imagined asking, have you ever committed suicide? and felt, in the midst of everything, a laugh push up inside her throat. "It would be helpful to know," she said, "if you'd ever had any . . . psychological problems—you know, trouble with your mind or . . . or with how you felt."

"Me? What are you saying? You don't know me, you have no idea how hard I worked for my children."

"All right. I'm sorry, Flavia. You're right." She was dimly aware of someone behind her muttering about needing the phone. "And he's never been like this before?"

There was a silence on the line, a considering. When Flavia spoke again, her voice was clipped and angry. "Are you telling me he's back with the drugs? Did you get him doing that again?"

"What drugs?" Miriam crossed her fingers.

"You know, like at the university when those drugs got him all excited."

"In college. Okay, that's helpful. Do you remember which year that was, and what the drugs were called?"

"Helpful? Drugs? Did you get him started on this? I knew—"

"Please." She forced herself to take a breath. "I didn't even know him then, Flavia—that was long before I met him. Can you tell me more? For the doctors, so they can make him better? Or if you want to, you can come talk to his doctors yourself."

"Just we saved and saved," said Flavia, "so he can go to Columbia University—they put him on the . . . the *dean's list,* you know? And then the hippies got him with their drugs, and he has nothing, no degree, just all this money we owe. Every month I pay for this, for the rest of my life."

"Did he get treatment, then? Did he see a doctor?"

She was answered by a mumbling—Flavia speaking, Flavia praying in Italian, maybe doing her rosary beads. Miriam listened, the phone pressed hard against her ear. She, too, would have liked to be able to fall into the comfort of old, rhythmic words, to feel beads and links of chain sliding through her fingers and have faith in a presence bigger and wiser than herself. But religion could not help her. Years before, it had stolen her father, and now, in some relentless, chattering form, it seemed to be stealing Francis, too. If belief came to her at all, these days, it was in the form of quiet, hidden superstitions—the charm from the Mexican market in the depths of her purse; her fingers, crossed, still, as she listened to Flavia pray.

And then a metallic hiccup came onto the phone, followed by a voice, harsh and jangling: *Please deposit—*

"I'm out of change, Flavia. I've got to go. Try not to worry too much—I'll call you tomorrow. I'm sure you can come see him then," Miriam said, but she got no answer, so she hung up and walked away, her fingers still crossed over her purse.

In the weeks that followed, big chunks of that night would disappear from her mind, leaving her with odds and ends: the sound of Flavia praying, the glossy polish of the doctor's black shoes, the hooded gray sweatshirt of a pregnant girl waiting for the phone—how frayed it was, how worn and soft. The busy sound of heels on linoleum, and waiting by the entrance to the locked unit where they put Francis for the first week, or was it for the first few days? Time itself kept playing tricks on her while he was in the hospital, the way it had while her mother was dying, and right after Eva's birth. This day or that day, her mother opening her eyes; Eva mewing, a blind, red animal; Francis lying clothed on a bed, his hands swimming through the air. He was— this day or that day—talking to someone she couldn't see; he was crazy, he had woken up one day crazy, because it *did* happen, she had been wrong about that, as she had been wrong about so many things. And this was not the first time; it had happened before, when he was in college. Eventually he told a doctor that, and the doctor told Miriam. It hadn't been drugs, the doctor said. Maybe drugs had set it off, but it was a thing in itself, an illness, a *mental illness.*

"But he didn't tell me," Miriam said. "How—" She pressed her palm to her forehead. "How could he not have told me?"

"He said he tried to. He was better for a long time. People want . . . they hope to start again. A long time had passed since the first episode."

"You think that's *all right?*" she asked. "Not to tell? You think that's . . . defensible?"

"No," said the doctor slowly. "No, I didn't say that. I think—"

She had an urge to slap him on his pink, scrubbed cheek.

"I think," he said, "that it's not for me to say."

In the early evening, for the six weeks that he was in the hospital, she left work and went straight there, leaving Eva with Ratha for an extra hour. A few times, his mother was there, praying by his bed or wedging Mass cards between the mirror and the wall. Flavia would say a brief hello but she never wanted to talk, and if Miriam hadn't known better, she would have thought Francis's mother didn't speak English. More often, Francis was alone, sitting clothed on his bed, murmuring or gazing out the window, or bent over a table in the common room thumbing vaguely through a magazine.

The first time Miriam came, she brought him a photo of Eva, which he glanced at, then let flutter to the floor. She's fine, Miriam said, needing badly to confess. She never had an ear infection—I'm sorry I told you that. And Francis nodded and said he would of course be taking legal action because they were all a bunch of liars, the whole slew of them, thinking they could pull one over on him; he knew about documentary sensitizing, about the wires and tryptophan and the echo system that let you calibrate a saint's syntonic thoughts.

Doors, she would remember—the swinging ones in the ER, the heavy ones on the locked unit; you rang a bell and were let in by a woman with a fistful of keys. And words. *Locked unit, four-point restraints, constant observation, privileges*—a whole new language to learn, the way, at other times, she had learned the languages of childbirth and law. *Checks. Meds. Group. Sharps.* She would remember the social work intern, Heidi, who was the only one who ever had much time to talk—her earnest face scarred by acne, her hunched shoulders and pale blue eyes, the gold cross dangling from her neck. Heidi liked Francis, took an interest in him. She had a lot of theories: Francis was ambivalent about Eva's birth; leaving the church had been hard for him; he had never really separated from his mother. At one point, as Heidi droned on and on, Miriam had to get up and leave the room. Francis loved Eva—anyone could see that. A "chemical imbalance" was the term the doctor used, and it made more sense to her.

Bipolar, like the North and South poles—two worlds where day and night lost their meaning and only the most intrepid explorers ever went. *Bi* like biannual, bifurcated, bisexual, binary, biological, biblical, binge. *Polar* like the bear, which looked like a toy but would tear you limb from limb if you got too close. At work, in bed, on the subway, the words kept tripping through her mind like an advertising jingle, persistent and unwelcome. Sleeplessness. Acute sociability. Verbosity. Increased sexual drive. Francis was turned, overnight, into a bulging diagnostic checklist. Yes and yes and yes. *Manic-depressive,* like Virginia Woolf, like Lord Byron and Vincent Van Gogh. One of the articles Heidi gave her kept naming names, as if to pedigree this illness and reveal its hidden gifts. But Miriam didn't care about genius and artistic temperament. She wanted him back. Francis. She wanted him the way he was before.

Give it time, said the doctors, the nurses, the medical students—all the people Miriam stopped in the hall and plied with questions. This isn't unusual, they said. It's only been four days. Or five days. Or six. Be patient, they told her. The lithium can take at least a week to kick in. The less harried among them handed her more pamphlets; they seemed to have an endless supply. *Lithium carbonate, a naturally occurring mineral salt. A delicate balance. Optimum blood levels. Soften the attacks.* Often it works, Heidi told her. But sometimes it doesn't. And if it doesn't? Then we try something else. And if that doesn't work? Try to be patient; there's a chapel downstairs if you want to pray. I'm Jewish, Miriam said sharply, and Heidi nodded. You might want to pray all the same.

At home that night, Miriam sat at the kitchen table with Eva sleeping in her lap. There'd been a message from Sarah on the machine, and one from a work friend, but they would want a report and she had no words to spare, so she didn't call them back. She knew she should eat but couldn't muster up an appetite. Instead, she shook a heap of salt into her hand and licked it up, wincing at the taste. She remembered a salt lick at the Central Park Zoo—the deer nosing around it, the deep groove down its center, slow-carved by their tongues. Francis had been beside her that afternoon, his breath visible in the winter air, his hand on the small of her back. Now she pictured salt traveling through her blood to her brain, stinging and healing her thoughts the way salt both healed and stung a wound. Not enough salt in his brain? It sounded like hocus-pocus, or like the mind was a stew in need of spice. *The illness involves a strong genetically transmitted vulner-ability.* Stroking Eva's sleeping head, she tried to shove the thought away, but back it crept. Her own mother, she knew, would have risen from the chair, made some tea, washed the dishes, checked in with Ratha, called the credit card people and explained why she couldn't pay the staggeringly high bill. She would have tended to Eva so that she might, with any luck, grow up healthy and sane. Her own mother would not have sunk into a stupor of self-pity and sat around licking salt; she had barely stumbled when Miriam's father left, almost as if she had expected all along that he would go. But Miriam wasn't strong like her mother. How could she be, when half her genes were his?

For a moment she allowed herself to picture what would happen if she, too, fell swiftly and totally apart—the dim, still room they would take her to, the drugs they would give her to let her sleep, the nurse who would bring her pills and wash her hair. At night the psychiatric ward would be quiet, the curtains drawn. Alone in her hospital bed, Miriam would throw back her head and wail until her voice grew thin. She would scream for everything that had left her and everything that was leaving her, for the mute girl standing in the schoolyard, her hair neatly parted, her shoelaces tied in double knots, her father—how she used to pray for it—dead like a hero, dead like a doorknob. She would scream for poor decisions and careless acts, for love that split you open, for plain bad luck. For Francis, she would scream. For, or maybe *at* him: the glitch in his brain, the words in his mouth, the way he had drawn her to him, handed her a life, only to snatch it away. *Bubeleh,* the nurse would call her, as if she was still a little girl. *Bubeleh, don't worry. You're sick, but we'll take care of you.*

Of course not, though. She was fine. She had a child to feed, a job to do, a husband to visit in the loony bin. In three weeks she would turn twenty-five. Somehow her mother had died; she had met a man. This had become her life. She looked down at Eva. Her new hair was coming in black and curly like her father's; her eyelids were twitching in a dream. A sour-sweet smell rose up from her. She needed to be changed. Stand up, said Miriam's mother. Miriam stood up.

The next day, *on the seventh day* (fodder for Flavia; Miriam chalked it up to chance) it began to work. Salt in his blood, seasoning his brain. *Lithium carbonate, effective in seventy percent of cases,* and Francis among the lucky ones. That day, his salted brain began to turn back from the North Pole, the South Pole, to trudge—but he was frost-bitten, but he was shell-shocked— toward some kind of middle ground. When Miriam came into the room, he was in bed under the covers, the shades drawn. For the first time since he had been in the hospital, he reached for her hand and held it limply in his own.

"Miriam?" He sounded as if he wasn't sure he remembered her name.

"Hi. Hi, Francis." She perched on the edge of the bed, afraid to get too close. He's doing better but be careful not to upset him, Heidi had said in the hall. Don't say anything that might worry him, or talk too fast or loud. Earlier in the week, Francis had lunged at Miriam, howling, his hands aimed at her neck. Gently, now, she squeezed his fingers, then worried she'd done it too hard. "How . . . how are you feeling?"

"How?" He dropped her hand and shut his eyes. "I'm . . ." He opened his eyes and looked straight at her. "I'm in the nuthouse, Mim. Me and my mother and all the other loony tunes. They've pumped us full of crazy drugs, you know? To clean out the germs or something. To—" He groped for words. "*Entice* us."

"To make you better. That's what they're trying to do."

"Maybe. If I could—" Abruptly, he sat up, and she stood and looked toward the doorway. "Where's Heidi?" he asked.

"Out there, I think. I'll get her, do you want me to get her?"

"I've got to ask her about—" Just as abruptly, Francis lay back down. "Focus," he told himself sternly. "Focus like a camera." In his voice, Miriam thought she could hear Heidi's, and she found herself oddly jealous. Francis made a circle with his thumb and index finger, shut one eye and used the other to peer through his fingers at her. "Miriam," he said again.

"Francis."

"Plus Eva Baruch DiLeone. Is she okay, is she . . . ?" He shook his head rapidly back and forth.

"Eva's good, she's fine."

He made a clicking sound, as if he were taking a picture. "Is she talking yet?"

"Eva? No, not yet."

Click click—he took imaginary pictures of the room. "Baby Girl Baruch. Of course she's not talking, she's still just a little Tootsie Roll."

Miriam smiled and had to stop herself from crawling into his arms. "She misses you, though," she said. "She'll be glad when you come home."

But he was gone again, shutting his eyes. She watched, wondering if he was asleep or about to speak. A minute passed, then another. "Francis?" she said softly, but he only shifted and sighed. She leaned closer. *Come back*, she wanted to call out. Instead she touched his shoulder through the sheet.

And then a nurse was at her side, leading her away. "Is he better?" Miriam asked in the hall. "He seems better, do you think—"

The nurse nodded. "It looks like he's coming around, but you can't rush it, it'll take time. He's been to the moon and back. Now he needs to take his meds and get his beauty sleep."

Francis stayed in the hospital for six weeks. Sometimes she would arrive to find him curled in bed, or she'd come upon him playing cards with another patient or sitting in a group meeting complaining about how filthy the bathrooms were. Or he'd be off seeing a therapist and she would want to put her ear to the wall and listen in—always the outsider, the visitor, in this place. It was a whole world in there, an off-key yet surprisingly unremarkable universe with its own elaborate set of rules. She could see Francis getting involved, making friends with the other patients, putting down the strangest, most ragged sort of roots. She had thought psychiatric wards would be full of drooling, screaming people, but most of the patients on Francis's ward just seemed a little *off*—abstracted or distracted, deeply sad or perhaps deeply drugged—and many of them, somehow, were too fat or too thin. Francis worked on crude crafts and gave them to her when she visited, for Eva, he said—a doll made from a clothespin, a stone paperweight he had painted with a purple face. Gone were his quick hands, his quicker tongue, and while his sense of humor still showed itself, it surfaced in unexpected flashes and quickly disappeared. His skin looked stretched over his bones; his left hand trembled; he got up constantly to pee.

Side effects, the doctor said. We're still playing with the doses. His slow speech, his sleepy manner, his upset stomach—side ef-

fects all, but they felt to Miriam like some nasty barga.
devil: *I'll take away the voices and give you this.* How long
have to take the medicine, she asked. The Haldol, said the doc.
was probably only temporary. If all went well, he would be on it
just for the next six months or so. And the lithium? The lithium
is his lifeline, said the doctor. As long as it keeps working and he
stays compliant, he'll be on it for the rest of his life.

Inside Saint Vincent's, things felt calm, mostly. The hospital
was full of check marks and signatures, printouts and diagnoses,
people with advanced degrees, the floors so clean that as you
walked down the hall, you could see yourself, waxed and polished,
looking back. It was outside, as she moved through the city, that
Miriam began to see crazy people everywhere she looked. They
were rummaging through garbage cans, rearranging objects in
plastic shopping bags, rocking and murmuring, picking at their
skin. They were stretched across subway seats with their flies unzipped, surrounded by a wall of their own smell. The rest of the
city dropped away from her during those days, and she saw only
old women talking to the air and men with faces jumping from
twitch to twitch, their palms stretched toward her. Before Francis
got sick, she would sometimes fish around in her coat pocket and
pull out a handful of change for such people, or she'd glance in
their direction and smile apologetically as she walked by, whispering *sorry* under her breath. Now she stiffened; now she
couldn't look. Who *are* you, part of her wanted to ask. Where
did you come from? Did you used to be, you know, *normal?* Have
you been treated? What did they give you? Why didn't it work?
Did you have a family? What became of them? What were you
like as a child?

But she couldn't ask. They might grab her by the collar and
pull her close—Hey lady, smell my breath. *Come,* they might say,
becoming her future. Or else, *go away.* Put them somewhere, she
found herself thinking. Just get them out of my sight. And as she
moved through the city, she gripped her purse so tightly that by
the time she reached her door, her knuckles ached.

*　*　*

Pink pills like Valentine's Day candy, the lithium sat in prim, white, pleated cups. It turned out Francis had been on it before, after his first breakdown in college, but had stopped taking it after a few years because he thought he was cured and disliked the side effects. There was a word for this: *noncompliance*. Miriam read about how to encourage your family member to comply. A weekly pill box. A regular schedule. *You might try giving an affectionate pet name to the medication,* suggested one article. *Try making the medication regimen a ritualized part of time you spend together, cuddling or talking about your day.* The old Francis would have made a snide joke of it; the new one was too spaced out. Going over things with Heidi, Miriam realized how scared she was to have him home again. Would it be like having two children? Would Eva be safe with him? Would he say unforgivable things to Ratha? Should they maybe live separately for a while and just see?

"You need to try to have faith in him," Heidi told her.

"Oh do I? How am I supposed to do that?"

"He's the same person he was before."

"I didn't know him before. He . . ." Her anger stopped her cold. "He left things out."

"You did know him, though. This is just one piece of him and it's under control. He's doing really well. He loves you."

Miriam shrugged. "He never tells me anymore."

"Imagine," said Heidi, "how scared he must be."

The day he was scheduled to come home, Miriam took a day off from work. She cleaned the apartment, put fresh sheets on the bed, dressed Eva in red corduroy overalls and a flowered turtleneck, then sat holding her on the couch, her stomach tight with hope, or was it dread? We're going to pick him up, she told Eva as she zipped her into her jacket. Your daddy. For a second she felt like a young wife in an old movie, her husband returning from a far-off war. But where was Francis returning from? A burning, haunted, restless place; she could see the outlines, as if on a postcard, but not the lived life inside the walls. Would he reach for Eva when he first saw her? Would he remember that, before, he had called her goose? Would he remember Miriam's body as a place to curl himself, spooning, before sleep? He'd only been gone for six weeks, and she barely remembered it herself.

16

What could a baby remember? Over the years, watching Eva growing up, Miriam both wanted and was afraid to know. Five months old and Francis has snatched Eva from Ratha's arms, he has run upstairs with her, put her in a bath (how hot?), begun to scrub her skin (how hard?) with antiseptic soap. He is talking Can she hear that his words are too fast, his pitch too high,. though she does not know *fast* or *high, pitch* or *words?* Can she hear that his voice is one she knows but also unfamiliar? In her plastic bathtub, her muscles might be tighter than usual, her eyes even more watchful; she is an animal on the alert. *Cunt,* he is saying about her babysitter. *Bitch dirty twat disease.* Or maybe Eva is bathed now, dressed, sitting in her bouncy seat. Maybe he is jiggling her with his foot. It's a familiar motion and she likes it, and perhaps now the day feels like any other—these are, after all, the walls she knows so well after five months, this quality of light, of air, this father's face. She can see now, according to the books, clear across a room, and this is the room she sees clear across when she turns her head to register the world.

Later, glinting objects. The silver badges of the policemen, all the lights turned on, her pupils—all their pupils—shrinking down. The feel of her mother's arms around her, gripping her too hard. How she is passed from arm to arm and finally taken down to Ratha's, and she probably doesn't cry, then, for this is a place where she goes each day, but now it is night and does she notice that her parents aren't with her, does she hear the cruiser start up outside the window, her father jabbering inside? Ratha puts her—where?—probably in the crib with Charu, each girl's head at an opposite end, the way they often napped during the day.

There were no baby pictures of Eva at five or six months old. In her baby book, a gap, the pages blank and clean, as if she had bypassed that period the way precocious children skipped a grade. Her clothes during that time grew tight on her; Miriam had no time, no energy to shop. Work, hospital, home. Sometimes hospital, work, hospital, home. The baby in the bed with her; she needed to keep her safe, but more than that, she couldn't stand sleeping all alone.

Eva, Miriam hoped, remembered none of this, and none of it was told to her. *And then*—but always these omissions. *And then your father thought Ratha was trying to abuse and kill you, and the police took him to the hospital where he was put in restraints and drugged into a stupor, and he stayed there for over a month, and during that time you started waking in the night again and you refused to breastfeed and would only drink from a sippy cup, and there were a few nights where I let you cry and cry, left you in your crib, I was just too tired to calm you down, and anyway Francis had always been better at it and you seemed so furious to me, so helpless and unhappy, and I thought the whole thing was a giant mistake—meeting him, getting pregnant—and meanwhile one of the saints had told him I wanted to kill you, and the next time I saw him, he lunged at me and they had to tackle him to keep him back.*

No. This was not a story for a child—for anyone—to build a life on. Hard enough that he had died.

And then your daddy drew you pictures. And then your daddy sang you songs.

17

He wasn't expecting her. It wasn't Thanksgiving or Christmas, she hadn't called ahead, and her knock, when it came on the side door, sounded just like Eva's—two staccato raps. "In here," he called. He was at the kitchen table paying bills and didn't turn around. Eva showed up almost every day now, wanting him to drop everything and take her out to the hives. It doesn't work like that, Burl kept having to explain. Mostly, for the bees to do well, you had to leave them alone; the more you opened the hive to prod and poke, the more likely they were to swarm or kill the queen. Leaning over the table, his back to the doorway, he could feel her presence, tense and watchful. "Hi there. Give me a couple minutes," he said.

And then a warm, sure hand—stroking the nape of his neck, causing first a shiver, then a panic to zigzag through him. Eva, touching, *stirring* him like this? Only when he turned around, shrugging her off, he found Alice, who laughed a little and squinted at him.

"Hey," she said uncertainly. "I was in town, I—"

He stood and pulled her into a hug, her shape so familiar to him, from the first time she had guided his hands inside her shirt one August evening after she finished bathing his grandfather and helping him from his wheelchair to his bed. From sponging Burl's grandfather's body to tasting his own—she had been the one to turn the ache of watching into action, a year older than he was, and he too awkward to know where to begin. He was about to go off to Princeton, she to a nursing program at the local community college. Both of them had figured they would move on to other things, and they had, but always, somehow, this return, this homecoming—he, in an unexpected twist, the local farmer now, and Alice a doctor, her hips wider after Meg, her blond braid shot through with gray.

"You're home." He pulled away so he could look at her.

"Back," she corrected and sat down.

"Back." Burl sat, too. "But it's not a national holiday. Is everything okay?"

"You didn't hear?"

"What?" he asked. Alice's family lived all around the county —cousins, parents, brothers, everyone but Alice—and got word of local news almost before it happened. It seemed to Burl that Alice had never quite grasped what kind of life he lived out here.

"Dick had a stroke last week."

"Oh no. Is he—"

She shook her head and Burl floundered—did she mean her father wasn't alive, or that he wasn't dead? "Dick"—the way she had always referred to him. As a teenager, Alice had called him Big Dick and lifted her shirt to show Burl where he whacked her when he was drunk or simply out of sorts. Their fathers had been so different, Burl's father all restrained, papery-dry, aristocratic rage, Dick's anger right out in the open, like his laughter, which was full and deep. But now Alice came back to see her parents on holidays, when the most Burl did was send a birthday card to the posh Assisted Living Home in Philadelphia, or call once in a while to make sure his father was still alive, talk for two minutes and hang up. Was it the difference, he sometimes wondered, between daughters and sons, or between each of their fathers? Or maybe Alice was simply more generous than he was. She had, after all, devoted her life to nursing other people's wounds.

"The funeral's this weekend." Her voice was matter-of-fact.

So Dick was dead. What could he say? "How's your mother?" Burl asked, then kicked himself—at least say I'm sorry; he was her father, after all. He wanted to move toward her again, to hold her, but there were too many hovering unknowns. At Christmas, her last visit, things had seemed different from the other times since her divorce, their sex less casual and friendly, more urgent, and he had felt himself—but what was new?—both compelled and wary.

After she left, he had gone into a funk for a few weeks, then started seeing Florence from the Beekeepers' Association—a pretty, spacey trust-fund hippie who had taken him home, gotten him high and offered him her bed. But he had found himself coming back from Florence's and heading straight to his computer, wanting not Florence, but Alice—even virtual, even thousands of miles away. Her e-mail messages had been frequent and friendly, sometimes even sexy in a joking way, but other than talking about Meg, they almost never mentioned the daily facts of her life. Nor had he mentioned Florence, but why should he have; she hadn't interested him, not in any way he could sustain, and things had quickly fizzled out. In April he had suggested to Alice that he fly out to Colorado—he who hated airplanes and believed in finding the world in your own backyard. Her response had been cryptic: *Let's wait a little—it isn't the greatest time.* Now she was here, unvirtual, actual, standing in his kitchen, and he felt like a bumbling, pimply-faced teenager and wished for a world like the bees', where there was a dance for everything.

"My mom's a mess," Alice told him. "She can't balance a

checkbook, and now her eyes are going, so she can't really drive. He was . . . well, you know what he was like, but they're—they *were*—joined at the hip. He was nicer to her than he was to anyone else, even when he was smashed. They were married for over fifty years. Can you believe that?"

He shook his head. It seemed a thing of the past, the fifty-year marriage, like record players or rotary dial phones. "Can I help?" he asked. "I could drop off groceries for her. I do it for two other widows."

But while his mouth was offering aid, already his mind was running. Alice would move back from Colorado, live with her mother until she died, too, then come live here with him, moving in a little at a time. They could expand the farm, make it like it used to be, get more hives, put in a serious garden. She could join a local practice; there was a shortage of doctors in the area. She knew when not to crowd him, knew all about him—his trouble spots, his past, his deep, abiding attachment to this place. It was getting clearer and clearer; he didn't want anyone else. He had tried now and then, but it never worked. He wanted Alice. For years he had wanted her—he had just been too . . . too *something* to act. And Meg? For a moment he had forgotten about her. Last Christmas she had clung to her mother and seemed sulky and shy, but with time, he would win her over. He wasn't so bad with kids. She could be friends with Eva; they couldn't be more than a few years apart.

"Is Meg with your mother?" he asked.

She nodded. "She's probably on her hundredth brownie by now. People keep bringing food."

"How's she doing?"

"She's okay. She liked the plane ride but it scares her to see my mother so upset. She . . . oh, I don't know . . ." She shrugged. "I'm kind of talked out. Do you think maybe you could just hold me again for a second—I mean, if it's not breaking any rules?" She reached across the table and placed her hand, for the briefest second, over his.

In silence, then, they stood, and he wrapped his arms around her, wanting to ask more: How long are you staying? Are you seeing anyone? Did the divorce proceedings finally end? What's it like to lose someone who treated you badly your whole life but was still your father and loved you in his way? Alice did this to him, turned him talkative, almost girlish, as if he was storing up words for her the whole time they were apart. He stayed quiet, though, rocking her, pulling her tighter, feeling a shudder pass down her torso, a long, exhausted sigh.

"I'm glad you showed up," he said into her hair and felt her nod against him.

"You were surprised that it was me," she murmured. "Did you finally meet the farm girl of your dreams?"

He shook his head. "How about you?"

"Could I take a bath? They don't have tubs like yours in Colorado."

I asked how about you, he almost said again. Instead, he took her hand and led her up the stairs. In the bathroom at the end of the hall, he gave her one of his grandmother's old bathrobes and ran water in the deep, rust-stained tub. For a moment he saw the room through Alice's eyes—the walls that needed painting, the tattered bathmat, the toothbrush holder hanging by one screw. The shiny steel bar on the wall was still there, out of place among so many peeling, aging things. When Burl's grandfather had been well enough, he had used it to lower himself down.

"Any bubbles?" Alice kicked off her sandals and lifted one leg, then the other, out of her shorts, letting them drop to the floor.

"Bubbles, uh, no. I've got dish soap, in the kitchen."

"That'll do." She smiled as she stood before him in her underpants and T-shirt, and he looked away and battled back a thick, insistent rising of desire. With anyone else, he would have taken the act of undressing as a clear invitation, but Alice was slippery, always had been—part lover to him, part sister, part old friend, part mystery. He never quite knew what it was she wanted.

I'm slippery? he could hear her retorting: If I'm slippery, what does that make you?

He went downstairs, took a few gulps of orange juice from the carton in the fridge and stood in front of its open door, trying to clear his head. Alice moved in and out of his thoughts so regularly that now that she was actually in the house, he had the feeling he was still daydreaming. And yet her father's death, this he couldn't have predicted, nor her hand on his neck, nor her sudden rush for the tub. It was probably filthy; he should have checked before he ran the bath. He kept his honey equipment spotless, repainting the empty hive bodies and scrubbing the extractor until it shone, but cleaning the house felt like removing traces of his grandmother (Give me a break, you're just lazy, Alice would say), so he left it alone to settle into old age. When he came back upstairs, the bathroom door was closed. He stood outside and knocked.

"Um okay, come in, I guess," Alice called over the running water. He opened the door to find her sitting in the tub undoing her braid. He squirted some soap into the stream and swirled it around to make the bubbles rise. She sank down deeper, letting out a long, contented moan. He noticed a wet hand towel hanging from the steel bar; she had already wiped out the tub and folded her clothes over a towel rack. When they were teenagers, he had been fascinated by how she handled his grandfather's body. She was just a kid herself, but somehow she had lifted him in and out of this deep bathtub, somehow she had cleaned and soothed him, not bothered by the knotted joints, the rubbery penis and loose skin. Burl's grandfather, he knew, had been a little in love with Alice, who was Allie before she left home. Gotta ask my head nurse, he used to say. That Allie might be skinny but she's stronger than an ox and twice as smart.

Now, without asking, Burl kneeled beside the tub and began to sponge Alice's long back, behind her ears, the pink, flexed bottoms of her feet. She tipped her head back and shut her eyes, and then he could really look at her—the line of her jaw, the way her shoulders rose and fell as she breathed, how the suds sat on her breasts like mounds of snow. The noise of running water was insistent and drumming, the noise his bees made when he opened up a healthy hive—lulling, surrounding him with sound. After a few minutes he stopped sponging, leaned against the radiator and let his muscles go slack, remembering himself in this tub at four, at eight, at eleven. At eighteen—he used to lie here fantasizing about Alice, her cheerful gaze and forthright gestures, the bloody, bitten-down fingernails that gave her away. He would touch himself, trying to imagine her—sweaty, lanky—in the bath, but they could never actually do it there, not in this room where she bathed his grandfather, not with his grandmother humming tunelessly downstairs. Later, over the years, they had been able to have sex wherever they wanted, free in the empty house. Before her marriage, and then each time she came back since it had ended two years ago, Alice had been drawn to the kitchen floor, the hayloft, the hammock on the screen porch, but Burl preferred the ordinary comfort of a bed.

When the tub was full enough, he shut the water off, then regretted the silence, which turned things solid again. Alice opened her eyes.

"Can you believe he's dead?" she murmured, sinking farther into the bubbles. "He drank himself to death. No one will say it, but it's what happened. Should I get it carved on his headstone? 'Big Dick, He Drank Himself to Death'? God, listen to me, what a pig I am."

"How about, 'His Daughter Stuck By Him, Through Thick and Thin'?"

"More like 'His Daughter Fled, His Sons Stayed.' "

"You didn't flee. You came to visit all the time, from across the country, which is more than I do for my father."

"A lot of good it did. Give me that." She took the washcloth from him and jammed it into the inner corner of her eye.

"Are you—?" In all the years they had known each other, he had only seen her cry once, and he hadn't handled it well.

"Lemon Joy. Don't panic." She smiled wanly, flopped the washcloth over the side of the tub and reached over to pull his shirt off. "Come here, you. No don't. Shit, I really shouldn't—" He leaned toward her but she shook her head. "I just want to look at you for a second, that's all. How come the rest of us get old and saggy and your stomach still looks like a washboard?"

He shrugged, feeling his stomach muscles tense. "Lifting honey supers, maybe? You're not old and saggy." He reached toward her, but she flicked a clump of soap suds at him and batted his hand away.

"How are they?" she asked.

"Who?" His hand traveled toward her again. This time she caught it in midair and held it there, lacing her fingers between his.

"Who? The bees, of course. Your little kingdom."

The bees. Right. He tried to remember. "They . . . they're fighting hard. I'm trying these herb concoctions for the mites— you'd probably tell me it's quackery if I showed you. They say these new packages are mite-resistent but it's bullshit. But maybe this year'll be better than last."

"You're not getting tired of it? It seems like such endless, repetitive work."

"Not really." He took his hand away from hers and leaned against the wall again. If she wanted to chat, they could chat, but not from five inches apart. "I have a helper."

"Really? Paid? You must be doing well."

"No. Volunteer. Sort of an apprentice." A reformed thief, he almost said, but something made him stop.

"Male?"

He shook his head.

"Oh? Is she pretty?"

"She's a kid."

"But pretty?"

"I guess. She's a live wire—you'd like her. I'm not sure what her deal is. She just shows up here and always wants to see the bees. She..." He didn't know what else to say. "She has this crazy mop of hair."

"Careful," Alice said. "People in rural America get lonely and desperate, and then they commit criminal acts. You'd know if you watched more TV. Is she at least sixteen?"

"Eleven."

"Ouch. I got here in the nick of time. Do you want to take a bath?"

"Isn't it getting cold?"

"We can run more hot."

"Or you could get out and we—"

"Or you could get in."

She gave him a challenging look and he remembered how, whenever she was around for more than a few hours, they had these battles of will. Today he would let her win. He stripped, turned on the hot water and unplugged the tub so it wouldn't overflow. Downstairs and in his bedroom, the phone rang five or six times and stopped. Burl settled in, sitting at the opposite end from Alice, her feet adjusting themselves around his legs like nudging, friendly fish.

"Oh god," she said, running her fingers up the insides of his calves.

"What?"

"I wasn't going to do this."

"Why not?"

"I—I thought, I'll just get away from everyone for a while and say hi and try to unwind by having a bath in the old tub." She bent over and kissed first one of his kneecaps, then the other. "Or that's what I told myself, anyway, but I was full of shit, wasn't I, of course I was. I shouldn't be doing this. I'm—" She swiped at her eyes again. "I can't stay long. I told Meg two hours tops. Her cousins might eat her alive."

He bent forward to kiss her but she had leaned back again. "You two can always stay here, you know."

"We'll be all right there. I told my mother I'd stick around for a while to help her with the paperwork and his stuff."

"Did Meg know you were coming over?"

"I told her. That Bee Man, she keeps calling you, even though she knows your name. Then she says how much she *despises* bees. It's her new favorite word."

He reached to turn the water off and plug the tub again. "How charming. She despises me?"

"Don't be so prickly—it's not you. She's always like this, you know that. It's been hard for her. She'd prefer me to be a nun."

He could have asked again—is there someone else?—but what if Alice said yes? Instead he drew her toward him, their bodies unwieldy against the slippery, steep curve of the tub.

"No, come this way," she told him. "The faucet will jam into our heads."

Dripping, then, they turned, resettled, sank down. Even with her living in his thoughts, he had forgotten how nice the actual thing was, like swimming underwater at the pond but different, her borders calling him. He ran his mouth from her jaw to her shoulder, from her nipple to the hollow of her underarm, across her belly and down. Alice arched to meet him, running her fingers up his spine. He tasted her soapy and sweaty, familiar and strange, her hair darker now that it was wet, floating like kelp in the tub. For a few minutes, then, they stopped moving and lay quietly, their breath rising and falling together, her head resting on his chest. It occurred to him, not for the first time, that he was glad to be a human. Drones only got to have sex once, rupturing their penises (the books called them *endophalluses*) inside the queen bee, then falling, split and broken, to their deaths. The queen was luckier, living a long life for a bee, but still she had just one nuptial period of a few days, and who was to say if she found pleasure in the hordes of drones giving up their lives for her, driving her deep into the sky?

But mammals, but people, but Alice, how nice they were, warm-blooded and smooth-skinned, cursed and gifted with language, troublesome, yes (as a species, he thought people did more harm than good), but she was back and he had missed her. From somewhere far away, he thought he heard his name being called, and then there it was again on Alice's lips—*burlburl*. Turning, he tried to stretch out above her, pulling her closer, but okay, she was saying, okay, you win, my back is breaking and we need a condom, let's move to the bed.

18

Salt of the earth, it worked. Each day Francis washed the pink pills down with a glass of water and they traveled through him, mending, seasoning, changing the balance in his brain. The pills didn't bring him back. He was never the same again (or was it that Miriam knew too much by then?), but he was *there*, living with them; he had, in some sense, returned. Gone, now, were the saints, the scrubbing, obscenities and sleepless nights. In their place was something else—a deliberateness, a plain, unadorned *surviving*, but also a sadness, stiller and more watchful than anything Miriam would have expected from him; it seemed more like the inside of her own head. Sometimes she would catch him staring down at his hands as if they belonged to another body, or he'd forget a name and his face would freeze, for an instant, into panic—or was it shame? Other times, a laugh would emerge unexpectedly from his mouth, harsh as a dog's warning bark, both of them listening, the question left unspoken: Could it be coming back?

Francis looked older after he came out of the hospital. The medication slowed him down and made him gain weight, but that was only part of it. *Twice burned* was how he put it to her later, when finally he began to talk about what had happened. I mean, you think you have it whipped and then . . . Miriam took his hand. But now it's over; the lithium is working—you just have to keep taking it. I know, said Francis. Why did you stop before, she was half-tempted to ask. And why didn't you ever tell me about that time? But she couldn't ask. Even the thought made her too angry, and if she was angry she might yell, and if she yelled he'd get upset, and if he got upset he might not take his medicine, and then he'd go crazy again. Or something like that, the dominoes clinking, the dominoes falling, a life—three lives—collapsed. So she said nothing, just swallowed down her words the way Francis swallowed down his pills.

For a few months after Francis came home, Miriam went to see an elegant, white-haired psychiatrist named Dr. Katz, who prescribed Ativan to help her sleep and offered her antidepressants to *take the edge off things*. Miriam took the Ativan and refused the other drugs. I'm fine, she told the doctor. I just have a little trouble falling asleep. In truth, each night was a new, enormous obstacle, her mind endlessly revisiting the same events and spinning into the future—what if? During those moments she caught a glimpse of what Francis must have gone through, the self turned to a stick figure, whipped round and round in the vortex of its own repeating thoughts. Most of the time, though, she was all right. People kept asking her. No, I am. Really. When her insurance coverage ran out, she told the doctor she wanted to stop her weekly visits and only come in for new prescriptions. Dr. Katz thought this wasn't a good idea but Miriam didn't care. She wanted a life—to let it unfold, to live it without telling it. She wanted Eva to have one parent who wasn't in psychotherapy and taking mind-altering drugs Anyway, they couldn't afford it.

"You're going through an extremely difficult period," the doctor said. "It seems to me that you could use the extra support. I have a sliding scale. We could find a fee that wouldn't be too burdensome to you."

Miriam let her gaze travel from the plush Oriental rug to the original paintings on the walls. Earlier, on her way to the bathroom at the other end of the doctor's office suite, she had glanced into an adjoining room and seen, next to the computer, a framed photograph of a smiling young couple (the doctor's daughter and her husband?) holding a baby, everyone looking prosperous, radiant, whole, *just starting out*. The baby, she thought, probably already had a college fund. The woman in the photo had a living, breathing mother; the man had his mental health. Or maybe the picture was a fake, planted where patients could see it, designed to push their buttons and make them lose control. She had taken psychology in college and knew the doctor would want to hear these thoughts—transference, projection, even paranoia—but Miriam focused on breathing and kept her mouth clamped shut. Finally Dr. Katz asked if she would think it over. Yes, she said, knowing she would not.

Sometimes she caught sight of herself in a mirror and was startled at how she, like Francis, looked older—tired, coping, resigned, almost—more like her mother every day. Even Eva grew thinner and less infantlike while Francis was gone. After he came home, time seemed to gallop, and suddenly a white chip of tooth had erupted through Eva's bottom gum, and she was crawling backward, then forward. Her first word came early, at eleven months, and was bell-clear and aimed carefully at Francis: *Daa-dee*.

Eva's first word, the naming of her father. Goose, he still called her, as he had before, but it wasn't the same goose; it was a whole different picture, a whole different life, this one as deliberate, cautious and breakable as the other had been headlong and impulsive. At first, after he came home, he wouldn't feed or bathe Eva and seemed not even to notice when she cried. Miriam worried that he had lost interest in being a father, that he had *lost* Eva somehow in the hospital, given her up like a changeling handed to the saints. But then she would catch him hovering over the crib watching Eva sleep, or he would take roll after roll of photographs of her, portraits where she stared deep into the lens, deep into her father's face.

"*No*," he snapped once after Miriam asked him for the second time that week if he wanted to give Eva a bottle. "Not yet, I—" He ran his hands over his face. "I knew I'd fuck this up. I told you."

"You're not, though. She loves you."

He looked at her as if she had missed the point. "But she saw me. . . . Don't you remember? She was *there*."

"I know." Instinctively, Miriam scooped up Eva from the floor. "I just want you to feel—" Her voice grew taut. "I want us to be a family, that's all. Is that too much to ask? If it is, just tell me because I—"

Francis muttered something.

"What?" she asked.

"I'm trying," he said quietly. "You have no idea how hard I'm trying."

"No," she told him. "I do. I think I do."

"Then why can't you be more patient?"

"I will," she said. "I'll try."

And so they stumbled along, their progress halting, if it was there at all. It was more Miriam's style, really, this tentative new life. It made more sense to her and felt more familiar, even as she liked it less. Ratha and Sarah kept telling her how well she was doing, how anybody else would have fallen apart, and here she was juggling her job, her baby, Francis. What choice do I have, she asked, and Sarah, who had just broken up with her boyfriend, said plenty of women might have left him, or gone to pieces themselves, or taken it out on the kid. I'm not doing it alone, Miriam said, and it was true. Francis's mother kept his paycheck coming even when, for months and months, he didn't go to work. She sent him more Mass cards: *This is to certify that Francesco DiLeone has been enrolled for FIVE YEARS in SAINT PATRICK'S MISSIONARY CIRCLE and will be included in three special Masses offered daily as well as in sixteen Novenas of Masses each year.* I pray and pray, she said, and once a week she brought over delicious food, and ruffled dresses and tights for Eva—not Miriam's taste, but she dressed Eva in the clothes just the same.

"Without a mother, how do you know what to do?" Flavia asked one day as Miriam wiped pureed peas from Eva's face.

Miriam looked up. "I had a mother."

"But not now."

Eva writhed, twisting her face away and Miriam caught her chin and guided her back. "No, not now."

"So?"

"So—I don't know—I . . . I miss her, that's all. But she already—she taught me a lot, I guess." Sometimes, still, she talks to me, Miriam almost added, but she knew that Flavia would turn her mother into a messenger from God.

"It was very hard for you, to lose your mother," said Flavia, and for an instant Miriam thought they could be friends. Then Flavia jerked her chin toward Francis, who had gone into the bedroom to nap. "It's not right for him to take drugs like that."

"Shhh." Miriam raised a finger to her mouth. "He's on medicine, Flavia. Not street drugs. It's helping."

"Maybe, maybe not. Who can say?"

"No, it is. It's scientifically proven, there are lots of studies—"

"Today it's all science, but the mind is a gift, not a science. That boy's mind was a gift from God. As a boy he was so fast, so beautiful. There was *nothing* wrong with him. He was the smartest boy in his class. You see how those drugs make him slow."

Miriam cringed. "Please," she whispered. "Don't ever tell him that—he needs to stay on his medicine."

"*I* never took any medicine."

"Were you sick?" Miriam put down the spoon. "Like Francis? Did they try to give you medicine?"

"*They they they*, who is this *they?*"

"The doctors."

"I have three doctors," said Flavia, and her smile—charming, elusive, there then gone—was Francis's smile that first day in the store. "The Father, the Son, and the Holy Ghost."

Miriam kept track. Each night when Francis wasn't looking, she checked his pillbox to make sure he had taken his pills. The lithium made him gain weight, so she brought home low-fat yogurt and skim milk. The lithium made him forgetful, so she left him notes. *Doctor's appointment at 3. Please pick up baby food, cereal, meds.* You're not my nurse, he said once, but mostly he didn't seem to mind. At night they cuddled but rarely made love. It was a whole new thing, the way they lived together now, and though the strong undertow of desire had disappeared, Miriam felt something else—a tenderness, a quiet regard mixed with vigilance. She would guard him, watching carefully for slips. She would keep him. For himself. For Eva. For herself. She and the pills—together they could do it. Each night she checked, and the empty cubbies in the pillbox were a place where she could rest her thoughts.

And so the months passed. In February Francis went back to work, first half-time, then three-quarters time. One night as they lay in bed, he asked Miriam what he had said to Ratha the night the police came.

"I know it was bad," he said, "but I don't remember the details."

"It doesn't matter anymore," Miriam whispered. "I've explained the whole thing to her. She understands."

"No she doesn't. She can't even look me in the eye."

"She's . . ." Miriam sought words that wouldn't unsettle. "She's probably a little embarrassed, that's all. She might need more time."

"What did I say?"

Could he really have forgotten it all, the words lodged forever in her brain? "You thought—I guess you thought she was hurting Eva. It doesn't matter, Ratha knows you were sick. She has a relative in Delhi who has a similar—"

"But what did I *say?*" He sat up.

"Please, Francis." She sat, too. "Can't we just forget it? It's over. It wasn't you—it was like you were—" She shook her head. "Possessed."

"I want to know," he said carefully, "so that if it starts to happen again, I . . . and so I can . . ." He touched her hand, his voice almost wheedling. "Come on, Mim, just tell me."

"I don't remember."

"Of course you do."

"You . . . you called her . . . you called her a bitch, okay? And you thought you heard her in the baby monitor. All right? You really don't remember?"

"No. What else?" His hand on her arm was pressing her on, forcing her back.

"Stop," she told him and shoved his hand away. How dare he drag her through this, he who had been so full of secrets, so jammed with things he hadn't said? "What's *wrong* with you?" she said before she could stop herself.

He lay down, facing the wall.

"Francis, I'm sorry. Please—I'm really sorry. I'm just . . . I'm upset." She lay down next to him. He twitched, and she felt the wave pass through her. "It's over," she repeated. "You're okay."

"You don't know that."

"Yes I do," she said, but in her mind she saw a treacherous night landscape, foggy and dark, filled with bulky shapes that might be chasms, or might be cliffs, or might be anything at all. The doctors had done a CT scan of his brain and it had looked like that, dark and eerie, made of nothing she could recognize. Living with Francis now, she realized, was like living in an earthquake zone. You could gird your buildings and cross your fingers, but then you had to behave—for your child, if for nothing else— as if you lived on solid ground. Besides, she was sure there was a good reason why the illness had made him forget what had happened, and hadn't Francis been the one who had disapproved of—what had he called it—*muckraking* the past?

The next day, he brought home tea roses for Ratha. The day after, he brought home irises, and then, in the days that followed, marigolds, day lilies, a white orchid in a nest of bark, and other flowers—drooping bell shapes, pink-petalled cups with heart-shaped leaves.

"Tell him it's all right—he can stop," Ratha said to Miriam after a week of bouquets, but her apartment was festooned with flowers and she had tucked a frilly orange blossom in her hair. Francis kept up with the flowers for a month, and while Miriam fretted about how much they cost and whether this was the beginning of another spending jag, she held her tongue. Ratha had grown more formal since the breakdown—not less kind, but a little distanced, wary, or maybe Miriam was just too lost in her own troubles to let a friendship grow. After he started with the flowers, Miriam and Ratha began to take the girls on a short walk each day when Miriam got home. Ratha would talk about her life in India—her ailing father, her sister who was already a professor, the way her marriage to Mahesh had been, as she put it, *sort of but not entirely arranged*. The walks were wistful times, the babies sleeping in their strollers, Miriam and Ratha taking each other to distant places as they walked the familiar city streets: Delhi; Mexico; *the day I gave up my spot at the university; the time—I must have been around seven—that I fasted with my father on Yom Kippur.*

177

They didn't talk about Francis, hardly at all, and their walks quickly became a daily ritual that Miriam couldn't do without.

At home, as soon as she walked through the door, her mind returned to Francis. Sometimes she worried that he was hiding his pills instead of taking them, and she found herself looking in crevices, peering, even, into the toilet bowl, imagining the lithium swirling through the sewers of New York. She had to trust him, though. What choice did she have? It's over, she had said, but it was over and not, just like he was Francis and not, just like this was a life she could want and regret at the same time.

The only simple thing was Eva. Francis loved her. Miriam had said so to his social worker in the hospital and she had been right. After only a few weeks, he started inching toward being her father again, and Eva reached out and yanked him back into the world. She was—well, what, for him? Maybe she was newness, starting over. Certainly, Miriam thought, she was playfulness—in her sidelong glances, in the keen pleasure she took in putting on a show. Down she would fall, flat on her diapered behind; then she'd let out a belly laugh and reach for her father to haul her up so she could do it again. Eva and Francis even looked the same. Flavia brought over pictures once, and they could have been the same baby—the same glint in their eyes, the same mop of abundant, grown-up hair, their heads a little too big for their bodies, a heavy weight. When Francis was slow from his medication or tired from a night of restless sleep, Eva could cut through. She was the reason—or so it seemed to Miriam—that he got up each morning; she was why he went to work and why he came home, why he had his blood levels checked and took, each day, his pills.

And so each time Miriam thought that maybe this was a life too full of compromise, too likely to explode, she was drawn back by the two of them together. Because what a gift this was for Eva, to have a father like him—it was both something Miriam had never had, and something she could never be. And Eva, what bright powers she possessed, able to lure Francis away from his

gray, dry-mouthed world. So if sometimes Miriam felt like an
interloper, wanting each of them for herself, the feeling never
lasted long. Anyway, they needed her; she knew that. She was
the zipper-upper, the filler of cupboards, the one Eva reached for
when she bumped her head or woke up in the night. Miriam was
the one who brought the needle to the flame, held the finger
steady and got the splinter out: *There, you see? All gone.*

And so the months passed, and so the years. Eva turned one,
then two, then three. Miriam got a raise at work, and another,
and she and Francis slowly paid off the credit card bills. You'd be
a good lawyer, her boss told her one day in passing, but she found
herself doubting his sincerity. Anyway, being a lawyer belonged
to another life, just as having a second child did. Every once in
a while Francis brought it up—what about another baby, a buddy
for Eva? No, Miriam always said. You know we can't afford it,
and we don't have enough time for her as it is.

Her real fears stayed unspoken—that she couldn't bear to risk
it, his getting sick again, the way it had all started after Eva's
birth. And more than that, worse than that, the thought as impossible to banish as it was to think. Had he already forgotten
that it could be *passed on*, that it *ran in families*, like brown eyes,
like curly hair? In the months after he came home, she had sat
in the public library during her lunch hour, trying to make sense
of the dense, beige textbooks filled with other people's underlin-
ings and question marks. *Relatives of early-onset bipolar probands
have a morbid risk of 9.6 percent for bipolar illness. . . . Depression
and other psychiatric disorders of childhood have been noticed repeat-
edly in many offspring of patients with affective disorders.* What were
probands? She had looked it up in the dictionary but it wasn't
there. The graphs had confused her. The books were as thick as
the Manhattan phonebook and filled with words she didn't know.
As she read, she had chewed on her pencil until she gagged on
graphite and rising fear, then she'd coughed and switched to the
blue plastic cap of her pen.

A few weeks after that, unable to contain her worry, she had mentioned what she'd read to Francis, who had dismissed her findings with a baffling offhandedness. Eva? Don't worry, she'll be fine. Miriam couldn't imagine how he could speak with such confidence. Was he fooling himself or fooling her, or was his reaction somehow part of the disease itself, a blind spot, a loop with no exit? They couldn't have more children. Of course not. They would have to be out of their minds.

So the only simple thing was Eva, but also not. Miriam worried over her, and she worried over Francis taking care of her, and eventually, as Francis got better, he began to grow irritated. Mellow out, he would tell Miriam. Or worse, he'd turn to Eva: Tell your mom to take a chill pill. It was around that time, Eva three and always on the go, that the fights began. They were usually about the same thing, with minor variations. It was a Tuesday or Thursday, Miriam at work, Francis home in the afternoon with Eva. Around three, she would call to check in. No answer. Then she'd call at three-thirty, four, ten after, quarter past. Next, she'd call Ratha and ask her to go upstairs to check on them. Out. Twenty minutes later—still out. By the time Miriam got home from work, she was always in a state. Where were you, she asked one Thursday after she opened the door to find them there, playing on the floor. Where were we when? Earlier—I tried to call. In the park, here and there, exploring. But it's raining, she has a cold, I kept calling and no one was home. Francis frowned, bent over a pirate ship: We were out, she wore her slicker. Well, I wish you'd tell me when you went out. Why? Because I worry. About what? About—No words sufficient, her terror at once too huge and too insubstantial to name. Francis stood. You don't trust me, do you? For Christ's sake, I'm her father. Shhh. Miriam looked at Eva, who was trotting a plastic pirate up a mast. No, said Francis. No, I won't shhh. I'm her father, dammit, I'd *kill* anyone who tried to hu—

Eva, come—we're going out. And Miriam grabbed her, took

her outside in the rain and walked with her: calm down, everyone try to calm down. It wasn't the first time, or the last. Sometimes she couldn't help herself—she'd start crying on those walks, Eva wiggling in her arms. Because didn't Francis see how much he scared her, talking like that? Didn't he know he sounded crazy, angry, nuts? Or was this different from before? Because maybe he was right; he *did* take good care of Eva. He had never forgotten her or let her wander off, get hit by a car or kidnapped by a stranger. But it might happen—he was absent-minded, and the cabs in the city would mow down anything in their path, and more than anything, Eva loved to run.

"Don't you think that if you want to stay with him, you have to let him be her father?" Ratha asked Miriam one Saturday as they sat drinking tea and the children napped.

"But what if something happens?"

"I don't know. Something can always happen. You let *me* take care of her, don't you?"

"I trust you."

"And not Francis?"

"No, I do, I think I do. I just wish they'd stay home more—they're always going off. It's just . . . you saw him. I can never totally forget."

"I know," said Ratha. "But that was how many—almost three years ago."

"It can happen again, I've read about it. He was worried, too, at first. Then it's like he totally forgot, or else he doesn't tell me what he's thinking."

Ratha blew on her tea. "You can find anything in a book if you search hard enough. Did you know that Mahesh is too tired after work to take the children to the park?"

"Meaning what?"

Ratha shrugged. "The walks are nice for her. He shows her things. They talk to people. Eva tells me about it."

"So you think I shouldn't worry? She's not even four yet. God knows who they talk to—it's a crazy city." The word *crazy* hung in the air like something she shouldn't have said. "Would you let Charu go with them?" she asked suddenly.

Ratha stared into her mug, steam floating up around her face. When she looked up, her face was pained. "I might. I hope so." She reached out and touched Miriam's arm. "But I would worry, too."

The worst part of the fights was leaving; the best part was coming back. When she took Eva and headed down the stairs into the city, Miriam sometimes had the feeling that they might never return, or that, by leaving, she was setting off a chain reaction and would arrive home to find the police at the door, carting Francis off. Sometimes when she was five or six blocks away, another image would come to her—of a clean and simple life, an airy loft. No pill bottles anywhere, no mess, no sticky notes, just a basket for Eva's toys and a medicine cabinet filled with skin care products—astringent, lotion, bath oil, a pumice stone to rub away the rough spots on her feet. Sometimes a lover would arrive in her thoughts, slipping in and out of bed with her—silent, simple—and leaving no trace of himself after he was gone.

The lover was always followed promptly by her guilt, and with it, her turning back. Because where, she had to ask herself as she hoisted Eva higher on her hip and began the walk home, was Francis in this picture? And how could she have been so hard on him? He was a good father; she was jealous, that was all. She had to control everything. She didn't know how to live among people and should have led a solitary, ordered, lonely little life. He would get worse, was probably getting worse as she thought about it, and if he had another episode, it would be her fault. They had a word for her in the medical lingo: she was a *stressor*. By the time she got home, she was always filled with remorse, and longing, too, almost as if *he* had been the one to walk out the door. I'm sorry, she would say. I don't know what gets into me—you're right, I have to mellow out. Then Francis would say he was sorry, too, and draw her near.

These were the moments that felt most like their early days, her skin aching for him, the way he always felt just slightly out of her grasp. Often they made love on nights after a fight, and so the more they fought, the more they made love, and the more they made love, the less she thought of him as someone who was sick. Had he finally (could she let herself believe it?) returned?

One night, without thinking, she blurted out the question. "Why," she said, "didn't you tell me you'd been sick before?"

Francis didn't hesitate. "I should have told you. I tried a few times but you didn't seem to want to hear, or maybe . . . I don't know—maybe I just didn't have the guts. I thought—I hoped I was all better, but I wasn't sure you'd believe me."

"I would have," she told him.

"You would have been wrong."

"No." She stumbled. "No, I mean, believed *in* you."

But as soon as she said it, already she was doubting. Would she have believed in him in those early days? Should she have? Did she believe in him now? She thought she did. You have to have faith in him, Heidi had said when Francis came out of the hospital, and slowly Miriam had begun to, though in some ways it went against her better judgment. After he answered her question, though, believing got a little easier; she wasn't sure why. She stopped calling so much from work. She took a chill pill. It wasn't easy, but she made herself. If you need to call someone, said Ratha, call me.

And then there were fewer fights and they were, for a while, happy, in the most mundane, daily sense of the word, though she never completely let down her guard. Sometimes phrases came to her out of nowhere: "Rounded the bend," "turned the corner," "out of the woods." "Once, long ago." *Once, long ago, he was sick, but that was years ago.* Despite herself, she began to relax, and as she relaxed she fell in love with him again, not as his nurse or mother, not as the younger self who had tumbled into bed and gotten pregnant by mistake. This time she fell in love with all the tangled fibers of his being—with his sickness and health, his jokes and stutterings, his brain of night colors, his body which was no longer so young and firm. She hadn't known she wasn't in love until it happened, and though the change frightened her, she found she couldn't help it.

As her spirits improved, so did his, as if mood were, in fact, contagious, and not, as the textbooks claimed, a chemical concoction of the brain. One day she came home and saw that he had taken his electronic keyboard out of the closet and plugged it in. The next week, he bought a box of pastels. To make a sale sign for the store, he said, but then he drew Eva—a quick, loose sketch in black and red, Eva caught inside a scribble, her cocked head, her wry gaze. You're really good, Miriam told him. No I'm not, he said, but a few days later he brought home wood, spread out newspaper on the living room floor and built two easels— one for Eva and one for himself. He made a new set of cherry shelves for the stereo, a wooden wall rack for Miriam's scarves. He carved walking sticks marked with each of their initials from wood he and Eva had scavenged in Central Park.

We took you to the zoo—do you remember? We rode the Staten Island ferry. We went on vacation to the Adirondacks and rowed a rowboat backward because we didn't know how. All the way across the lake, each of them in an orange life preserver, Francis laboring, laughing, bent over the oars.

And Eva turned four and started nursery school, turned five and started kindergarten. *This is how tall you were when you were five* (she is seven, she is eight, a stringbean, prone to nightmares, tracing her finger over the marks on the closet door).

And Eva turned six.

When I was six, my father had a heart attack and died.

19

In her mother's bedroom, Eva pranced and paraded, happiness sparkling in her throat. "Guess what, we have a dinner invitation," Miriam had told her a few nights before. It was from a guy named Simon who worked at the newspaper across the hall from the law firm. He had two kids—a thirteen-year-old boy and a girl Eva's age, and, yes, they'd be there, too. What about their mother, Eva had asked. Divorced, said Miriam, so then Eva knew it was a date but she didn't care as long as she was invited and there'd be other kids. A few times in New York, her mother had gone on dates while she stayed downstairs with Charu, but Miriam had never liked the men. Not for me, she'd say afterward, or, I should have stayed home with you.

Now, though, her mother was opening dresser drawers and picking through the carved wooden box where she kept her earrings. Now she was holding up filmy scarves and glass bead necklaces, a fistful of silver bracelets from Ratha, the amber bug necklace from Eva's father. "You're getting big enough," Miriam was saying, "that if we roll up the sleeves you might be able to borrow one of my shirts," and Eva was thinking yes, maybe a silky one, purple or turquoise, but also worrying about how to hide her brand-new body as she changed.

"Try this." Her mother handed her a stiff white blouse with pearly buttons.

"I'd rather have silk."

"Oh you would, would you?"

Eva nodded. Her mother had draped a whole bunch of scarves around her neck and looked like a clown or magician, her eyes happy, a hairbrush in her hand. This was how it was supposed to be, how it used to be—the two of them doing projects together, going through Miriam's stuff: *I got this in Mexico from a man with a monkey on his shoulder. You like this one? Sarah strung it for me after you were born. That one was my mother's—it's made entirely of shells.* They could have been on a TV show about a single mom and a kid who were best friends and wore each other's clothes.

"Can I try on the one with the silver buttons?" Eva asked. "The bluish-purpley one, you know?"

"Really? That's my nicest shirt. You won't spill on it?"

Eva felt a prickle of irritation but managed just to shake her head. And then the shirt was in her hands, so slippery and soft, a dusky, smoky color which changed depending on the light. She turned her back, wiggled out of her T-shirt and slid, in one quick motion, into the shirt, which smelled like her mother and felt like running water on her skin. When she finished buttoning, she turned around and looked at the floor, suddenly shy.

"Oh it's much too big," said Miriam. "I was afraid of that."

"No it's not." Eva stroked the fabric. "I can roll up the sleeves."

"It's as long as a dress, sweetie. You're lost in it. Maybe in a year or two."

"But I could wear it as a dress, like with leggings."

"You think?" Her mother looked doubtful. "I guess you could give it a try."

Eva ran to her room to get her black leggings, shimmied into them, ran back. Her mother had put on the white blouse while she was gone. It made her look exactly like a nurse.

"Oh." Miriam looked her up and down. "You're right, that was a good idea. We can tell them it's the latest fashion in the city. Here, try this." She draped a necklace around Eva's neck—chunky blue and purple glass beads. "You like that? The colors are pretty with your hair."

Eva nodded, fingering the hard shapes.

"How about me?" asked her mother. "What do you think?"

"Maybe a different shirt."

Miriam looked down. "You think? I thought this was . . . summery. Or something." She sighed. "I don't know."

"Wear silk, like me."

"But it's just a casual dinner and we don't want—we really don't need to be dressed up at all."

"Then silk and jeans," said Eva. "Your black silk shirt. And this—" She plucked the amber necklace from the box.

Her mother took the necklace, looked at it for a moment, put it back. "Silk and jeans?" She frowned. "It sounds like a perfume ad."

"And perfume, and for me too—" Eva ran to get it from the dresser.

"All right, but calm down; let's not get too excited. You might not like these kids, the dinner might be boring. I don't want you to be disappointed."

"I won't." Eva stood on tiptoes. "Lift up your hair." She sprayed a burst of perfume on her mother's neck and a spurt on her own wrist. "Now you do me."

She handed the bottle over and lifted her own heavy mass of hair. Her mother leaned forward and planted a kiss on her neck, making a shiver travel through her.

"Look at you, pretty girl," Miriam said. "You're getting so tall—soon you'll be all grown up."

"Oh no I won't."

"Oh yes you will. Before you know it. Before I know it."

Eva stepped away. She thought she might be about to cry. But then her mother was coming toward her again, gathering up her hair, aiming the perfume bottle, letting out a squirt. "How about a scarf in your hair, wound like a headband?"

"Maybe," said Eva, and the smell in the room was of a long, long time ago—her mother bending down to say good night, a babysitter there, her room with its goose-shaped night-light, the radiator hissing, her father bending down to say good night. He had been nice, her father. Hadn't he? He had been funny and nice, sad and sick. She thought so. She wasn't sure. Good night. *Buenas noches.* Something like that, or was that Spanish? Once she had known some Italian; now it was gone.

Her mother handed her a scarf.

The dinner, as Eva later informed Miriam, sucked. No kids, bad food, lice. She sat and sat, so bored she wanted to lie down on the scratchy orange carpet and die. I thought you had kids, she said to Simon as the three of them perched in his living room, the grown-ups eating olives and spitting out the slimy gray pits. I thought I did, too, he said. Ha. It turned out the kids were at their mother's house because they had lice which they had gotten that week at camp. *Lice*, like orphans got in books. "We didn't want you to get it," said Simon. "And we didn't even know you had that gorgeous head of hair." Simon was bald and wore clogs and jeans with a red patch on one knee. His house was filled with boats: pictures of boats, model boats, books on boats, a boat steering wheel. At first he acted as if he thought Eva might be interested—look at this one, a clipper ship—but she didn't even pretend to care, and pretty soon he started ignoring her, then kept it up for the rest of the night.

You might have been friendlier, Miriam said later when Eva complained. He made an effort but you didn't exactly encourage him. But Eva wasn't *feeling* friendly as she sat there all dressed up with no one to talk to, imagining her scalp crawling with lice from some camp where she didn't even get to go. Simon asked lots of questions and her mother blabbed: the city, blah blah, tax law, thinking about applying to law school, wrote away for applications, maybe public interest, not really sure. . . . At dinner Eva poked at her food—chicken, rice with rubbery brown mushrooms on top, and salad covered with moldy cheese—while her mother drank one glass of wine and then another, her cheeks rosy, her eyes bright, her mouth announcing plans that Eva had never heard about and anyway didn't believe were true. She's too old for law school, Eva was tempted to say. She's only trying to impress you, don't you see? She felt, as she sat there, as if she was having dinner with two strangers. Why didn't you tell me, she wanted to cry out. If you're applying to law school, why didn't you tell me first? Really, Simon kept saying. Really? Then he'd make some joke Eva didn't get, and her mother would laugh and have another sip of wine. Wow, she'd say. Really, from Maine to the Virgin Islands? Did you hear that, Eva? And you brought the kids? What a wonderful experience for them.

"Do you have a TV?" Eva cut in finally.

"Eva!" Her mother laughed, a fluttery, high trill.

"We do," said Simon. "And some videos you might like. Have you had it with the grown-ups? I don't blame you. I'm really sorry Chloe and Jake aren't here. We'll have you over again, or take a picnic to one of the state parks. Do you like canoeing?"

She shrugged.

"She's never been, but I'm sure she'd love it," said her mother.

"Great." Simon clapped his hands together like a grown-up on Sesame Street. "For now, should we set you up in front of the TV?"

Which he did, leaving her with a bowl of ice cream, and she sat in a room behind the kitchen and watched a movie about a man who woke up one day in a kid's body. Maybe it would have been funny if she hadn't been in the worst mood of her life.

Round and round, Eva stirred the ice cream, turning it to mush, then soup. Finally her mother came in, Simon standing behind her in the doorway.

"Hi goose. Is it good? Do you want to watch the rest? I can wait."

Eva pressed *Stop* and *Eject* on the remote and stood up.

Her mother glanced back at Simon. "It's late for her."

No it's not, Eva wanted to say. I'm up this late all the time—I'm almost a grown-up, remember? *Before you know it.* She made an effort, though, to pull herself together. She brought her ice-cream dish into the kitchen and put it in the sink. Thanks for dinner, she told Simon. Thanks for the video. 'Bye. During the car ride, her mother tried to talk: I think he seems nice, you have to give people a chance . . . it's too bad his kids weren't there . . . he's been all around the world . . . he did the Peace Corps in Ghana.

Eva didn't ask what's the Peace Core or where's Ghana or say yeah, you're right, he does seem nice. Are you really applying to law school, she asked, and Miriam said she didn't know, it was just an idea, it was probably too expensive, what did Eva think of Simon's photographs? Mmm, she mumbled as her mother rambled on, and after a while Miriam's words started to run together and become a string of sounds. Pretend to sleep, Eva told herself blearily, though she knew she should keep an eye out for oncoming cars. Pretend to sleep. *Ninna-nanna, ninna-oh.* And then her mother was shaking her by the shoulder. Wake up, goose, just for a minute. Time to go up to bed.

The next day, she went to see the bees. Or was it the bees she was going to see? My friend, she found herself thinking as she rode toward the house. *Mine.* She would never have invited her mother to Burl's, gotten all dressed up with her, then ignored her for hours. She wouldn't even tell Miriam about Burl; no, she would guard him the way the guard bees protected the hive, patrolling, checking things out, sometimes falling—she had seen it—on another bee. She kept trying to forget about the night before but she couldn't stop seeing her mother drinking red wine with her cheeks stained pink, leaning forward, her eyes huge because of the mascara she had on. The way she had said good-bye to Simon, all shy suddenly. She had seemed so *happy*—that was what bothered Eva the most. Her mother was hardly ever that happy with her, always too tired or worried or just so serious, but last night she had been laughing in her silk and jeans, earrings swaying from her ears. As she rode, she pictured how her mother would call her into the kitchen, ask her to sit down, tell her she was marrying this man, this Simon (Simon Says Jump, Simon Says Fuck You), that she was happy and hoped Eva could be happy for her, and Eva would say okay but I want to move back to New York now, and her mother would nod and hand her a bus ticket. So then Eva would go back there and live by herself, finding her food in dumpsters and sleeping in abandoned buildings on the floor. *There but for the grace of God goes every one of us.*

By the time she got to Burl's driveway, she had worked herself into a state (her mother's phrase), remembering all the orphans, all the sad, sad girls—the Little Matchstick Girl, Mary in *The Secret Garden*, Anne of Green Gables, Heidi, the Little Princess, the girls in China who got thrown away because they were girls. The world was full of orphans, it hurt to think of it, yet still she egged herself on with worse and worse thoughts. And then there was that TV show about the five kids whose parents had died, except they weren't sad, they had a big house, a Jeep and great clothes. They had one another—big brothers and little sisters and a baby boy to haul around. Eva would have given anything for that, but of course she was an only child.

So when she parked her bike, walked up the driveway and saw a sad girl sitting cross-legged on the grass, she felt as if she had walked into the inside of her own head. An elephant would have surprised her less, or a giant, talking bee. She moved closer but the girl didn't look up. She was so blond and so pink that you could see her scalp through her straight, yellow hair. She was frowning and staring into a small toy that made a beeping noise, her face puffy as if she had been crying. Eva came nearer, wondering if maybe this girl was deaf; there had been a deaf boy, Tony, in her class at school; you could come right up behind him and he wouldn't know. But then she coughed a small, fake cough, and the girl looked up and let out a yelp.

"You scared me," she said flatly, looking up at Eva.

"Sorry."

The girl returned to her game. What's that, Eva wanted to ask. Can I play? Also, who are you, what are you doing here and *are* you sad? Or no, maybe she didn't want to ask, because maybe she didn't want to know. What if Burl had a daughter? That could be why he let Eva hang around so much—he had a daughter who lived someplace else, and he missed her but now she had come to stay. This girl's skin was pink, like his, and she was sitting on the grass as if she owned the place. Then why had he lied, saying, that first day by the hives, that he had no kids? But why not? People lied all the time; she should know. Maybe he thought his daughter didn't love him, or maybe somebody, just to be mean, had lied to him and told him his daughter was dead.

"What's that thing?" Eva asked.

The girl was talking to the object in her hands, whispering words too soft for Eva to understand. She didn't look up. "My pet."

"What?"

"My virtual pet. You know, from Japan. You don't have those here?" Her voice was verging on scornful, but then she stood up and handed over the thing and Eva saw from her height that she was just a little kid, maybe seven or eight; she barely came up to Eva's chin.

Eva turned the pet over and looked at its tiny screen. Holding it, she remembered seeing toys like it before, a grade or two ago. Kids got in trouble when their pets beeped in the middle of class.

"Oh yeah, I forgot," she said. "My friend had one. How's it work again?"

The girl took it back. "It makes noise and there's stuff on the screen, like if it's hungry or needs discipline or wants to play."

The screen was gray, blank. "It's not doing anything."

"Sometimes it just sits there, like a real pet. I just fed it."

"How?"

The girl used the edge of the pet to scratch her arm. "There's a knife and fork."

Eva wanted a virtual pet of her own; they were just that snatch-able size that made her fingers itch. She pictured a plastic bin of them in the store, her arm diving down among the shapes, her fist closing around the one meant especially for her. "Where'd you get it?" she asked.

"In Denver."

"Was it expensive?"

The girl shrugged. "It was my cousin's but she got sick of taking care of it."

"Where's Lissa?" Eva asked. All at once she missed her bulk, her dogness.

The girl eyed her suspiciously. "How come you know Lissa?"

"I—" How come she knew Lissa? "Um, I'm staying in a house near here. Sometimes I help with the bees."

"I despise those bees," the girl said violently. "They act like they own the place."

So Eva had been right—it was all making sense now; this girl hated the bees because they lived with her father while she lived somewhere else, probably with her mother, far away. Burl was divorced, he just had never told her. The poor little girl was kind of like an orphan, too, or a half-orphan like Eva. Eva wanted, then, to sit the girl down in front of her and braid her hair, which was exactly like the hair of Lissa the farmgirl.

"My father died when I was six," she said. She hadn't told

anybody in a while and had decided not to tell the kids at her new school, but she thought knowing might make this girl feel better.

"So did my grandfather," the girl said. "A couple days ago. That's why we're here."

Inside Eva, then, a falling, a fast, wide opening of a space she hadn't even known was there. Because could Burl be this girl's grandfather, meaning that he was dead? How old was he, anyway? She didn't really know, knew only that Charu's grandmother, visiting from India, had been so young and pretty that she had looked more like an aunt. Not that, no, not dead again, not Burl. Enough. She found a twig in the grass and knocked three times. "So is Burl your grandfather?" she asked.

The girl shook her head. "Dick's my grandpa. *He's* dead—I just told you. That's why we came."

"So is Burl . . . is he your *father?*"

The girl made a face. "My father's in Denver. He's a doctor, a . . ." She sounded out the word with care. "Gastroenterologist."

"Oh." Eva was more confused than ever. Where was Burl, anyway? She kept expecting him to come out the screen door or appear from around the corner of the barn. "Is Burl . . ." She realized that maybe she should say Mr. Somebody, but she didn't even know his last name. "Is he around?"

The girl looked over at the house. "He's in there with my mom. I think maybe they're fighting." The pet in her hand beeped, and she pressed some button to make it stop.

"Is it thirsty?" Eva asked, her own throat dry.

"Hungry. It's supposed to be different things, but it's always hungry. I think it might be broken."

"Why are they fighting?"

"Because they're losers." She looked like she might start to cry.

And then a woman's voice called from the kitchen window. "Meg, sweetie, if you're out there, come on inside—I made you a sandwich."

"That's my mom," said the girl, and Eva wanted to ask if she

194

was sure, because the "sweetie" had sounded so much like her own mother, though the rest of the voice was different.

"What's your name?" the girl asked as she turned to go.

"Eva."

"Too bad you don't live in Denver. I have another pet there, a purple one. I'd let you take care of it."

"Meg?" came the voice again.

"*Coming!*" Meg shrieked, and closing her fist around her pet, she wheeled around and ran up to the house.

After that, a lot of things didn't happen. Meg didn't invite Eva in to lunch. Burl didn't appear at the door and offer to show Eva the queen. Eva didn't wait until Meg was inside, then go knock herself, or ask if Meg could play after lunch, or find out where, exactly, Denver was, and was it very far away? She didn't go visit the bees, who didn't recognize her anyway, or whistle for Lissa, who only came running for Burl. She didn't think of her mother dying and need to steal something. She didn't even knock on wood.

She stood there. For a long moment she stood and felt very young and very old at the same time—herself, Eva, Eva DiLeone Baruch, standing alone with her feet planted firmly on the ground. As she turned to go, she noticed a red car parked up by the barn, the same car that had been in the driveway three days ago. That day, she had called for Burl outside but hadn't found him. The kitchen door had been open so she had stuck her head in and called for him again, but he hadn't answered so she had given up, leaving his mail on the porch. The car was bright and new, gleaming like a cough drop, and now, as she looked at it, it made her heart hurt. If she had known how, she would have stolen that car, crossed its wires like they did in movies and driven off down the road. That would show them, but of course she didn't know how to steal or drive a car. There were—it made her tired—too many things she didn't know.

She brought her wrist to her face and smelled the perfume

there, left over from the day before. It was the smell of her mother—of flowers and soap, lipstick, lotion and sweat. She licked her skin, tasting salt and something metallic.

What had her father smelled like? Once she had known; now the smell was just beyond her grasp. A strong wind might carry it back to her, the way strong winds carried things in fairy tales— magic carpets, babies in baskets, news both good and bad. Eva would face into the wind and fill her lungs. Breathe in; now let it go. Yes, she would say, like she was being interviewed by a detective, like her father had committed some sort of crime. Yes, I'm sure—that's him.

20

She remembered how her mitten felt against his glove, and how he scared her when his face was covered with shaving cream because he looked like someone else. She remembered a small box divided into the days of the week—the shiny white plastic, the black letters, one on each compartment, and below the letters, little bumps so blind people could tell what was inside. Once when she was four—or was it five?—he had sat with her and traced her finger over the letters on the box, M like M&M's, like Mom, like Monday. Is today Monday? No, it's T-T-Tuesday— Tuesday with a T. Then he opened up the T cubby of the box, swallowed down the pills and gave Eva her vitamin, which he fished from a jar. Is yours a vitamin, too? Sort of. Can I have one? No, they're not for kids. But can I have just one, *per favore?* Raising her face to him, knowing that he liked it when she used Italian words. She wanted a pill that lived beneath a letter, wanted to swallow the same thing as her father. No, he told her. They make me healthy but they would make you sick.

She remembered being told *shhh Eva, Daddy needs to sleep*, how he took naps on the weekends even after she stopped taking them, and her mother made her sit with a coloring book in the living room and stay quiet. She remembered a gray box in her parents' bedroom. The sleep machine, they called it; it made noises like rain and wind but it was not a toy. She remembered going to her grandmother's apartment at Christmas. Everything there was red, and Jesus was on the wall, and her grandmother brought out toys that had been her father's when he was little, but when Eva tried to play with them, she swooped down and took them away.

A guitar. A sweater, its yarn coming loose at the hem, making her want to tug. Somebody crying, maybe her mother. Don't forget, don't forget; she remembered that. But don't forget what? To pick Eva up at school. To take your medicine. To call your mother back—I left you a note. Sticky notes on the fridge and the bathroom mirror, curling yellow flags she wanted to peel off and collect. A bee sting in the park. Someone had held a popsicle to the sting until it stopped hurting, the syrup dripping slowly down her leg. Brave girl, now you can eat the rest. And sometimes fights between her parents—a door shutting, her mother pulling her out into the night. She couldn't remember the words of the fights, just the watery feeling in her stomach as she listened, and the way her mother would hold her afterward like she was still a baby. Once the two of them had sat on the edge of a fountain in the middle of a snowstorm. Eva had wanted to squirm away, to get up, but she had known to stay very still while hundreds of snowflakes pricked her neck like pins.

Dinner on the bird plates, the napkin rings shaped like animals—bear, anteater, lion. Her father catching Charu by the waist, flying her up and down as Eva watched, trying to stop herself from yelling *me me me*. Or was she picturing something else, Charu's father, maybe, or some father she'd seen on TV? Because her own father's face, when she tried to see it, to actually picture him, was blurred like a watercolor she had smeared before it dried. Or like a dead person, or a wrinkled, rotting peach. Once she had asked Ratha if she still remembered India. Of course, Ratha said. But don't you forget after a while? No, Eva; it's my home, it's in my blood.

She remembered the songs her father used to sing, but they always came to her in her mother's voice because Miriam had kept singing them after he was gone and had written down the words in Eva's baby book.

Fate la nanna coscine di pollo,
la vostra mamma vi ha fatto il gonnello
e ve l'ha fatto di buccine d'aglio
fate la nanna coscine di pollo.

Beddy-bye chicken legs, mama's made you a skirt of garlic skins. And another one: *Ninna-nanna, ninna-oh, questo bimbo a chi lo do?* This one was in her head as nonsense. If she had ever known, she no longer remembered what it meant.

These, then, were Eva's half-memories. Of words but not their meanings, of a sweater but not the face above it. Of a box, the corner of a room, the scratch of wool, but never a whole father, or even a whole mother the way she'd been before. These were among the things she hoarded, like the nail files, key chains and pink erasers she kept hidden in a shoebox, her loot. Because mostly, she didn't remember. Or not in words, anyway, not in sentences, pictures or scenes. If this kind of un-memory existed at all for her, it was as something she could sense but not quite say, an unmapped island in her brain, a grainy texture in her bones, a *thing*, mute and blind, that lived between her ribs and teeth, in the roots of her hair, in the slick, wet walls of her throat.

She asked her mother questions, and her mother answered, and the answers both soothed and itched, so Eva asked again and yet again.

A hand, a pillbox, a lamp with her name painted on it, a once-upon-a-time inside her mother's mouth. A heart like a piece of candy, or no, like the smashed squirrel she had biked past on the road, its insides all squeezed out. The heart was a muscle to pump blood; they had seen a plastic one in school. *Apis mellifera*. If you said it again, you might not forget. The brain weighed three pounds and was full of water. The heart beat four times for every breath. Her father had loved her; that much she knew. Her mother loved her, too, but she was too near, too far, too near. Eva could never forget her—not her voice, not her face, not her smell.

21

This time, when Alice came through the door, he sprang up, went right toward her and leaned forward for a kiss, as if to say *see, I mean it, things have changed.* She kissed him back, then stood holding him, her mouth pressed up against his neck. Burl took it as a good sign—she had made up her mind, she would stay. He had asked her on an impulse—why don't you move in here with me, you and Meg—but it was an impulse born of long waiting, of the heft of accumulated years. Two days earlier, they had been sitting, talking, Meg off playing with Lissa in the dining room, and suddenly he had found that he *had* to ask her, even though the words were grindingly hard to say: I don't know how to put this . . . for a long time I've . . . Finally, he had arrived at a stilted version of what he meant: Why don't you move in here with me, you and Meg?

Alice had looked at him for so long that he'd felt a blush creep up his neck and across his face. Then, quietly, she had spoken.

She should have told him before, but she was seeing someone, a pediatrician in Denver, it was—well, actually it was pretty serious, they were thinking of moving in. You're right, you should have told me, he said, and she said yes, she knew that, it was crummy not to, it was just that with their long history and her father dying and the way things always seemed so casual . . .

"Maybe for you," Burl interrupted.

"Oh please," Alice said loudly. She lowered her voice. "You can't just turn around and—" She got up and went into the dining room; he heard her tell Meg to go play outside. When she returned, she sat down heavily. "It *is* casual between us—you know that. You set the terms here a long time ago, remember?"

"All right, maybe, but I've never felt casually about you, I just . . ." He rubbed his brow. "Can't people change?"

"Can they? I don't know. First of all, you have lousy timing, but also I'm not at all sure I believe you."

"Which part?"

"That you'd really want this, that you've changed."

"Why not? I never asked before, and now I am, I—"

"But you like your life. I have a kid. They're a lot of work and I don't think they interest you that much. Also, why would I want to move here? I hate it here—I spent years working to leave. You, of all people, should know that."

He remembered her at nineteen, heating a compress on the stove while he—the rich, out-of-town boy—leaned against the coolness of the fridge and watched. Even then, she had been so sure of what she wanted, talking to him through a haze of steam as she fished his grandfather's dripping compress from the pot and folded it inside an old towel. Her skin had been damp and flushed from the heat, her voice confident. *I'm going to be a nurse and go far away, maybe even to another country. Eventually I'll go to medical school.*

He took the easiest path. "I do like kids."

"At a distance."

"No, up close. I . . ." What to say next? He wasn't sure. Something about Eva, maybe, how alive he found her, how brimming, but that wouldn't work; Eva wasn't Meg. Something about growing tired, finally, of the life he had chosen, the deep grooves of habit he followed day by day. Something, yes of course, about Alice. I love you? Too cliché, and they had never said it, not once, each of them as careful as the other, except with their bodies—there they let their longing speak. Marry me? No, that would be jumping the gun, and as far as he knew, Alice wasn't even officially divorced yet.

"Will you at least think about it?" he said finally, and she nodded and asked if he had anything for sandwiches, it was time for Meg's lunch. It had felt, suddenly, like a test, and he had wished he could open the fridge and pull out a platter loaded with cold cuts, sprouts and fancy cheeses, homemade bread. He went to the cupboard. "Peanut butter and honey, or jelly," he told Alice, and as he spoke, he knew, for a brief, crashing moment, that it would never work. "Or maybe there's some tuna somewhere. I could look."

"Don't." Already she was up, opening the utensils drawer, rummaging for a knife. "PB & J is fine."

And she had gone to the window to call Meg in.

Now she was back. Now, apparently, she had thought about it. She pulled away from him and sat down. "Listen," she said. "What you asked me about—I . . . how do I say this? I—" She blew air out her mouth, making strands of hair fly up, an old gesture, one he loved. "I can't do it . . ."

She looked at him as if she expected him to say something, but he wouldn't help her.

"I just—I can't come back here." She touched her lips. Her nails were badly bitten down and he wondered if they had been like that earlier and wished he'd noticed. "For one," she said, "I don't like farms. Too much muck. When I was little, that's why I wanted to be a nurse. Did I ever tell you that? People think it's some sort of Mother Teresa thing, but for me it was the white shoes. Also, though, I can't take Meg that far away from her father, I mean, he lives ten minutes from us, he's very involved and his whole family lives around there. I couldn't—" Her voice was nervous, too fast. "I'm sorry. It's not that I don't . . . I just—" She reached across and stroked his arm. "In another life, I'd live off the land with you and eat only honey. And I'll always wish I could touch you."

"You can. You are." He reached for her, but she withdrew her hand and sat back in her chair.

"I know, I know . . . I really have to stop. Anyway, you wouldn't give up your life to move to Denver. I asked you, or did you forget?"

She *had* asked him—some ten years ago when she was in medical school, before her marriage, Meg, her divorce. He hadn't been gentle, hadn't given it much thought. He had panicked, his peace with himself too tenuous, his life on the farm too new. She had cried—violent, gasping, un-Alice-like tears—and left. He had written her a few times but she never wrote back, and the next thing he knew, Ed Strum was standing at the honey table reporting that Alice was getting married.

"I might consider going now," he said, surprising himself. "I mean, if you wanted me to."

She raised her eyebrows. "Would you? I don't think so."

"Would you want that?"

Alice traced her finger along the linoleum table, round and round. "No," she said finally. "Not anymore. You wouldn't transplant well. Our place is a townhouse, no dogs allowed. I like it—there are kids right next door for Meg and there's hardly any upkeep and it's sunny, but you'd hate it, and then you'd resent me for making you come there, just like I'd resent you for making me come here."

"Plus let's not forget the esteemed pediatrician."

"I can picture it better. He already lives there. He's divorced with two sons. He . . ." She shook her head. "Actually he's great. You'd like him. He loves to hike and paint and—"

"What, did you meet him through the personals?"

"Please." She sounded weary. "Don't be nasty."

" 'Divorced doctor loves to hike and paint,' " he announced. " 'In spare time, saves the lives of children.' For god's sake, Alice, you *fell* for that? Doesn't he at least have bad breath or scaly skin or . . . or lousy politics or something?" He held up his hand to try to stop the anger rushing through his veins. "Never mind. I'm sorry—I'm—" He swallowed. "I wish you the best. I do. I bet Meg thinks he's Superman."

"No, she's not wild about him but I'm hoping she'll come around, if things work out. I've really screwed up badly—what a jerk I am. Oh god, I'll have to tell him what happened here."

"He might not forgive you."

She nodded. "I know."

"But I would."

Alice smiled faintly. "For sleeping with you?"

"Or him, or anybody, as long as it doesn't happen again. And I'll throw in a lifetime supply of honey and fresh eggs, what do you say?" Part of him was feeling desperate, almost reckless. Another part was thinking, All right, enough of this—if you're going, go.

She shook her head. "I can't, Burl. Don't you see that? My life is somewhere else."

"And you've always been a realist."

She nodded. "Just like you've always been a romantic, underneath your quills."

He felt a pang at how well she knew him. "I'm planning to mellow out. *Qué será será.*"

"No, don't mellow," Alice said. "Not too much."

"All right, then, when the good doctor dies, when they're all dead from environmental blight except for you and me, will you come back here to live out your old age? I'll give you baths. The tub has that steel bar."

"It depends on where Meg's living. And you'll be old, too, and you'll have met someone else and forgotten all about me.

Anyway, why do we get to survive? But okay, yes, if we're the last ones left—on one condition."

He waited.

"Don't let me sleep with you in between, not if I'm with someone else."

"Excuse me," he said. "Who got undressed and hopped into my bathtub. Who took off my shirt?"

"I know, of course, it's up to me. It's just—" She puffed air out of her mouth again. Already he felt himself watching her through a fog of nostalgia, as if her gesture belonged to the past. "This was the last time," said Alice. "It's not fair to him, or you, or anybody." She looked at the clock on the stove and stood. "Damn, I said I'd be quick. I have to go."

And then, before he could tell her that the clock was fifteen minutes fast, she had kissed him on the forehead and turned to leave.

"Wait—" Burl got up and reached for her; he couldn't help it. He bent to kiss her on the mouth.

"No." Alice's voice was cold. "I just told you, you're not even listening. Let me go."

"Fine." He dropped his hands. "Go."

And then, of course, it was she who leaned in to kiss him, her mouth salty and sweet, probing and retreating, the complicated taste of home.

"Go," he said again, pulling her toward him.

"I am," said Alice and was gone.

Into a funk he fell, then. He gave into it—no chores, no bees, no work on the deck book. Screw it. He could wallow if he felt like it; what was to prevent him? Like a hippo, he could groan, roll and sink down in the mud, die there even; someone might find him in a week or so, or maybe not. He went into the basement and pulled out a six-pack of his homemade orange mead. In the kitchen, he poured a bottle over ice. As the ice steamed and crackled, the smell rose up—cloves and cinnamon, allspice and orange, black tea, yeast and honey. He'd drunk some of it with Alice last New Year's Eve. Like teenagers, they had taken it to the barn and sipped it there, huddled under blankets without a watch. Happy New Year, Alice had said sleepily at one point, guessing, and they had clinked bottles in a woozy toast.

Slowly, he thought, now, as he lay sprawled on the couch nursing the mead, slowly he had been making some sort of inching progress with regard to the human world. He didn't do it the way many of his fellow Americans did—no psychotherapy, no happy pills. He had no marriages or children, raises or better neighborhoods to mark the milestones of his life. His progress was unspoken, glacial, unremarked upon by anyone but himself, but still he had arrived somewhere, hadn't he? In his mind, at least, he had, from the closefisted lawyer who had come to this farm so tightly wound that he would wake in the middle of the night with both legs seized with cramps. That first year, he had chopped inordinate amounts of wood, much more than he could use, needing to feel the thwack of the ax on the tree trunk, to see the split middle and smell the sap. Briefly, it had calmed him; then he would need to lift, swing and make contact again. He had written letters to his father, long, self-dramatizing, rage-filled explanations of why he had quit his job, why he wouldn't follow in his father's footsteps, why he was returning to this place. He sent the first few letters and received no answer, just cards at his birthday and Christmas, the checks folded neatly in half. A year passed, then another, and he stopped sending the letters, then stopped writing them. Forget it, he used to find himself mumbling like a mantra. Forget it forget it forget.

His third spring on the farm, he had noticed the hive bodies stacked up in a corner of the barn. He had a cow by then, and a few chickens. He'd remembered his grandmother spooning honey into his cream of rice cereal, how she had let him tend the honey table, trusting him to make correct change when he was only eight or nine. "My son, eat thou honey," she used to quote to him, "because it is good, and the honeycomb, which is sweet to thy taste." He had remembered seeing her in her bee suit, small and busy. When the first men landed on the moon, the astronauts had reminded him of nothing so much as his grandmother—bundled in white, slow-moving, focused on their tasks. Near the hive bodies, he had found a wooden fruit crate, and inside that, neatly folded, her bee hat, gloves and suit. The suit was too small for him so he had ordered another from the supply place in the phonebook and signed up for a course at the university extension service. Bee school, they called it, and for the first time in his life, he had sat down to do his homework without feeling torn in two.

For thousands of years, people had attributed marvelous powers to the bees and their honey. The Greeks claimed they used mad honey to turn the enemy army into dazed fools. These days, bee stings were said to help people with multiple sclerosis and rheumatoid arthritis (his grandfather might have walked again, his twisted limbs uncoiled). Health food nuts ate royal jelly by the spoonful, claiming it made them strong. Burl didn't know about any of that, but he knew that he had found something out here—necessary, unexpected, hard to explain. The more he drank, lying on the couch, the clearer it became. Alice was right. How could he move to Colorado and live in a townhouse? He had become untransplantable, like an exotic, temperamental flower.

But what about Alice? Wasn't she more durable? Why couldn't she come to him, now that, finally, he had asked? Bad timing, he told himself, starting on another bottle, but he knew it was more than that, her own demons as plentiful as his, and everywhere in this air. And who didn't look durable from the outside—look at him, even, a strong, smart, fit man of forty-two, esteemed author of *How To* books, prize-winning beekeeper, not to mention (so, he remembered) in the ninety-ninth percentile on his high school SATs? That was outside; inside was different—inside Alice, inside himself. Inside Eva, that much was clear, though what exactly lay in her thoughts he couldn't begin to guess.

Only inside Alice (there—his self-pity again, wet-nosed as

Lissa, who had abandoned him hours ago, sick of lying around), how moist and dark it was, how nice. He drained the glass of mead and reached for the shoebox full of photos on the end table by the couch. Sifting quickly, he made his way past his grandmother as a girl, his mother as a girl, himself as a baby, a few people—some grim, some smiling—that he didn't know. Alice was in here somewhere, a few photos from not long ago. He remembered one of her sitting on the porch railing, squinting into the sun.

The first picture he came across was not that one, but an earlier photo, Alice when he first met her—she must have been nineteen. She was standing in the grass next to his grandmother, a coffee can in each of their arms; they must have been picking berries. The photo was taken from low down, probably from his grandfather's wheelchair, and both Alice and his grandmother looked oddly long-legged, their heads small and far away. But her knees, they were the ones he knew, the slightly bony cast to them, and her collarbone jutting out above the V-neck of her shirt, and the golden color of her skin—it always seemed to hold the heat, like sand. What had been wrong with him? Why hadn't he scooped her up and gone somewhere with her? Because, you fool, he told himself, she wasn't scoopable and you weren't scooping.

If only he was still eighteen and had that younger Alice in his arms. Touch me, she had told him the first time; then she had shown him how. Sleepy now, and dizzy from the mead, he slumped down on the sofa and propped the photo next to him, sliding his hand inside his shorts. His grandmother stared back at him so he took another photo from the box and placed it, face down, over her half of the picture, the fan playing across him, the picture propped now on his thigh, now falling to the floor. But it didn't matter; his eyes were shut, he was back with her, eighteen years old or thirty-one or last week, all rising blood, all falling hair. His hands were her hands, the low sounds coming from his mouth were hers (would they ever again? she would marry that doctor), and he was just about to come when he sensed something and opened his eyes to see Eva standing in the doorway with his mail.

"Jesus Christ—" He sat up, tugging down the hem of his shirt. "What're you—"

But already she was gone, his mail scattering across the floor. He pulled up his shorts, then stayed bent over his knees, immobilized by a blush so strong it hurt. He shut his eyes, trying to will what had just happened to unhappen, then sat up, put the photograph in the shoebox and shoved the box under the couch. Still his skin burned; still his tongue was coated with the milky taste of shame. He stood, tucked in his shirt and looked around, trying to shake off the sense that he was being watched. But no, Eva was gone. Everything was gone—Alice, Eva, the peace he had worked so hard to find. His hard-on. Gone, all of it, and he pictured Eva fleeing on her bike, filled with disgust and fear, and Alice on a plane with her arm around Meg, going back to the life she was choosing with open eyes. His bees were still outside, but did he really give a shit? When had he become so pathetic, fixated on his hives, jerking off to a photo of Alice at eighteen?

But he did—he gave a shit—pathetic or not. He collected the mail from the floor and went to the sink to splash water on his face. Today he would extract again; there were at least four honey supers full and ready to go. He would check the mite detectors he had made from freezer paper and Crisco and left on the bottom boards of a few hives. He would feed the animals; they were hungry so he would feed them. For a second he imagined Eva helping, but she was probably home by now, calling her mother at work—*and then he took out his thing*. A lawsuit would follow, complete with newspaper headlines: "Beekeeper Molests Girl." Nobody watches her, he'd be forced to tell the court. The kid runs wild, totally uncared for. Yes, Your Honor, she stole my honey and didn't even know enough to knock.

The extractor, clean and silvery shiny. The frames, each full of honey, which was the purest and most sterile of all foods. The jars; he had washed them the night before, hand-drying each one, checking for smudges and lint—big, medium, small, plus the bear- and mug-shaped ones. The heat box he had built to keep the honey from crystallizing. And other things; he pushed his thoughts toward them. The pole beans and raspberries ready to be picked, the lettuce needing to be thinned, the chickens scrabbling for food. Tasks to be done. What was he waiting for? He got to work.

22

The saints were talking. In his head and in his ankles, in the chalk of his bones and the air around him. Quick as a thought, as a life, they rose from their salty, doctored, pink-washed sleep, *come come*. Saint Christopher of Travel, Saint Elizabeth of the Hospital, Saint Anthony of Lost Objects, Saint Jude of Hopeless Causes, Saint Francis—they landed like pigeons, beaked and hungry. *Here*, they were saying. *An iguana for your daughter. Here, some places to hide. Come come—don't tell.* And Francis, what was he saying? *Back off*, maybe. *Get the fuck away.* Or maybe *come*. Through the whir of wings, through the fast-folding, shuddering collapse of hope, he was telling himself—what?—to call for help, maybe, 911, or Miriam at work, or his mother, but he couldn't because the numbers, too, were talking—spiked and spoiled, barbed and wired, changing places with each other, *come*. Hold on, he might have told himself, hold on hold off hold on, but there they were again, pecking inside and out, those birds the truest thing that he had ever seen.

No, she had never let herself believe—even as she watched him lean over the oars, over the bright water, even as the years passed and things began to feel more comfortable, more seamless. She had *thought* she believed; she'd told herself she did, but now that it had happened, she was strangely unsurprised. Happened. It had happened. The dominoes clinking, the dominoes falling.

On Eva's sixth birthday, they went with Charu, Ratha and Mahesh to an Indian restaurant on Sixth Street and the girls clambered up to where the sitar player sat and leaned over his lap to pluck the strings. Suddenly Francis, too, leaped up—can I play, can I try?—the whole restaurant clapping as he crooned and plucked. Ratha squeezed Miriam's hand under the table: Look how happy he is. I know, said Miriam, but did she know? A week later, she woke in the middle of the night to find him not beside her, to find him in the living room, drawing, surrounded by a ring of crumpled paper. The next day she called his doctor, who said that Francis had been in to see him, there was a problem with the dose, not to worry, not to worry. And so they tweaked the dose (*breakthrough hypomania, happens all the time, common common, not to worry*), but a few days later Francis came home with an iguana, dumb and blinking. Take it back, Miriam told him, Eva already stretching toward the beast—I want it. No. Miriam put herself between them. You don't.

Like this, it might have gone:
He leaves the pottery store early. Eva is downstairs at Ratha's, Miriam is at work. He opens the door, steps inside. In his hand, a plastic bag; in the bag, a pill jar. There, his pills. The first of the month, a new month's worth; they rattle like candy, like rattlesnakes: *come*. They are his salvation, what lives inside him

and keeps him living, pink as pork chops, as petunias or petalled panties, pink as a tongue or a throat or the words that call him, that undo him, pink as the saints with their flickering tongues, and his pastels are in their box on the shelf, then scattered on the floor (later she will find them), and the faucet is running, a slack, open mouth, and he can't remember anything, much less how to shut the water off.

And so he fills his glass. And so (over and over, afterward, her dreams will force her there) he fills his mouth, swallows one pill, then another, doubles the dose, just one more to be safe because this is what saved him and now he can't *stop* swallowing, now he wants more, to be coated with it, salted, cleansed. One more to right the balance, to tilt him back. To them—Miriam and Eva— love lifting his hand, making him gulp down another, then another. A string of beads, a necklace of pills—*and this and this and this*. But was it love lifting his hand, and not its opposite? Was it life and not its opposite? She needed to think so.

Nobody knew; nobody was there.

Or this: key door bag pills, but in his thoughts they are no-where, Miriam and Eva. They are nobody and nothing, gone from him, unseen and unseeing, wiped clean. In their place, just fear— the galloping pull of it, just giving in, letting go, the quick col-lapse of it, one more to be unsafe—one more and then another, death lifting his hand: *come come*. A mouthful of glass; on his tongue the pills bleed pink. Francis tips his head back, swallows, sends them down.

Lithium Carbonate Overdose. The coroner's report.

A heart attack. What Flavia told her church, what Miriam told Eva in a heartbeat, without even stopping to think. It wasn't a lie, exactly. Too much lithium and your heart stops beating. More salt, he took, and more again, thinking, maybe, that it would make him better; thinking, maybe, that it would let him go. Miriam found him, Eva still downstairs, the water running, pastels lying on the floor. A sudden acute mania, said the doctor afterward. In rare cases, the lithium just stops working. Miriam might have sued, but you didn't sue a psychiatrist over a heart attack, and she couldn't seem to lift her body from her bed. A heart attack, yes. The story sent down roots, twined around her brain. This, the new shape of things, bearable, possible. Probable. She, for whom belief came hard, found herself in a new place, where words turned, heedless, into facts. Poor Daddy. Poor Francis. A broken heart, his or maybe theirs. A heart attack. She began to believe it.

After a time, she put one foot on the floor. Her friend Sarah stood watching, a glass of water in her hand. Get up—a child is waiting. Miriam put her other foot on the floor and leaned to gather up the child, whose hair and breath, whose skin and eyes were his. Where to begin? She didn't know. They had lost him. It was the worst thing but that didn't mean it couldn't happen, and somehow their own hearts kept pumping—stubborn, stupid fists.

23

Eva rode. Down the gravel driveway, onto the tar street, out in the opposite direction from her usual route, her legs pedaling, taking her anywhere—it didn't matter—her bike carrying her away. To *someplace*, she would ride, any town big enough to have a bus station—Ithaca or Utica, Syracuse or Albany; she knew the names if not the places. One ticket, please. New York. Taking the money from the red wallet, handing it over—if you acted sure enough, they wouldn't ask. One way. Thanks.

How long would it take her mother to notice? *Simon says he wants to go canoeing, Simon's daughter skipped a grade so she might be in your class at school.* The phone ringing after Eva was in bed, her mother talking too softly, laughing too loud. Eva hated it all—Simon, his daughter who had skipped a grade, the boats, the lice. She hated her mother gone giggly and stupid, far away and happy, home from work yesterday almost an hour late, her kiss hot and sugary with wine. Behind Eva, now, a car honked, but she wouldn't move over (metal against metal, the girl flying off her bike, the wheels still spinning, the mother bursting into tears), except then, somehow, she was steering over to the side, riding past one mailbox, then another, past cows in a field, and most days they raised their heads to look at her, but this day (why is this day different from all other days?) they didn't even turn.

What did you do today, goose? Watched Mrs. Flynn do her crossword. Watched you not get home from work. Watched a man touch his thing. Deep pink, it had been, veined like the chicken neck hidden inside the chicken along with the other disgusting parts; it had made her want to gag. His dick, his cock, his weenie—she knew the words from school: *you dickhead, you cocksucker*—knew what he was doing, jerking off—*you jerkoff*—and his eyes when he saw her had been full of hate. Hey Eva, he said usually, then let her follow him around. A few times, in her most inward moments, she had pictured him kissing her—his hand on her ankle, tying her into the bee suit, his palm on the top of her head, and then he would kiss her like a father or maybe like a boy, except he was too old, and she too young. One time, he had stood behind her, one hand gathering up her hair, the other grazing her shoulder as he tucked the veil into the bee suit, and Eva had wanted to let herself fall back into those hands.

Never, though, even in her most secret thoughts, had she pictured his thing, but now she couldn't stop seeing it. Everyone needs a little privacy, Miriam said once when Eva asked her why she sometimes slept with her door shut. Fine. They could all have it, their cars and fights, dates and privacy, their hulking bodies full of sweat and hair.

Up one road she went, down another, wishing she remembered how to get to Ithaca. It was far—she knew that much; when she went with her mother, it took half an hour in the car. At one point she considered abandoning her bike and hitchhiking, but she realized she couldn't do that—either the people who picked her up would be maniacs, or they'd want to know where her parents were and why she was hitchhiking alone.

I'm going to stay with my father, she might tell them. My mother beats me. My mother steals from me. And your father? My father. . . . But how could you describe someone who wasn't anybody at all? Like Saint Francis of Assisi, he was, maybe. On one of the prayer cards, Saint Francis was holding something white and droopy to his eyes, his other hand bleeding red. Or maybe her father was like Jesus, with long hair and a puffy red heart. A heart attack—that's what her mother had told her. In the picture, Jesus' heart was on fire, covered with twigs. *In Loving Memory of Francesco Paulo DiLeone, Entered Into Eternal Life*. She kept the card in her wallet. Her father's name was printed in fancy, raised letters underneath a picture of Jesus. Under that was a poem. *I am going to prepare a place for you, and then I shall come back and take you with me, that where I am you may also be.*

After he died, she had sounded out those words, then waited— would he come back for *her*? Or for her mother? She had been afraid of either thing—steadily, unspeakably afraid—at the same time that she had wanted to slip between the slats of the fence, step into the graveyard and lie with him (no, goose, he's buried on Long Island) in the grass. Now, once a year on the same day he had died, they lit a candle and her mother whispered a Hebrew prayer, even though he had been Catholic and she supposedly didn't believe in god.

Ladybug, ladybug fly away home—Eva thought it as she rode. Ratha would let her sleep there. Hal would give her bagels, or she'd take things from stores—a bag of chips, a Slim Jim, leathery and spicy in its yellow sleeve. She'd *steal* them, not to ward off anything but because she was hungry. So what if they caught her—a hand on her neck, a silver badge, her mother driving in from the country, yelling and shaking her, then smoothing her hair and holding her: I was so worried, baby; I didn't know where you were.

Eva was growing short of breath but still she rode, past a barn with a giant peace sign on its side, past a parked yellow schoolbus and a house with no roof and no front door. One hill was so steep

218

that her legs gave out and she had to get off and walk her bike, but she wasn't going to stop now, not even for a break. She wanted a road sign to tell her where she was, but there were only names on mailboxes—Newbury, McDonald, Maziarz—she recited them as she passed by. One of these families had to have a girl her age. She had told Mrs. Flynn she was going to Lissa's. All right, dear, Mrs. Flynn had mumbled. As long as you're home by four.

She rode her bicycle for what seemed like hours and hours, miles and miles and fell, after a while, into a kind of moving trance. So when she saw a field that looked familiar, she assumed it was because all fields looked more or less alike, and when the bends in the road began to feel predictable, she thought the same thing. But then she saw the horse she always visited on her way to Burl's, and this was a horse she knew—the white splotch on his head, the way his tail was chopped off halfway down, his quivering nostrils, the questioning look in his eye. How had it happened? She had made a circle, going forward only to end up going back. And after the horse was the gray metal barn, and after the barn was the curve in the road, and there—the rusty mailbox with no name or number, the honey table, the sample jar with its same old label: TASTE.

She stopped and got off her bicycle. She leaned the bike against a tree. And then she could feel it, keen and focused—it was *anger* that was making her move. She went over to the table, unzipped her backpack and started to fill it with jars of honey. This time she took three jars, wrapping them carefully—one in a pair of panties, one in a shirt, one in a pair of socks. She didn't look around to see if anyone was watching, didn't glance over her shoulder or into her heart or mind. She took the jars and zipped the backpack shut. And she might have been on her way then, taking what she felt to be her due, except that something made her stop.

Later she would wonder—had she heard a noise coming from the mailbox, or seen something on the edge of her vision, since the mailbox had no door? Had she sensed a presence there, a trapped and buzzing life? At the time, she simply pulled out the mail and began to look through it, and then there it was again, hope, because she honestly felt like there might be a letter for her—from Charu or that girl named Meg, from Ratha or Dimitri, or even Burl. From her father: *I shall come back and take you with me*. Or from her mother, but what would that letter say?

Instead, she found a small cardboad box with holes punched in its sides and green lettering on the front: FIRST-CLASS MAIL, LIVE QUEEN BEES, FRAGILE, HANDLE WITH CARE. She put the rest of the mail back and held the box by one corner, away from her. Could there really be a bee inside, sent through the regular mail? She knew Burl ordered bees from Hawaii and Georgia, but she had pictured some kind of special delivery, a team of men in bee suits knocking at the door. She looked up the driveway—no truck. Burl had probably gone to town, taking Lissa with him, or maybe he was somewhere with the mother of that girl.

She held the box to her ear and heard a rising, anxious buzzing, put it down on the table, looked at it, picked it up again. Her Majesty the Queen. Burl had promised to order a queen for a hive that needed a new one and to let Eva introduce her to the hive. That was the word he had used—*introduce*—and she had thought of bees at a party shaking hands, or was it legs? Each time he'd opened up a hive, Eva had searched for the queen, but she had never been able to pick her out. Where *is* she, she would ask him, and he'd shrug. Don't know, hiding somewhere down below. All that felt like ages ago, before the red car in the driveway, before Burl never wanted to hang out with her anymore, before this afternoon.

She put the box on the table again, looked up and down the road and driveway. All clear. Maybe she could take a peek, then she'd return the box to the mailbox, or maybe take the queen with her to New York. Would other bees follow, drawn by this First-Class Queen? Eva pictured them flying in a cloud behind her bike, following her all the way to New York, where there were cockroaches but probably not a lot of mites. She hid her backpack under a bush and grabbed the box and another honey jar from the table. Then she stepped into the pine trees, dumped half the honey out onto the ground and stopped for a moment to watch the ants gather at the feast.

A few feet from there, Eva put the jar on the forest floor and left it open—a place to put the queen when she came out. Again she lifted the box to her ear and heard the buzzing noise. Still alive. Bit by bit, facts Burl had told her kept returning to her: how the queen bee lived longer than the others; how she was the only one who didn't die when she used her stinger. Careful, she could hurt you, Eva told herself sternly, then laughed out loud. She tore open the tape and opened the flaps; she put the box down next to the jar and backed away. Would a head appear first, or a tip of wing? Would the queen look up at her or fly straight at her, ready to sting? She squatted, cupped her chin in her hands and tried to stay completely still.

Finally, when nothing appeared, she grabbed the box and held it at arm's length, shaking it until a chunky object fell out, flipped over and landed on the ground. Eva leaned forward to see. Of course—she should have known. A queen bee was only queen among her bees; people made her travel like a zoo animal or a prisoner, in a cage. She picked up this smaller, wooden box. It was slightly longer than her middle finger, with screens stapled like windows to its open sides. Inside, she saw, were *lots* of queens, at least five or six, all frantically trying to get out. Had Burl ordered a whole bunch at once, hoping to have some kind of competition? Maybe he was doing that with Meg and Eva—the better girl can be my friend. Or maybe each queen was for a different hive, but what about the queens who were already there?

As she stared, she grew able to separate the insects from each other and saw that one was bigger, marked with a red dot on her back. The other bees kept gathering around this one, clinging to her legs, it looked like, and smelling her, and fussing around her wings. Of course. It was the queen and her servants, the queen and her daughters. Eva turned the cage over and saw, written on the bottom, a name: STARLINE QUEEN. Pretty.

As she crouched in the shade breathing in the smell of pine, she knew what she had to do: give the queen a home, put her inside a hive. She couldn't take her to New York; the city was no place for a bee, just as the country was no place for Eva. You couldn't just plop people down anywhere and expect them to be at home. You couldn't make them leave their best friend, their room, the place where, once upon a time, a girl, a mother and a father had been so happy (over and over Miriam told her so, and Eva wanted badly to believe). She could send the queen back to the return address in Georgia, except she might not survive the trip, and her death would be Eva's fault.

She put the cage back in the cardboard box and went to the barn, where she found Burl's grandmother's bee suit on its hook, with the hat, veil and gloves near it in a neat pile. She zipped and tied herself into it the best she could and picked up a hive tool from where Burl had left it in an empty super. There, that smell again, held fast in the fabric of the suit. Beeswax and honey, rain, sun and dust. She might miss it when she left.

She took the queen's cage out into the field. Standing to the side of the hives (*never approach a hive head on—the guard bees get worked up*), she watched. Some hives looked busier than others, their fronts covered with bees. Finally she decided on a hive that looked less hectic and was a little shorter, too, easier to reach. She took a breath and began moving slowly toward the hive.

At first, when she took the brick off the top and tried to lift the lid, it wouldn't budge. She tried again. Still nothing. Then she remembered what Burl usually did, and she took the hive tool and began to unstick the goop caked around the edges. Round and round she went, the queen waiting in her cage in the pocket of the bee suit, the bees in front of the veil, rising and falling, flying close and away. They made her dizzy; they made her happy. Round and then again she went, wedging, unsticking, like working a knife around the edge of a brownie pan. She leaned forward, using all her strength, and tried to remove the lid. This time it gave. She pulled it off, let it drop to the ground and lifted off the inside cover of the hive.

And there they were, the queen's subjects, the queen's family—a whole crowd of them, though not as many as she had seen in other hives. You could see bare space here, the wood of the honey frames exposed. Still, the bees looked busy, cleaning and hauling, landing and taking off. Not dead. She had seen an open hive before but never by herself, and for a moment she just stopped and watched. Most of the bees, she saw, looked fine, but some had gotten crushed when she took the lid off, and a few of these were dead or dying. One dragged a wing painfully behind.

She set the queen's cage down on the top of the hive. Slowly, as she watched, the bees began to come over—first one, then two, then nine or ten. They sniffed at the cage, crawled on top of it and up its sides. Somehow they knew that the queen was important. Were they dancing for her, or calling out her name, or interviewing her for the job? Eva didn't know if she was supposed to find a way to let the queen out of the cage, or just leave her here like this, or drop her farther down into the hive. She picked up the cage, squinting through the mesh.

Somehow a bee got inside her veil.

At first she felt only the slightest itch on her neck, but then she heard a close-by buzzing, different from the outside noise, and soon the sound was in her ear, loud and insistent, trapped and furious, boring through the tunnel of her ear. She flung the queen away from her and swatted at the veil. *No*, her mouth was saying, *no no*, and then she was screaming, her own sound red and raw; then she was backing away from the hive, hopping from foot to foot, shaking her head but she couldn't shake the noise away because it was inside her—a dentist's drill, a siren's shriek. Flailing, she ripped off the hat and veil.

And then the bees were coming at her from all directions—concentrated, lowering in attack. She felt a sting hot on her lip, another on her neck, her nose, her eyelid. They were in her eyes and on her face, on her neck and down her back, tunneling inside her hair.

She turned and ran, tripping over the cuffs of the bee suit, catching her balance, propelling herself forward, the pain searing on her scalp. She ran and ran but still they followed her, still she heard their buzzing in her ears. Far in the distance, she saw a truck pulling up, a man getting out, his mouth moving, his arms waving, but she couldn't hear him, her own voice too loud, the pain too bright, and now her throat was closing up, the world was shutting down; she couldn't breathe. Mom, she thought but couldn't say and then he was stopping her: Stop, Eva. Stop.

It was Burl. He had come home. Already his fingers were working through her hair.

24

As Miriam drove up and saw him kneeling in the grass, she was tempted to mow him down. Her foot on the gas pedal, her eyes shut: Take this, you fucker. Take that. An accident or not, it didn't matter; let someone else pick up the pieces. She got out, leaving the engine running, walked over like a neighbor coming to call. He looked up at her. She spoke. Anaphylaxis. She said the words to this so-called beekeeper, the same man who had been lurking in the hospital waiting room the day before. Anaphylaxis—the word awkward in her mouth. In the years since Francis's death, she had avoided speaking out loud of illness, but now here it was again, Eva with an IV jammed into her arm, hives blotching her skin, her breathing labored, her eyes swelled nearly shut. They were keeping her in the hospital, to *watch*. Watch *what*, Miriam had asked. Her blood pressure, her breathing—we just want to make sure she's completely stabilized before we send her home. Don't worry, the doctor had said. Her reaction wasn't severe, she'll be just fine. And one second Miriam knew he was probably right, but the next she wondered. Who could she trust, how could she know?

"You," she said to this stranger, who was bent over something on the grass. She pointed her finger, towering over him. "How dare you let this happen to her?" As she spoke, days folded, years. Lives folded, losing breath. She was screaming at some stranger, screaming at herself—so *stupid*, she had been, so careless and unseeing, the worst kind of mother, when all along she should have known. "How dare you?" her voice kept screaming, miles from her but also rising, pure and distilled, from her own throat. "How could you let this happen to her? She's a child!"

She couldn't help herself, was losing it, *losing her mind, losing her marbles*, all of it rattling loose inside her. Because how could he have let Eva get stung like that, bees on her skin, on her eyelids, lips and neck, crawling inside her ears? I've been learning about bees, Eva had admitted almost proudly from her hospital bed. A whole secret life she'd had, and all this time, Miriam had thought she'd known. She had never known. Not Francis, not Eva. Is that beekeeper your friend Lissa's father, she had asked yesterday, trying to get a hold on what had happened. Is that how you know him? Eva had looked at her through bleary, slitted eyes. No, Mom—Lissa's a dog.

Now he was straightening up, this so-called beekeeper, this *Burl*, wiping sawdust from his hands, sweat from his brow. "But I thought . . ." he said. "Eva told me you knew she came here."

"Knew? Of course not, I would never—"

He didn't let her finish. "I called the hospital this morning. They told me the same thing they said yesterday, that she had a relatively mild, generalized allergic reaction. It wasn't life-threatening. It was never that—I asked specifically. She'll—" He shook his head as if he wasn't quite sure, "be fine."

"You called the hospital about her? That's confidential information, for family, you can't just—"

"I'm sorry," he said. "I was worried, I wanted to be sure she

was all right. They knew it was my bees who stung her so they—"
He shrugged. "I happen to know her doctor. He told me she's
fine."

"Fine?" Miriam found herself shrieking. "Fine? She's not fine—
she's covered with beestings because some *idiot* took it upon himself to let her into his bees without asking me! She could have
died, for all you knew; she couldn't breathe, they had to give
her—" She searched for the name of the drug. "Fluids for shock
and . . . and other things," she finished lamely.

"Please." He stepped closer to the house. "Please. I'm really
sorry she got hurt but she's all right now, and I wasn't *there* when
it happened. I'm extremely careful, I would have never let her—"
He rubbed his beard. "She told me she'd been stung before. I
thought that meant she wasn't allergic, but I guess I was wrong.
It's all right, though. Dr. Lee said they can give her treatments
that will completely eliminate any allergy. It's an amazingly effective treatment, her symptoms are—"

"Symptoms? Eva doesn't *have* any symptoms!"

The words rushed out of her; she felt food rising in her throat.
And then she was running to the car, climbing in, leaning over
the steering wheel, crying in ragged, nearly silent gulps. Because
all at once she could taste it, the knowledge she had always carried with her, a hard, dry seed: it was only a matter of time before
you lost them. Already, right before her eyes, it had begun. Eva
will be fine, all these people kept saying—a simple sting, a simple
cure—but meanwhile they had no idea. There had been so many
signs over the past year, so many symptoms: her stealing, her
tantrums and lying, the way she swung in an instant from laughter
to tears.

In secret, Miriam had read the medical textbooks and Internet
sites, using her paralegal skills to track down information like a
spy. In secret, too, she had read the testimonies of parents losing
children to brains gone haywire: *Brian had always been a loving
boy, an honor student, and now and now and now.* Halfway houses and
hospitals, drugs legal and illegal, voices and lawsuits, a daughter

who came over for pancakes and held a gun to her mother's head. *It's been four years since we lost track of Rita's whereabouts; it's easier for us to think of her as dead.* And other stories, better ones—of medication working, lives kept afloat; of a family where, though one child got sick, four others turned out fine. Miriam had known she shouldn't keep returning to these places, but back she had gone, again and again. If only she could know, she had kept thinking, if only she could read and watch, find and master, somehow she might keep Eva safe.

So on her lunch break and late at night while Eva slept, she had researched the signs of early onset bipolar disorders. Impulsivity, she had read. Rapid mood cycles. Increasing withdrawal. Hyperactivity. Irritability. Religiosity. Shoplifting. In the city, she had snuck into Eva's room and read snatches of her diary, but after the first few weeks in the country, the diary had disappeared. *I think Jesus talked to me in my dream. Maybe knocking on wood is Superstition but maybe not.* And cryptic lists of letters: n.p., k.c., b., c.c., with checkmarks in different colors next to them. *Sometimes I wish my mother would—.* The rest vigorously crossed out, a purple smear.

At first, when she'd felt Eva start to slip away from her, Miriam had hoped. Growing pains. A vivid imagination. A normal reaction to a not-so-easy life. Don't hover, she had told herself. Don't let her know you're worried, it'll only make things worse. Until the stealing; then she had known she had to act. So she had taken Eva from the city to the country. Clean air, a new view out the window, a place where a girl could walk barefoot in the grass. The Geographic (who had she been kidding?) Cure.

She could take Eva to Timbuktu, she could take her to the moon, but it wouldn't help because it *ran in families,* a glitch in her genes, a time bomb waiting to go off. Now it was happening. Crazy kid, the allergist had said, shaking his head and laughing like the whole thing was a childish prank. Crazy kid to open up a hive like that. You have to wonder what was going on inside her head.

*   *   *

Miriam rolled the windows up and rested her forehead on the steering wheel. She sat in her car for a long time, grateful for its windows, walls and roof. When she heard a tap, she didn't respond. Then a waft of cooler air passed over her; he had opened the door, he was leaning in. "I'm sorry," he said. "But you've been in there for a while and the car is running—the fumes—it's pretty hot out—I thought—"

With a snap of her wrist, she turned the motor off. *What* did you think, she was tempted to ask. *What?* That I'd do it, too, leaving her alone? Well, think again; I'm not a coward. I know that if you bring a child into the world, you stay with her—that as long as she lives, you live.

Except Francis hadn't. Francis couldn't, or wouldn't. She would never forgive him for what he had done to them, just as she would never forgive herself for not being able to forgive. Round and round she had gone as the years marched on, doing her best to keep Eva from shouldering the same sour, heavy load. Tight, she had become; she knew it but couldn't help it. Unseeing and, from guarding so much, unseen. Somebody else, she knew, would have been braver, smarter, more able to look things in the face. She had done—had she?—what she could do.

Her own father, though he was still alive, had left her nothing much, had left her nothing. When Miriam was in eighth grade, her English teacher had called her mother and said she'd heard about how Miriam's father had died serving in the Israeli army and she just wanted to say how sorry she was. Miriam's mother had sat down with her that night, shaking her head: Why did you tell your teacher your father was dead? Because I wish he was, Miriam had thought. "So they'd feel sorry for me," she had said. But Francis was different. He hadn't left them, not like that.

He had left them.

She didn't know.

He painted you this, he called you that, he loved, loved, loved you, until she had turned Francis from a man with a broken brain into a saint with a weak heart.

She got out of the car and stood there uncertainly, her hand still on the door. Behind her, she heard a clanking noise and turned to see Burl lifting Eva's bicycle into the hatchback. He shut the door and came around to where she stood. He was looking at her, *studying* her—the hysterical mother, the lady who's lost her grip. She met his gaze and he looked down.

"I put her bike in there," he said. "I could get . . . um, would you like a glass of water?"

And because drinking water seemed relatively simple—the one thing in the world she could imagine doing next—she let herself be led inside the house.

She drank. She drained one glass of water, he gave her another. She finished that one, he handed her more. Do you have anything stronger, she asked, and he disappeared and came back with what looked like a beer bottle but contained something else. She sat down at the table and drank it anyway. It was bitter and sweet and so full-bodied it seemed, as she gulped it down, like food. I might faint, she thought. At the hospital she had forgotten to eat breakfast, then lunch. She took another sip of the drink, then another, and felt it fill her stomach, some kind of ballast.

"I need to know what happened," she said finally.

He was standing by the sink, looking out the window. When she spoke, he turned. "I really don't know," he said slowly. "I wasn't here. I drove up after. I did find a queen cage by the hive, I think maybe she—"

"A what?"

"A queen cage. The queen bees come in wooden boxes—you send away for them. Eva wanted to help re-queen. I promised her, but then I got busy . . . I had a guest—" He was, she noticed, blushing again. When he spoke, he sounded slightly annoyed. "I guess she found the queen in my mailbox. She must have opened my mail and then picked a hive, totally at random, which isn't—"

"But why was she over here in the first place? How long has she been coming? She has a babysitter. I thought she was home or . . . or with a friend, but now she tells me Lissa's a *dog* . . ."

She had a flash of all the babysitters she hadn't interviewed, of Mrs. Flynn sitting in a stupor on the porch. She could have found Eva a camp; she had tweaked the truth about that, as she had about so many other things. She had called around, but a few of the camps had been full, and one was miles away in the opposite direction from her job. Anyway Eva didn't know how to swim, much less ride a horse or build a fire. Miriam had worried that she'd feel out of sync, even if she managed not to set her hair on fire, get caught stealing or take up with a wild band of kids. In the end, even the idea of camp had been too exhausting, and her search had been half-hearted at best. The summer, she had told herself, was almost over. At least with Eva at home, she could—or so she'd thought—picture where she was.

Meanwhile, she herself had been at work, meeting people, researching cases, eating lunch with the other paralegal in the park behind the law firm, getting asked out on dates. After the first few weeks in this new place, she had felt herself beginning to open and stretch. A new life? For the first time in years, it hadn't seemed unimaginable; she was, after all, still young. Only at home with Eva had her old life pressed hard upon her, Eva screaming, Miriam coping, but not really, not well; she saw that now. She could have tried harder, been less selfish, taken better care. She could have panicked less and orchestrated more. Because hadn't they come here in the first place for Eva's sake, or had that, too, been an illusion, a tale she'd told herself? Twice this week, she had gone out with Simon for a quick drink after work, Simon who seemed good-natured and smart but talked a little too much about his ex-wife.

"It's my own fault," she told Burl. "I should have kept closer track. She started telling me I smother her, she thinks I don't trust her so I tried—I guess I tried to give her room, and we just got here, I was still working things out. . . . I needed to find something better for her to do, it's my own fault, I should have—"

"Nobody's perfect," he said, and although it was a stock phrase, somehow it settled her. She looked up at him leaning against the sink. This time he didn't look away, and she found herself lowering her own eyes. Who *are* you, she wanted to ask. What do you know about my daughter that I don't know? A raw picture came to her, then: a grown man, a small girl, he lures her into his barn, into his hands; she lashes back by opening his mail and then his hive. "Why did Eva come over here?" she asked again.

"I've wondered the same thing. She just showed up. One day I was out working and," he shrugged, "there she was."

He sat down across from her and explained how Eva kept coming back and wanting to know more about the bees. She would stay for an hour, maybe two, he said. Often she asked if she could call her mother, so he had assumed it was no secret that she was there. He didn't really mind her coming over, not most of the time. He liked teaching about the bees and she wasn't a lot of trouble, actually she even helped sometimes—

"But does she seem—" Miriam couldn't stop herself. "I don't know, *all right* to you?"

"She'll be fine, the doctor said—"

"No." She went to the window. Outside, a dog was rolling in the driveway, raising dust. "I mean before yesterday, even, the way she invented a friend and . . . does she seem like, you know, a happy kid?"

"Eva? I think so, I mean, I'm no expert, but sure—to me she seems fine. Sometimes I guess she's a little," he hesitated, "maybe moody or something. I guess moving is a big adjustment."

She winced. "The move wasn't easy for either of us, but also she's been through . . . I don't know how much she's told you, about her father—"

"Just that he's Italian. She seemed sort of touchy about it. I thought maybe he was in Italy."

"No." She let out a breathless laugh. "He's, well, actually

he . . . he died—four, no, god, already over five years ago, when Eva was six."

"Oh. I see." He cleared his throat. "I'm sorry. She never mentioned that."

Miriam knew she should sit but she couldn't stop moving, pacing the kitchen, running her hand over the countertop and the backs of chairs.

"How did he die?" Burl asked. "If you don't mind me asking."

Later she would realize that he couldn't have had any idea what a bold, what a giant question it was, how directly to the source he'd gone. At the time, she simply touched her neck and tried to speak. "He, it was—he . . ."

Burl stood and pulled a chair out. He filled her water glass, set it on the table, pointed for her to sit. "Here," he said, sitting, too. "Sorry. I didn't mean to pry. Never mind."

Miriam sat down and closed her hand around the water glass. "No, no, it's just that I'm so—" She shut her eyes, opened them "I'm so worried about her, that something's really wrong—it can happen to kids her age, I've read about it, and I just don't know what I'll do if she's sick—"

"Eva? She seems pretty healthy to me."

"Really, she does? She seems okay? I don't mean physically, her father had a lot of . . ." She stopped. "I'm sorry—I don't even know you. It's been a difficult few days, I should go." But then she didn't move, and he didn't speak, just sat across from her looking down at the table.

"She didn't say anything else about him?" she asked after a few minutes.

"Who?" He seemed genuinely confused.

"Her father. Eva's father."

"I don't think so. She didn't tell me he had died. I'd remember that."

"What do you . . . when she comes here, what do you talk about?"

"Nothing much. The bees, mostly, or I tell her stories about when I was a kid or, I don't know, I guess I explain things about the farm. She asks a lot of questions."

Miriam nodded. "So she never brought him up?"

"Not that I remember. But that's not surprising, it must have been pretty hard for her—"

"She doesn't know," Miriam said.

Like a laugh or a sneeze, the way it left her—that unexpected, that involuntary: *She doesn't know.*

"Know what?"

"I couldn't—" Her voice jammed, and then the words rushed out of her, water carving out a wider path. "It was sort of unclear what happened, whether it was . . . we, I told her it was a heart attack, which it was, he took too many pills, he might have thought it would help but it turned out that he had . . . he'd been diagnosed with bipolar disorder but then he was okay, the lithium worked for a long time and for years he really was fine, we were fine and after, I couldn't—" Her voice grew firmer, stronger. "We had to move on. I had to raise her by myself and let her have a life that was at least seminormal, that wasn't *about* that, and anyway he loved her, he was a good father, he tried to be—"

Suddenly she missed Francis more than she had in years: the way he fixed things, the songs he sang, his hands on her skin, giving her permission to reach, to yearn. "I—I guess I'm hoping Eva's forgotten the bad parts. That's all."

And now tears were spilling from her eyes while another part of her looked on appalled, ashamed. "The thing is," she managed to say, "it's inherited. His mother might have a milder version of it—it was never diagnosed, or I don't think so anyway, and even my own father, even on my side, he's not the most stable person—"

She let out a gulping sob, and he got up and turned away from her, toward the sink. She knew she was out of control but she couldn't help it, and for a second she thought she understood what Eva had felt like as she went into the beehive—*just let me open it; just let me fall inside.* Then, just as quickly, her pieces reassembled. "It's crazy to walk into danger like that," she said. "It's not a normal thing to do, even for a child. It's impulsive and stupid and . . . and *crazy*."

He came over and handed her a paper towel, and she had a brief urge to stand and lean into him—the broad, solid weight of a male chest. Instead she noisily blew her nose and wiped her eyes.

"I don't really know anything about it," he said, sitting again. "But Eva seems all right to me. She took precautions—she was wearing the bee suit. She just didn't tie it on well enough. It was a fluke, it could happen to anybody."

"You don't know her. Already, in the city, she used to . . ." Miriam's gaze caught on the jars of honey on the windowsill. I'm sorry, she thought to Eva, then plowed on. "Has she ever—did she ever take anything from you?"

"No." He followed her eyes. "I've given her a few jars of honey."

"But she never—"

"No."

"Because a few times in New York, she took things from stores and she *is* extremely moody, and I read about how these . . . how this illness sometimes starts in early adolescence, plus she's so much like her father, it's uncanny, I look at her and I . . . I can't help thinking—"

"But she's a teenager, or almost, right?" Burl said. "Isn't she supposed to be moody? I swiped baseball cards when I was her age, and money from my mother's purse. Also I figure she's had a rough ride, with her father dying and her not knowing what really happened. I mean, she must have sensed—"

"I couldn't tell her." Miriam felt, suddenly, as if she were in a court of law. "She was six years old. She didn't even understand what death was, I just couldn't—"

"But are you planning on telling her eventually?"

"Maybe when she's old enough for me to explain it in a way that makes sense." She started herding the crumbs on the table into a heap and knew, as her fingers grabbed and gathered, that such a day would never arrive. "It could be too much for her to handle. I have no idea what she would do."

"I don't know," he said. "Eva seems pretty tough in her way. She's become—" He looked down. "She's become a friend to me. I know that might sound unlikely, but it's true. As her friend, I—I guess I think you should consider telling her what happened, I know it's not my place to say but—"

"I'm her mother." She said the words, and felt her whole body tighten. Just gather yourself, she told herself. Gather yourself and go.

"I know," he said, "of course you are, but you seemed to want advice. I'm sorry. Should I shut my mouth?"

She nodded.

"Okay, I will, I'll shut my mouth, but I don't think anything's wrong with Eva. I'm no expert, but I really don't. I think Eva's fine."

Miriam stood and pushed in her chair. "Fine? Oh really? She could have died. I could sue you, you know, for everything you're worth. You should be apologizing, not giving me this . . . this uninformed, half-baked advice."

"I'm sorry about what happened," he told her, "like I said before. But I wasn't even here, she—"

"I have to get back to her."

"Please," he said. "Say hello from me and tell her I put the queen in a hive."

As Miriam reached the door, she turned back into the room, which already looked dollhouse small and far away. "I don't want her coming here anymore. She needs to spend time with other kids, not with—"

"No problem." He held up his hands. His voice, when he spoke again, was clipped and bitter, reminding her of something, though she couldn't say what. "Good," he said. "Makes sense to me. She's the one who kept showing up here unannounced. And if you're planning to sue me, you might want to remember that *she* went through *my* mail, and vandalized *my* hives, and barged in whenever she felt like it."

"Well," said Miriam stiffly. "She won't anymore."

And then she was walking—one step and another—out of the house, into the too-bright, burning day. Where were her car keys, where was she going? To Eva. She was going to Eva. You're fine, goose, she would tell her, and in telling, would make it so. Everything is and was and will be fine.

25

Eva played queen bee. Drowsing in her hospital bed, she thought of her thousand daughters and how they each had a million eyes but could find her without looking, by her smell. Now, outside the hospital, they were making their way toward her. They were stingless and friendly and dusted with pollen, coming to see their queen. It had to be a quiet game, a secret one—she knew she couldn't actually call the nurse a worker bee or tell the doctor he was a drone. She lay in bed swollen, stung and oddly happy while the bees fed her royal jelly, swabbed her with ointment and gave her special air to breathe. Deep inside her hive she lay, and the morning light poured through the slats the color of honey, and the air conditioner buzzed. It was a big, hushed city in the hospital—people coming, people going, their shoes squeaking on the floor. In the middle of it all, Eva let her thoughts grow slack, folded back her wings and slept. There was no wood in her room to knock on, but she didn't mind. She was precious and hurt and the center of everything, and often she would wake to find them bending over her—these nice, wide women, these busy bees. How are you feeling, dear? Time to check your blood pressure. Do you prefer ginger ale or Coke?

She knew she was supposed to hate hospitals the way her mother did, but she found too many things to like: the tray table that swung on a long arm over her bed, the TV crouched high on its perch, the way someone was always passing by her door, peeking in or bringing food. It was a little kingdom there, built just for her, and though she caught glimpses of the other patients—bald kids, pale kids, kids with casts and slings—only grown-ups ever came inside her room. She liked the doctors and nurses, liked the old lady, Mrs. Correlli, who came with coloring books and crayons, which Eva didn't have the heart to tell her were for little kids. She liked, too, all the *stuff* of the hospital: the blue paper slippers, the plastic bracelet with her name typed on it, the blood pressure cuff, the way dinner came in three compartments covered with a shiny foil hat, and on the tray, twin packets, P and S, like *P.S. I miss you* or *P.S. write back.* Once a nurse let Eva follow her into a supply closet, and it was a whole hidden store in there, the high shelves filled with boxes of Band-Aids, rolls of gauze, stacks of hospital gowns folded into pastel squares, cartons marked FRAGILE, STERILE, HANDLE WITH CARE. She spotted an orange toothbrush and was briefly tempted, but she had no pockets. Then she felt the nurse's hand on her shoulder: Okay kiddo, back to bed—we don't want to wear you out.

Bed was where she drifted, where she thought and slept and tried not to scratch her stings. She was pleasantly surprised to be alive, so sure had she been, as she fled the bees, that her throat was closing up for good. She remembered almost nothing of the ride with Burl—just her tongue too big inside her mouth, a slicing, vivid pain on her head and neck. *I can't breathe*, she kept gasping, and from far away, she'd hear Burl answer: *Yes you can, goddammit, Eva—breathe*—and feel his palm thump against her back. *Where's my mother, I want my mother*, she had tried to say, but then she was doubled over, puking all over his truck. At the hospital he had carried her through some swinging doors. They had put her on a stretcher, stuck a mask over her mouth and given her shots—one c.c. of this, two c.c.'s of that—a true Emergency, like on TV. Later they told her she'd had an allergic reaction, and while it became clear that she wouldn't die, she still had to stay there for a few days. By that point she was sort of liking the hospital. Her body hurt—it wasn't that it didn't—but somehow she welcomed the feeling, and when her doctor said she was doing great and would be home in no time, she found herself thinking, No, just let me stay.

Did I mess up the bees, she asked her mother on the second day, and Miriam said, Don't be silly, it's the bees who messed you up. Eva knew she was supposed to be scared of bees now, but discovered that she wasn't, just as she knew she was supposed to be scared of the nurse sticking a needle in her arm, but found that she didn't mind at all. I remember, she thought instead, surprised to find a memory rushing at her as she watched the needle slant under her skin and her blood rise, dark and red, inside the vial. I remember, though she wasn't sure *what* she remembered, just an arm, some blood, a tan rubber strap like a popped balloon, hands beneath her armpits, lifting her up so she can push the button on the elevator—5 for how old she is, or maybe L (*L is for Lobby*), and on the way home they stop at Love's pharmacy (*L for Love's*) and he buys her something. A chocolate bar? Some sidewalk chalk? A candy necklace strung on white elastic, each bead a sugary, tart pill which she catches, then releases with her tongue.

She might have stayed in the hospital forever, dozing and dreaming, making up riddles for her doctor, watching TV, peeling back the foil on her food tray, like opening a present three times a day. She forgot about running away. People were nice in the hospital, everybody liked her, she made them laugh. Hello Merry Sunshine, said Jane, the nurse who blew mist in her face from a cute little contraption called a Handivent. Another nurse told her she was a dark beauty and said it was considered fashionable among models to have bee-stung lips.

Only the visits from her mother made Eva nervous, despite the fact that Miriam arrived with presents and hugs. I'm so sorry, she said, over and over, even though Eva had assumed that *she'd* be the one in trouble, the one expected to apologize. Then Miriam would pull out a present—a turquoise ring the first day; the next, a book called *A Wrinkle in Time*. Thanks, Eva said when she saw the ring, her mother leaning toward her: Do you like it? If you don't, we can exchange it. Eva's fingers were so swollen that the ring would only fit on her pinkie. She put it on, displayed her hand—no, it's great—and it *was* great, so why did she feel, deep in her stomach, the vaguest, most confusing sort of dread?

Too soon, her blood pressure and breathing returned to normal. Too soon, after only a few days in the hospital, it was time to go. We have a present for you, her doctor said. For a second she thought he might mean it, but it turned out the present was a bee-sting kit so she could give herself a shot if she got stung again. He showed her how to use it—like sticking the tip of a ball-point pen into your thigh—and gave her a black zippered pouch to keep it in. Her mother sat furiously writing down everything the doctor said, but Eva was having trouble listening. Why, she wanted to ask, did the shot people make the EpiPen black and yellow, like a bee? Didn't they know that the colors would attract the bees, not make them go away?

"Do you think she can manage this?" the doctor asked her mother.

Miriam looked panicked.

"Yes," Eva said. "She can."

He kept looking at her mother. "Remember, it's only temporary. In a few weeks you'll bring her back in for allergy tests and we'll start giving her venom injections to desensitize her. After four or five months, she won't even need to carry the kit anymore. It's amazing how this field has developed since I first started practicing. She'll be better than new."

Eva laughed. What was better than new? "So I can go see the bees again?"

"No, of course you can't." Her mother sounded like she was either going to cry or yell. "How can you ask me that after what . . . I mean, are you out of your—" She stopped. "Of course you can't go see them, Eva. Never again."

"All right," Eva said. "Okay. I was only kidding."

Miriam looked up, her eyes moist. The doctor fiddled with his pen.

"I won't go see them," said Eva. Her mother looked too young, too uncertain, like a child who had lost her way. "I promise," Eva told her. "I won't go."

Miriam brought Eva's clothes in a new knapsack, blue with yellow trim. Standing there in her hospital gown, Eva remembered the red backpack filled with stolen honey. Where had she left it? By the table, or no, under a bush near the hives. Suddenly, too, she remembered Burl—his hand squeezing—and her mother giggling to Simon on the phone. Burl had sent her balloons, but he hadn't come during visiting hours, maybe because he was mad at her, or maybe because her mother wouldn't let him. That . . . that *beekeeper*, Miriam said whenever he came up, like the word beekeeper was a swear word, like it was all his fault. He's not so bad, Eva wanted to say but didn't dare. Better, anyway, for her mother to be mad at him than at her. She sat back down on the bed, holding the bag to her chest. In the corner by the window, the balloons were slowly sinking to the ground.

"What? What is it?" Miriam sat next to her.

"Nothing," said Eva, but then she leaned in and her mother slipped an arm around her. They sat like that for a moment, staring straight ahead as if they were on a date, watching a movie on the wall.

"How would you feel," Miriam asked, "about taking a trip, getting away for a few days? Your next doctor's appointment isn't for a week."

Eva pictured the atlas spread out in front of them—Silver Springs, the Great Lakes. More leaving, more coming and going; it made her tired. "To where?" she asked, then added, "Why?"

"To—" Her mother paused. "I thought maybe we could go back to the city, I mean, if you wanted to, if you feel up to it. Ratha said they could make room for us. Just for the weekend. We need—I know it's been hard, but I do think we need to give this more of a try."

"Will Charu be there?"

"Of course."

"And Mahesh?"

Miriam turned and gave her a look. "Yes, Eva. All of them."

"Can we go upstairs to our place?"

"To our . . . no, I don't think so. We should leave the subletters alone. We really just left. I know it seems like a long time, but it's not."

"Two months," Eva said.

"A little less."

She started to scratch her stings, and her mother reached out to stop her. "Why don't you get dressed, goose? Then we can go. I'll gather your stuff."

"Jane said I could keep the slippers and nightgown as souvenirs. And my hospital bracelet." She touched it. "And don't forget the balloons."

"They look a little sad," Miriam told her. "Let's get you some new ones."

"They're not sad," said Eva, irritated. "They're just losing air."

And she took the backpack and went into the bathroom to change where her mother couldn't see.

That Friday night, they took the bus. It was raining again. They sat near the front, and the swish of the windshield wipers and the sound of rain made Eva want to flop into her mother's lap and sleep. But she couldn't—she was too old, plus they were fighting again. Or not exactly, not out loud; something crackled in the air between them, as distinct as it was invisible. Miriam kept eyeing her as if she was a stranger, and then she'd lurch over and kiss her on the forehead. Thank god you're all right, she'd say, and stare again. Please don't scratch. Eva didn't know what she was looking at so hard. Was it the scabs from her stings, which looked like zits, or her puffed-up nipples showing through her shirt? She stayed hunched in the seat, her arms folded across her chest, her bee-sting kit strapped to her belt like the holster for a gun. She had talked to Charu on the phone before they left. The call had been all wrong, full of silences and bursting giggles, and she had hung up full of fear. Be the same, she had wanted to plead to Charu. See you tomorrow, she had said instead. 'Bye.

As the bus made its way toward the city, the rain stopped and night fell. She had no idea where they were, knew only that it felt as if the bus was being pulled by a magnet down the road. They were going home, if only for the weekend. Home. Second Street, where she had always lived. She saw her room waiting for her—the futon bed, the blue walls and red windowsill, the baskets full of stuff—and had to remind herself that they would be sleeping downstairs.

"What do you want to do tomorrow?" Miriam asked, breaking a long silence.

"I don't care. Hang out with Charu."

"There's a surprise on Saturday night."

"Okay."

Charu in a leotard lifting her dancer's arms, or dropping, like her legs were made of rubber, into splits. Ratha had wanted her to take Indian dance, but Charu had begged for ballet and finally won, and now she was the best dancer in her class.

"I was thinking that during the day I could take you both to the zoo, or maybe a museum," said Miriam. "Would you like that?"

"Maybe." Really what Eva wanted was a regular old Saturday, her mother and Ratha drinking tea while she and Charu dressed up Charu's baby brother, or made up a dance to the Spice Girls, or went outside, just the two of them, for a walk. They could drop in on Hal who would give them each a stick of gum, or do errands for their mothers. Bananas, apples and broccoli at the fruit stand, resoled shoes from the shoe man, his store smelling of leather and oil, the window stacked high with old, cracked shoes. Later, by herself, she could ring the buzzer of the church. It's me, she'd say, and Dimitri would move aside to let her in.

"There's something . . ." Miriam's voice startled her. "I need . . . I think I need to discuss something with you."

Eva looked out the window. Was she about to get into trouble? Outside, she could see nothing but a few far-off lights.

"Sometimes," Miriam said softly, "you know, if people are upset or they're going through a difficult time, or something's painful for them, then they might . . . well, at times they could be tempted to play with things a little and distort the truth, thinking it would make things easier for the other person, or maybe for themselves, too, but it's not always clear—"

"Just about Lissa," Eva burst out. "It's not like it even matters, I *wanted* her to be a girl, and if you'd asked to meet her, I would've—"

"No," her mother said. "No, sweetie, that's not—"

"And I was going to tell you about the bees, but I knew you wouldn't like it, even though it was totally safe except for that one time, but that was—"

"Shhh," her mother said, and Eva realized she'd practically been yelling.

"That's not what I—" said Miriam. "How can I say this? I'm not . . . listen to me, I'm not upset with you, okay? I'm . . . really, I'm upset with myself, and actually I've been meaning to talk to you for a long time, I just . . ."

You just *what*, Eva wondered as her mother's voice trailed off. She pressed her cheek hard against the cool glass and felt her mind narrow, a bright sliver of attention. Then she said it aloud. "You just what?"

Her mother sighed. "Maybe this isn't the best time."

"No, tell me. What?"

"Just that, I mean, I know it was a long time ago so it might seem kind of odd to bring it up, but when he . . . when your father died, sweetie, it was so hard for everyone, and we all had our different ways of getting through. You were just a little girl—it was a lot for you to take in, and I couldn't exactly sit you down and ask you what you wanted—"

"I wanted—"

Eva didn't mean to say the words; they just came out. What had she wanted? She had no idea. She remembered passing chips to her mother and some other people, the blue bowl large in her arms, remembered falling asleep beside her mother and waking later to find herself alone in the grown-up bed. *My father had a heart attack,* she remembered saying over and over, like *I live on Second Street,* like *My name is Eva.* She remembered a room full of plastic toys, someone handing her a family of little dolls with arms and legs that didn't move and asking her to make them talk. She remembered a koala bear with a baby bear stuck with Velcro to its back, how she would tear the baby off to hear the noise, and stick it on again, and rip it off, liking the crackly sound.

"What did you want?" her mother asked.

In front of them, someone was listening to a Walkman, the music so faint it almost wasn't there. Behind Eva, a boy kept kicking at her seat. "I don't know."

"It was a long time ago, wasn't it? Almost half your lifetime." Eva shrugged.

"Do you—" Miriam took her hand, holding on too tight, and Eva tensed but let it stay. "Do you remember much from back then?"

"No. A little."

"Like what?"

"Like . . ." Sitting there, she could feel herself barreling forward, leaving what she would later look back upon and know to have been her childhood. "I used to go with him to where they drew his blood, like they did with me in the hospital," she said, and then she could see the corner of a room, a pale green wall, a metal table, a woman leaning down. "And he had a box with bumps for blind people on it. Did he?" She took back her hand. Could her father have been *blind?*

"A what? I don't think so."

"With letters on it. In the kitchen."

"Oh, do you mean, are you thinking of his pillbox? He—he had some medical problems, he was sick, I guess you knew that—"

"I know. He had a heart attack."

"Yes, but also he had other problems, too. He—" Miriam made a choked sound, somewhere between a hiccup and a moan.

Okay, now stop, thought Eva. Now that's enough.

"Listen, sweetie," said Miriam. "I want to talk to you about some of this, but this doesn't feel like the right time . . . I should have waited until we had some privacy, I can't—"

"Just tell me." Eva presented her ear to her mother. "You can whisper," she whispered. "Go ahead."

"I'd rather wait until—"

"Okay, then *I'll* tell *you.*" She felt words waiting on her tongue and leaned close to her mother's ear, but when she tried to say the words, they disappeared. Miriam pulled away and looked at the seat in front of her.

"All right, all right," she said softly, almost to herself. "He . . . the heart attack, the one he died from, he—well, he had it because . . . the thing is, he was sick, and it was getting worse, and one day he took—there was too much medicine—"

"*What* day? I can't hear you. What do you mean there was too much?"

"He took too much."

"Too much what?"

247

"Shhh, not so loud. It . . . it was supposed to make him better, and it had, it was working, we were so thankful for that, it worked for a long time, really—"

"What do you *mean*? I don't know what you're talking about!" Eva smashed her fist down on the seat. The smell of the bus, like vomit mixed with perfume, was making her dizzy, but the window was sealed shut. "I can't even hear you, you just keep—"

"This isn't the time; I told you that, Eva, but you just push and push."

"I'm not pushing." Her voice rose, shrill, above her. "You started it—you can't start to tell me something and then stop, that's totally unfair, you don't just—"

"Calm down." Miriam took one of her deep-breathing breaths, a long whistle in and out. "We both need to calm down, all right? He . . . he had an illness, he was sick, and it made him . . . how do I explain this? It was a disease that played tricks with his mind so he, I—" She touched Eva's arm. "I didn't want you to grow up thinking he didn't love you."

"I know he loved me."

"He did, of course he did," said her mother, but she sounded surprised. "He loved you very much. But I wasn't sure you'd be able to make that fit with, you know—with what finally happened."

"What?"

"That he, I just told you—he took too much medicine."

"Oh." She sat up straighter. "So he didn't have a heart attack?"

"No, he did, of course he did, but it was because the pills—if you take too many pills it can make your heart stop . . ."

"So he did it to himself." Eva said it loudly, firmly. She could feel her mother stiffen; the whole bus would hear, people would turn their heads to see. "He—" she raised her voice higher, "killed himself."

As soon as the words left her mouth, she realized she had known them all along; for as long as she could remember, she had known and not known them at the same time. One two three four five six seven cubbies in the box, and the pills were pink, more pills than days in a week, and still he swallowed, and again.

"He killed himself, that's all," she said, and as she spoke, the old story shifted shape and turned into a new one: *When I was six, my father killed himself.*

"We don't know that." Miriam shook her head. "He took too many pills, that's true, but it's entirely possible that he thought it would help. We weren't there, nobody was there, we just don't know."

Eva twisted a lock of hair around her finger, pulling until her scalp stung, but it didn't stop her fury from pouring out—at her father, at her mother, at a world (she saw it clearly for the first time) that she would never be able to fully hold and understand, though she might forever reach and try. *Had* he killed himself? Sitting there, she could feel even that hard fact begin to crumble. *Nobody was there.* Better, almost, to make up a whole new story. *My father was a beekeeper who got stung to death by killer bees.*

Her mother touched her arm again. She jerked away. "Why didn't you tell me he took too many pills? You lied to me. You tell me not to lie but then you lied!"

"You were practically a baby still. What happened was—I guess I thought for such a little girl, it seemed impossible to understand, I could barely—"

"One time," said Eva, the memory rising in her as she spoke, "once Charu asked me and I said of course not, my mom would've told me, but you didn't—"

"I'm sorry," Miriam said, and the bus pulled into a rest stop in a town where other people lived, and someone got off, and someone else got on. "I'm sorry. I was trying—I wanted you to be all right and you—you were so little, I just—" She shook her head. "I can't explain any better, not right now. I'll try, okay, but not now."

Eva looked out the window. Outside, someone was waving as the bus pulled away, and she found herself waving back. She could feel her mother shaking by her side, silently crying. Eva turned to her and stroked her cheek, over and over, as if Miriam were a baby, or a pet. She herself felt far from tears, her mind jumping ahead to Charu, who always waved with a funny flick of her wrist—hello, good-bye—and back, to places she could only see in glimpses, if at all. Her mother's face was soft, was familiar, it was Eva's own face for a moment, and then not at all. Shhh, she said, stroking, and when her mother stopped crying, she turned and resettled in her seat. It's okay, she found herself saying. It'll be okay.

And then Miriam was reaching for her, drawing her near. Would you sleep in my lap, she was asking, so Eva tried to fit herself, too big, inside her mother's shape. She shut her eyes, though she knew she wouldn't sleep, but oh she was tired, tired and safe, at least for a second, a baby still, before everything. She gave into it and slept.

26

The other members of the Beekeepers' Association had tried to persuade Burl not to do it. Why, they had asked, would people want to see an exhibit on the varroa and tracheal mites when they could see baby lop-eared rabbits, dancing draft horses or a nine-hundred-and-twenty-nine-pound pumpkin, the biggest in New York State? You could work at the crafts table, they had suggested. You could do a shift at the observation hive. But Burl didn't see the point of hawking Pooh pillows and beeswax ornaments, and the observation hive depressed him, all those bees trapped for hours under glass. His exhibit, he had told the association, would be educational, substantive, even—he tripped over the word—fun. He wouldn't proselytize or preach, lecture or cajole. A little wall space in Building 14, the Honey House, was all he wanted, a place to set up shop.

In the end, they had granted him half a wall near the front entrance of the metal grange. Neil and Ruth Birnbaum had been

251

given the wall across from him to display their exhibit on honey and Judaism. AT ROSH HASHANAH THE JEWS DIP CHALLAH IN HONEY, read the posterboard across from Burl's magnified view of a bee's infested lung. L'SHANA TOVA: HAPPY NEW YEAR. On another board was a huge drawing of what looked like a white ship sinking into yellow water: AN APPLE SLICE DIPPED IN HONEY WILL BRING A SWEET YEAR. And next to it, a drawing of a sheep's head: ABRAHAM SACRIFICED THE RAM INSTEAD OF ISAAC; THIS IS THE HEAD OF EVENTS TO COME.

Burl's posterboards looked better, if he did say so himself, but then Neil and Ruth Birnbaum had a life to live, three kids, jobs at the elementary school, four or five hives which they managed with cheerful neglect and replaced with package bees each spring. Burl had devoted more time than he cared to admit on his exhibit, driving into town for color enlargements, fiddling with the layout, writing and rewriting bits of text. He had tried to make some of it accessible to children. WHO ARE WE? asked a mite on the first poster, and another mite answered, WE ARE THE MIGHTY MITES AND WE ARE OUT TO GET THE BEES. On the next two posters he got more technical, describing how the mites did their damage and providing national statistics on hive devastation and decreased honey production over the past five years.

After that, a careful observer, if there had been any, would have watched the exhibit take a more hopeful turn: the second-to-last poster focused on treatments, possible cures and the need for scientists to breed a mite-resistant honeybee. On the bottom half, he had glued pictures of other pollinators: the blue orchard bee, the horn-faced bee, the black carpenter bee, the alkali and leafcutter bees. WE CAN HELP WITH POLLINATION, they were saying in cartoon speech bubbles, BUT WE'RE DYING OUT AND NEED TO BE PROTECTED, TOO. Burl had worked the hardest on the final poster. THE YEAR 2000 AND BEEYOND (he had tried to resist the pun but finally cracked). Plump, healthy bees crawled through the zeros; the edges of the poster were lined with photographs of honeycomb, flowers and fruit. In the middle, he had written a long list of all the ways in which bees were necessary to the food chain, to happiness and health, to our future as a species on this earth.

Earlier that morning, as he wrapped the posters in garbage bags and put them in the pickup, he had felt happier than he had in weeks, pleased with his exhibit, looking forward to the bustle of the county fair. Driving there, he had rolled down the windows and inhaled the sharp October air. Now, though, as family after family passed by on their way to the honey and craft displays, a heaviness came over him, and he was tempted to pack up his wares, go home and finish medicating his hives. These people clearly couldn't care less about bees, science or the future of the earth. They wanted nothing more than to fork over their money for a jar of honey and go stand in line to see the enormous pumpkin, which sat like an obese, florid king in its glass case. As he stood watching them all—children, women and men, babies in strollers, old people with walkers and canes, everyone chattering with someone else—his vision jumped and he saw himself from outside, too—watching, always watching. He might, after all, have been his own exhibit: BITTER MAN, OUT OF TOUCH MAN, MAN WITH TOO MUCH TIME ON HIS HANDS.

He left the mite exhibit and went into the main part of the hall. The association had set up a glass-topped wooden stand with lightbulbs inside and displayed the prize honey on top, lit like the crown jewels, from underneath. The jars were shining, holding the light, each jar with its own fine gradation of color, from the water-white Minty Clover honey to the amber Spicy Herb. The winning jar, a Premium Clover, sat, queen for a day, wearing a blue ribbon on its own raised stand. Looking at it, Burl felt a small measure of peace return, though his own honey hadn't even placed this year. He had, he told himself, been too distracted by Alice coming, Alice going; by Eva getting stung; by handing in the deck book and then tearing down the deck. His grandmother had won first prize for her honey at least five times; Burl had placed second once, third another time. Her winning jars were still in the basement, their blue ribbons faded purple-white, their honey crystallized. Years after she died, he had found a handwritten page in the back of one of her bee books: "Strain the honey through pure silk NOT cheesecloth—my secret to winning First Prize—Don't Tell." Reading it, he'd had the feeling she was speaking directly to him.

He glanced across the grange to see if anyone was checking out the mites, but of course there was no one, so he wandered up and down the aisles, stopping, finally, next to the observation hive. A gangly teenaged boy (one of the Birnbaum kids?) stood beside it, explaining what honeycomb was to a father and two girls.

"If you want a break, I'd be glad to take over for a while," Burl told him after the family walked away.

The kid eyed him almost suspiciously. "Really? You sure?"

"Yeah, I—" He pointed. "I set up that mite exhibit over there, but it's—" He laughed, but the kid just stared at him. "It's pretty quiet and I'm signed up to work for a few more hours."

"I'm kind of starving," the boy admitted. "Thanks." He bobbed his head and disappeared into the crowd.

The hive, modeled after an ant farm, was the size of a large windowpane but only a few inches deep, and though Burl didn't like the way the bees got shut inside it for the whole day, he had to admit that they seemed unfazed, keeping house, feeding their young, doing the daily business of the colony for all the world to see. "What's that?" a boy asked. "Where do they go to the bathroom?" asked a girl, and although her mother told her she was being rude, Burl pointed and showed her—there, a nurse bee feeding the larva; here, a bee dragging debris. As he spoke, he lost himself in it, finding in the exchanges a kind of soothing rhythm—questions asked in clear, high voices or deeper, adult ones, answers delivered, accurate and true. Now and then, he would look up to see someone he knew—Stephanie Carr who ran one of the B&Bs in town, or the tall guy from the gas station, whose name had slipped his mind. Then he would nod, wave or say hello. It was hours later when the boy came back, a girl trailing behind him with a green stuffed rabbit in her arms. Burl offered to keep going for another hour and the kid said sure, that'd be cool.

By the time he signed out and got ready to leave the Honey House, it was after four.

"See you," called Neil Birnbaum. "You coming tomorrow?"

Burl nodded over his shoulder. "I signed up for the morning shift. It's when the mite crowd tends to come."

"So I hear," Neil said. "The rabbis, too."

Outside, the ground was strewn with popcorn bags and soda cans; the day crowd was thinning out. He could hear the rides going on the midway—tinny, jumpy music and the shrieks of kids. He stopped at a stand and bought some fried dough. The cinnamon and sugar parched his throat so he got in line at a hot dog stand to order a soda, and after that, an ice-cream cone. Even the cotton candy tempted him, diaphanous and pink, but he knew his stomach would rebel. Finally he began to make his way toward the parking lot where he had left the truck. Already he was slightly disoriented; every year, they filled up these fields with metal buildings, rides and horse trailers in a different pattern, turning him around. MORE THAN LAST YEAR, the flyers always proclaimed. MORE RIDES, MORE EXHIBITS, MORE FUN! This year's fair even had on-site ATM machines and a building marked Lost Children/Nursing Mothers. Would the lost children, he had wondered when he first saw it, be offered a sip of milk?

At the Trade Center, vendors were selling flagpoles, hot tubs and vacuum cleaners. Next door, antique tractors had been brought in and arranged in a figure eight. Most of the families with young kids had gone home and now the teenagers were coming out, whole bands of them, the boys jostling the girls, the girls laughing and telling them to cut it out. Burl passed the cow barn, the rabbit house, a sand sculpture of a charging bull. As he walked by a pushcart, a woman in a Hawaiian shirt handed him a cup of juice and tried to fling a plastic lei around his neck. He ducked away and drank the juice in one gulp. The sky had filled with clouds while he'd been in the Honey House. The wind had

ELIZABETH GRAVER

come up; it felt like rain. He walked past the sheep barn, getting
a whiff of wet wool, hay and liniment, past the pig-racing ring,
empty now except for a man dragging a rake across the dirt.

It was then, as he rounded a corner, that he saw her—Eva's
mother, Miriam, the one who had screamed at him in his kitchen;
the one—he had been right—he had spotted earlier in the summer in the health food store. A few weeks after Eva got stung,
her mother had left a note in his mailbox, her handwriting surprisingly round and loopy, like a girl's.

*I want to apologize for my behavior the other week. Things are
better now. Eva is getting allergy shots, but still needs to be very
careful. You were right about talking to her, at least I hope so. I'm
sorry for the trouble we caused you and would be glad to reimburse
you for any damage to your bees. Sincerely, Miriam Baruch.*

He had read the note a few times, unsure what to think of it.
Several times, since then, he had thought about calling or leaving
his own note or a get-well present for Eva, but there were too
many reasons to leave well enough alone.

Now, though, here was her mother on the other side of the
dirt walkway, standing outside a tiny white church with red steps.
At first he wasn't sure it was her—her head was bent—but then
she looked up and he saw Eva in her wide forehead, in the sharp
shape of her chin. She caught his eye and looked down again,
pretending she hadn't seen him. Knowing he should probably
keep walking, Burl went over and said hello.

"I—I got the note you left," he said. "I mean, a while ago. I
assume the allergy treatment is still working out?"

She nodded, perfectly polite, perfectly unreadable. She had a
yellow plastic lei around her neck.

"So things are okay?" he asked.

Again she nodded. He saw her swallow. "I think so," she said,
and then, more softly, "thanks."

"Is Eva here?" He scanned the crowd.

256

"In there." She pointed at the miniature church with a blue and red sign above the door. THE GOOD NEWS CHAPEL. CHILD EVANGELICALISM FELLOWSHIP. WELCOME ALL CHILDREN.

"Really? She's ... I thought—" I thought she was Jewish, he nearly said. "Why did she want to go in there?" he asked instead.

"I wouldn't let her go on the Gravitron because it makes her sick, so then I promised she could do the next thing she wanted and we walked by this." She rolled her eyes, and again he caught a glimpse of Eva in her, like a familiar word embedded in a foreign language. "No parents allowed," she said. "They're probably baptizing her as we speak."

Beside them, a mother ushered her twin boys into the church, then stood waiting outside, staring at the sky. Burl lingered, unsure whether to go or stay. He had wondered, over the past month or so, if Eva was even still living in the blue house anymore. One day he had run into Andrea Flynn, who told him she'd been let go and was back working at the consignment shop in town, which she liked better anyway. Never did warm up to that girl, she said.

A week after Eva got stung, he had found her knapsack in the bushes near the mailbox, splattered with mud and filled with clothes, honey and a diary he had been tempted to open but had not. He had retrieved his honey and put the backpack in the cab of his pickup, thinking he could drop it off sometime, though he wasn't sure if he was welcome. But nearly two months had passed, and the knapsack was still sitting on the floor of his truck.

He looked up to see her stepping out of the toy church—Eva, the honey thief herself—dressed in a tattered flannel shirt and baggy jeans, a pamphlet in her hand, a red lei draped around her neck. As she walked down the steps, her gaze traveled over him, then moved away, and he watched her shoulders tense. He wanted, suddenly, to shrink down into something pure, something outside a body—not male, not adult, not marked and riddled by his own particular history, his catalogue of cramped desires, lost causes, unimportant wounds. A presence, a being. Hello, it might say, and hers, another presence, bright and keen, could answer back: Hello. Instead he felt himself towering and awkward, all blushing skin and uncertain words. If anything, Eva looked shorter than she had two months before, a little whip of a thing, a tiny, unfamiliar child swimming in her clothes. She glanced at her mother, who reached out and touched her arm.

"Hi," Burl said.

Eva scuffed her sneaker in the dirt. "Hi." She took a step away from Miriam and looked at him. "What're you doing here?" she asked, and it came back to him—how bold she was, how she always broke right through.

"Me? I was—" He pointed toward the Honey House. "There's a beekeeping exhibit over there. Every year I work a few shifts."

Eva nodded. "We walked by it earlier. My friend went yesterday, and I wanted to go but my mom—"

"So what's it like in that church?" Miriam interrupted.

"I don't know. Anyway, I wanted to go into the—"

"You don't know? But you were just there."

"There's—" She sighed. "It's pretty stupid. There's a video about the lions and the lambs, and a boy who won't talk but gives you these." She held out a pamphlet with a red cover: *The Punishment of Sin is Death.* Miriam took it and dropped it into her purse. "Everything's small," Eva said. "Even the boy. He's—" She held up her index finger and thumb, an inch apart. "This big."

Burl and Miriam both smiled. "So how's school?" he asked.

"Okay."

"You made a friend?"

"Who told you that?"

"You said you had a friend who went to the Honey House."

"Oh." She tugged on the lei. "Bridgette. She's new, too, from Wisconsin. I don't—" She looked sidelong at her mother. "I don't have a lot of friends and I totally don't have a best friend yet, not like Charu in New York."

"It's early still," Burl told her. "You'll make friends."

Miriam gave him a small, grateful smile. It was starting to rain, the drops pocking the dust at their feet.

"Maybe," said Eva. *You were my friend,* he could feel her thinking, or was he imagining it? *You were my friend and now you're not.* As they stood there, the silence grew until finally it became too much for him; he could feel his skin grow hot.

"I'd better get home to the dog," he said stupidly.

Eva looked at him hard for an instant, and he had an urge to reach out and muss her hair. I have your backpack, he could say. I have your diary, which I promise you I haven't read. Or he could simply tell her he was glad to see her, or even ask if they'd like to come over for dinner sometime, she and her mother, as a late welcome-to-the-neighborhood, as an I'm-sorry-you-got-stung. But no. Either they'd rebuff him now or end up sobbing in his kitchen later, blaming him for things he couldn't help or didn't know anything about.

"Take care," he said, and walked away.

It was Eva, then, who ran after him, placed herself in his path and asked if she could see the queen.

"Which queen? You've already seen one. Haven't you had your fill of bees, after what you went through?"

She twisted a lock of hair. "I've never seen one, not in a hive. Bridgette said there's one at that honey exhibit, behind glass. I wanted—" She turned to look for her mother, who had caught up and was standing a few feet away, shaking her head. "I'm not allergic anymore," Eva said. "After two months of the shots, you're protected. They said that, Mom, remember? Anyway, I have my kit, and they're behind glass." She patted a pouch hanging from her beltloop and gave Burl an imploring look.

"It's probably not a good idea," he said. "It might scare—"

"It won't." She rolled up her sleeve and showed him a bandage on her arm. "See? They put venom in you, just a little at a time, so you get used to it. Plus they teach you how to give yourself shots."

"Eva." Miriam moved toward her. "Sweetie, it's getting late. It's raining and Dimitri will be hungry. We need to go."

"We got a kitten," Eva told Burl. "Dimitri. He'll be fine—I left him a whole bowl of dry. Please, Mom, can't we see the bees? I want—" She paused, as if wondering whether to go on. "I want to show you," she said finally to her mother, and as he watched, some kind of signal passed between them, though what it meant, he couldn't say.

Miriam turned to him. "Is there any way she could get stung?"

"No," he said. "Not from the observation hive. We take them into the elementary schools. It's completely enclosed in glass— they can't get out. I'd be glad to show you, but only if you think . . ."

And then they were following Eva through the rain, back past the pig ring and the Trade Center, past the entrance to the enormous pumpkin and the rabbit show. They were going into the Honey House—you could hear the raindrops hitting the metal roof—past his mite exhibit, over to the observation hive. It was almost closing time, the building nearly empty. Miriam hung back at first, her hand on the nape of Eva's neck, but after a minute Eva left her side, walked up to the hive and bent close to the glass. Hey, she said. It's me.

She began, then, to show her mother the bees, picking out the drones from the workers, the pupae cells from the pollen cells, remembering it all with an ease that made Burl flush with pride, though of course he had no claim. Miriam started out with her hands pressed to her face, her shoulders hunched, but after a while she seemed to absorb the fact that the bees couldn't get out, and she came a little closer, asked a few questions: What's this? Really? What's that?

"Where's the queen?" Eva asked. "Are you sure she's in there?"

Burl nodded. "She has a yellow dot painted on her back."

"I don't see her."

"Keep looking."

"I am."

He saw her first. She was moving sluggishly toward the bottom of the hive, wagging her long abdomen, the paint splotch garish on her back. He stayed silent and did not point, and a few seconds later, Eva saw her, too.

"Look," she told her mother. "That's her—that's the queen. She gets fed royal jelly and can live for, like, ten years."

"Actually more like three or four," Burl said.

"Four," repeated Eva. "Where's she going?"

She leaned in, pressing her forehead to the glass, and Miriam reached to grip her by the collar of her flannel shirt, as if she might fall through.

"Look," Eva said to her. "Do you see?"

Watching, Burl found himself trying to picture them as very old or very young—a brown-haired mother holding a black-haired baby; an old woman with a middle-aged daughter, they are walking down a sidewalk, the daughter taller now, grown into herself; she is talking, laughing, her head thrown back. She is strong and lovely and somebody's lover; she has forgotten every-thing—almost everything—she once knew about bees. *Who are you*, he wanted to ask them, then, for he knew too much and too little. *She'll be fine*, he wanted to say to Miriam, but what did he know about Eva, about anything? A man had lived with them once, an Italian prince, something like that. He had lost his mind and so his life. Still they had kept on, as people did.

And then Miriam had let go of Eva and was leaning in to look. "Where?" she was asking. "Show me. Is that her?"

"Wait—" called Eva, but already the queen was gone, covered by a swarm of daughters, searching and searching (though this place was only inches thick and framed by glass) for the deep, protected center of the hive.

ACKNOWLEDGMENTS

For gifts of time and space, I am very grateful to the John S. Guggenheim Memorial Foundation, Boston College, and the Blue Mountain Center. Kiki Herold, Jacky Garraty and Elise Frick lent me their hideaways. Kenny Harper was a patient and generous teacher, guiding me through the world of bees. Douglas Whynott, author of *Following the Bloom*, helped me with accuracy of detail, as did Dr. Richard Ball. Over the years, I have come to depend on Lauren Slater for the deep attention she gives to every word. I am extremely lucky to have found both rigorous readers and steadfast friends in Alexandra Chasin, Darcy Frey, Suzanne and Lawrence Graver, Ruth Graver, Michael Grunebaum, Suzanne Matson, Jim Pingeon, Bridgette Sheridan and Melanie Thernstrom. Thanks, too, to my literary agent, Richard Parks, and my editor, Jennifer Barth, for nurturing this novel at every stage.

READING GROUP GUIDE

1. From the first chapter on, Eva's desire to steal forms a central strand in the novel. Why do you think she has this impulse? How is it related to the events of her early childhood? To her present circumstances? What is it allowing her to work out or stave off? What do you make of the fact that Miriam also stole when she was younger, as we see in her memory of her trip to Mexico (page 23)?

2. *The Honey Thief* takes place both in Manhattan and in a rural town in upstate New York. How is this dual setting important? At one point, as Miriam considers moving to the country, she remembers Francis scoffing at what he called "the Geographic Cure" (page 22). Was Francis correct in thinking that changing location is no solution to life's troubles? What effects does the move eventually have on Miriam's and Eva's relationship? On their individual development?

3. What is Burl's role in the book? What does beekeeping mean to him? To Eva? To their growing friendship? What compels Eva to open up the hive toward the end of the book? The world of the bees and the social world of people in the novel intersect in many ways. How would you describe those connections?

4. "She asked her mother questions," we read of Eva, "and her mother answered, and the answers both soothed and itched, so Eva asked again and yet again" (page 200). Why is Eva so interested in hearing stories about the past? What happens to those stories (for example, the one about how Miriam and Francis met, in Chapter Five) as they are told or remembered over time? What is the function of stories or memories about the past for the different characters in the book?

5. There are many instances, in *The Honey Thief*, of people lying, skirting around the truth, or omitting key details. Eva neglects to tell her mother about Burl; Burl covers up for Eva when Miriam asks him if she ever stole honey; Francis withholds information from Miriam about his illness. Most important, Miriam misrepresents the past to Eva. How do you understand the motivations behind these various dodgings of the truth? Should Miriam have been more straightforward with her daughter? What made her behave the way she did? What are the obligations, in a family or friendship, to reveal or withhold the truth?

6. Author Elizabeth Berg wrote that "in *The Honey Thief*, Elizabeth Graver captures the mixed pain and pleasure in the mother/daughter relationship [and] illuminates the sharp-edged longings of adolescence." A number of recent novels explore relations between mothers and daughters, among them, Jamaica Kincaid's *Annie John*, Elizabeth Strout's *Amy and Isabelle*, and Kaye Gibbons's *Sights Unseen*. What links do you see between *The Honey Thief* and these books or other recent novels about mothers and daughters?

7. Mental illness is a specter throughout the novel, most directly for Francis, but also for Miriam as she watches Eva grow up and worries that the child may have inherited her father's disorder. How does the novel explore what it's like to live under such a shadow? How does Francis's illness bring out or suppress parts of him? Of Miriam and Eva? Why is Miriam so worried that Eva might end up like her father? What is your evaluation of Eva's mental health?

8. Why do you think Elizabeth Graver chose to tell this story from three perspectives, instead of, say, sticking to Eva's perspective? How do the fears, hopes, and longings of Eva, Burl, and Miriam echo with or contradict each other? Why are we never given direct access to Francis's point of view? The book ends with Burl's perspective, as he watches Eva and Miriam at the observation hive. What has shifted by the end of *The Honey Thief* for each of these three people? How have these changes come about?